THE MEETING POINT

Lucy Caldwell

WINDSOR
PARAGON

First published 2011
by
Faber and Faber Ltd
This Large Print edition published 2012
by AudioGO Ltd
by arrangement with
Faber and Faber Ltd

Hardcover ISBN: 978 1 445 85952 1
Softcover ISBN: 978 1 445 85953 8

British Library Cataloguing in Publication Data available

Printed and bound in Great Britain by
MPG Books Group Limited

For Tom, my rock, my love

Where you go I will go, and where you stay I will stay. Your people will be my people and your God my God.

Where you die I will die, and there I will be buried.

Ruth 1: 16–17

The land of Dilmun is holy, the land of Dilmun is
    pure.
In Dilmun the raven does not croak, the lion does
    not kill.
No one says, 'My eyes are sick, my head is sick'.
No one says, 'I am an old man, I am an old
    woman'.

Ancient clay tablet found in Mesopotamia, *c*.2000 bc displayed in the Bahrain National Museum

I

Theirs had been the first wedding of the new millennium to be held in the little church at Kirkskeagh. The smooth granite steps of the porch had been scrubbed of their habitual coating of creeping yellow lichen by the elderly sexton, and the ivy cut back in the places where it had begun to send curling tendrils inching over the low limestone wall. Wooden buckets planted with white hellebores and early yellow primroses had been placed on each side of the steps, and the papery petals, so bright against the dark soil and the grey stones, fluttered and shivered in the breeze coming in off the lough.

They had not intended to get married in February. Ruth had wanted an autumn wedding, some warm and lazy afternoon when the air would be filled with the scent of cut grasses and of hay drying golden in the fields; when the sun, golden too, would pour down like a benediction from a deep blue sky; when apples would be ripening on the gnarled old trees in the orchard and the first blackberries swollen in the hedgerows; the thrushes that nested in the rowan coppice down by the ancient rath burbling their liquid songs and the waters of the lough calm and shining silver. That was to be their wedding day. A day perfectly balanced between summer and winter, plump and sun-warmed, like an ink-skinned damson ready for the plucking. Euan laughed when she described their wedding day to him, and asked: what if it rained? But even if it rained, she would not mind the rain. She knew all the moods and nuances of the seasons in these parts. The sudden, spattered sprays of rain in early spring, and the fresh bright light that followed; the sullen shiver of raindrops on the lurid yellow whin bushes after a summer shower; the fogs that rolled in from a grey and seething autumnal sea; the tattered sky and sudden piercing shards of light on a bright winter's day that sent the wavelets glittering like quicksilver. And September was her favourite time, rain or no rain: the heifers weaned and grazing the last of the sea-meadows, the black-wrapped bales of silage fermenting in the barnyard; the sugar-frosts in the mornings and the nights drawing in; the last weeks, then days, before her father declared it was time to turn in for winter.

Everything, still, even on a modernised farm—which had computerised milking and identification systems to track precisely the yield of each cow, the number of days since heat and service and until a probable calving date—was done according to the seasons. The time to bring the herd in for the winter was after the second ground-frost; the time to plant barley after the first crocuses showed. You did not impregnate a cow before the summer, or else she would calve too early for the calf to grow strong on spring grazing. Everything, too, had its place in the order of things. Turnips were planted after harrowing, which was done three times after harvesting the barley; a field used for crops one year must be fallow the next, untilled, and used for pasture after that. A time to plant and a time to uproot, her father had framed in his office, a time to scatter stones and a time to gather them.

They planned the wedding for the last day of September, a Saturday: after the flurry of harvest was done, and before the winter wheat was sown. But when she discovered she was pregnant, they

4

brought the date forward: settling for a plainer version of the dress, a reception at the local golf club rather than the hotel on the marina up the coast, which only opened for six months of the year; a weekend in a country manor house in Sligo rather than a two-week honeymoon in Italy. But it was the marriage, they insisted to each other, the marriage, and not the wedding, that counted. What did one day matter when you would have all the days of your life with someone, and the days beyond that? They were to be blessed with a child, too: and unplanned, unexpected as that child was, a child was always a blessing. They told each other this, eagerly, relieved to hear it said and affirmed by the other. Saying it made it true; made you realise that it was true. It allayed, too, the quiet guilt each felt at not having waited until their wedding night, as they had planned to, as they had ought to; at taking the engagement to be married as the marriage itself, the intention for the action. A time to embrace and a time to refrain. But this was 1999, not '59, they reminded themselves: a generation ago, things might have been different, but the worst that happened to them was a ribbing from Euan's colleagues at Braemore Park.

And the weather was with them for their February wedding. January had been uncommonly nasty, even for these parts, which were exposed to the Irish Sea and used to fierce winters, with storms blowing up almost daily and thick, greasy fogs roiling in across the land. But a few days into February, a fortnight before the wedding, a cold snap set in. The days turned crisp and bright, the low skies lifting to show the heavens wide and cloudless above; blooms of frost appeared on the

5

dark bare fields like icing; cracklings of ice covered the puddles in the lane. As a result of the torrential rain, the waters of the lough were up, heaving black and oily against the shingle shore. But the danger that the sea-meadows would flood had passed, and at sunset the rippling currents blazed and danced like scattered handfuls of rubies. Every day, they prayed it would hold, and it did hold, the morning of the wedding dawning crisp and bright and brittle.

That was two years ago now; more than two years. Anna will be two this May, and the word *husband*, once so slow and soft in the mouth, has become easy, familiar.

*   *   *

Ruth shivers suddenly. She has been standing still too long, watching the sky grow ragged to the east where the night is thinning, dissolving into grey. This morning is the last morning: today the very last day. Finally, suddenly, it has come, and she is trying to see everything with new eyes, as if she can imprint it on her mind's eye and take it with her, as if she might never see it again. She can see the little old church from here, across the bay, the shape of it squat and mute, dark against the lightening sky. Services are rarely held there any more; weddings, because it is picturesque, or occasional funerals, candlelit carols during Advent, but that is all. She and Euan worship at the bigger church in Kircubbin, or the cathedral at Downpatrick to hear the Bishop of Down and Dromore, and she has not set foot in the little church for months. The thoughts, the memories it has brought back! She had not known she remembered so much of the

6

day; it was all such a blur; everything had passed so fast. But now her mind conjures up the groomsmen, stiff and upright and self-conscious in their morning suits, in a semicircle at the base of the steps; the bridesmaids huddled together, their bare white arms mottling in the cold as puffs of wind snatched at their flimsy shrugs and sateen fichus. Her mother and father and Euan's mother and father and sister, standing not quite close together enough; the waves of cheers and applause; the handfuls of pastel-coloured horseshoes and shamrocks and hearts, flung straight at them by the breeze; ducking and laughing and clutching at Euan's hand, married. No longer *Miss Ruth Bell* but Mrs Armstrong; Ruth Armstrong; the strangeness, solidity of it; the certainty.

At last the sun is rising now, slowly, large and red, creeping over the waters. A sharp crescent moon and one or two stars are still visible, and the waters of the lough glitter quietly, slapping and sucking at the pebbles on the shore. She nudges at a couple with the toe of her wellington, then picks up a particularly smooth one and puts it in the pocket of her bally old fleece jacket. It is icy cold. Her fingers curve perfectly around it. She will take it with her, she decides. A living stone, like Isaiah's stone, to lay in Zion; *the one who trusts will never be dismayed*.

She turns, walks quickly back across the fields, stamping her feet to warm them. When she reaches the lane, her footsteps ring out across the frozen ground as if her wellingtons are iron-soled.

In the farmyard, her father and the farmhand are already letting the first lot of cows into the milking parlour. Each cow knows where to go; she ambles

7

into her slot and nuzzles at her feeding tube. The cows are slow and heavy-bellied; thick with calf. In a few days her father will start separating from the herd those due to calve in the next four weeks, and cease to milk them so their milk can thicken, swell with the fats and antibodies needed by their newborns. She will not be here for calving, she realises. It will be the first year, the first time, ever, that she has not been here. Even last year, she had been able to leave Anna with Euan or with her mother and go down to the barn for an hour or so to help with the newborns, give bottles of defrosted colostrum to the two or three whose mothers couldn't or wouldn't suckle them, keep watch over the first-timers for the signs of impending labour. And even the year before that, big with child herself, she had kept vigil with her father, wrapped up in rugs and fleeces and oilskins, ready to help a cow in fear or distress. It will be strange not to be here.

By faith he made his home, she reminds herself, *in the promised land like a stranger in a foreign country.* She and Euan have been studying the passage from Hebrews all that week, to strengthen their faith in preparation for the task ahead of them. Last night, they concentrated on the final verses, the tribulations, the warnings. Those ancients who faced jeers and flogging, those chained and put in prison. Those stoned, or sawed in two; those put to death by the sword. Those left to wander in deserts and mountains, to hide in caves and holes in the ground. *They were all commended for their faith, yet none of them received what had been promised. God had planned something better for us so that only together with us would they be made perfect.*

8

What they are about to do, Euan assures her, will be the most important thing they have ever done. They must shore up their faith; they must pray for serenity; for courage. The bags are packed, the arrangements checked and finalised; all that is left to do is pray, and keep on praying.

The solid warmth of the cattle is comforting; the smell of them; the steam from their flanks and the scrape and clatter of their hoofs on the concrete floor. She slaps her way through them to find her father and he smiles to see her, surprised. She has not helped with the first milking since before Anna was born; since she was pregnant, and married.

'I couldn't sleep,' she says. 'This time tomorrow, you know?'

'Aye,' he says, the word puffing slow like smoke from his mouth. 'Aye.'

Rosie, the arthritic old Border collie, whines by his feet, and Ruth bends down to scratch her forehead and tug her ears. It suddenly strikes her that Rosie does not have much time left.

'Oh, Rosie,' she says, letting the dog lick at her hand.

'Come on,' her father says, as if he understands, 'no time for petting,' and he sets to slamming the gates and setting the pumps going. She falls in behind him, her limbs moving automatically in the remembered ways. Once, she had thought she might take on the farm one day, take it over. But God, it seems, has other plans. Sometimes she can barely credit it, that she, a farmer's daughter, should be chosen for such things. But that is the way, Euan says. The son of God Himself was born in a stable, and to a humble carpenter. And so she has been studying guidebooks, studying maps,

9

learning new phrases and customs, hardly able to believe that they are going, what they are doing.

Bahrain. She says the word to herself, the weightless aspiration of it like the billowing of silk in the air. *Bahrain.* She shivers again, this time with excitement. It is not just a new place, Bahrain. It is a whole new life: a whole new world. *Go into all the world, and preach the good news to all creation.* She feels laughter bubbling up inside her, the joy of the Holy Spirit.

Tomorrow.

II

1

Bahrain.

As the plane circled Muharraq Island, waiting for clearance to land, fear budded in her stomach. This was the furthest from anywhere that she had ever been. A school trip to Germany, and another to France; a weekend in Paris, once, for her parents' wedding anniversary; a two-week holiday to Disney World, Florida when she was thirteen. Day trips into Belfast, or down to Dublin, to go Christmas shopping with her mother; a week or so each summer with her cousins in Donegal. Until now, these have been the limits of her world.

When she was younger—nine, ten, eleven—she used to beg her parents to go skiing at Easter, or spend summers in the south of France or Spain. She cut out pictures from Sunday supplements and travel brochures and glued them into a series of scrapbooks; glossy photographs of honey-skinned models in straw hats and sundresses, dangling strappy sandals from their fingertips as they walked laughing through azure waters. They had reminded her of it at the departures gate this morning, her mother laughing and dabbing at her eyes, her father squeezing her arm and repeating each anecdote, each detail, until she feared they'd never make it past security in time. They had to jump the queue, in the end, with Euan praying audibly that they wouldn't be chosen for a random bag search.

Now, as the plane wheeled and tilted into another circle, she tried to ignore the raw-penny taste of fear and concentrate instead on the fact that God, truly, worked in mysterious ways. Her parents were right: her scrapbooks had been more than a hobby, almost an obsession. She had been desperate to get away, convinced that elsewhere, away from the dull, incessantly drizzly countryside, life was happening. *Marbella*, her calligraphic caption would read, or *Albufeira*. She would whisper the words like magic charms, sitting in the draughty front room with the heavy *Reader's Digest* atlas dragged from the shelf and propped open on the floor, imagining the starfish and sea horses such words conjured up, the palm trees and hammocks. Once, after reading an advert about safari holidays to Kenya (*Kenya*, the loop of the word round on itself at the back of your mouth), her scrapbook became a jumble of rhinos and elephants at waterholes, lions and zebras and all things exotic. She saved her pocket money to join the WWF, stuck the sad-eyed panda stickers in the cab of her father's tractor and begged her parents for a holiday in Africa. But it was too far to go; always it was too far to go. The one occasion they left the farm for any length of time—the Disney World trip—her father grumbled and fretted, spent most of the day finding phone booths to telephone the locum and farmhands who were left in charge of things. When they got back he vowed never to do it again. And if Ruth talked about the plight of the great apes or the evils of the ivory trade he told her to volunteer with the Ulster Wildlife Trust on the boglands at nearby Inishargy, and help conserve the marsh fritillary butterfly or the mistle thrush. Oh, how that had infuriated her! As a teenager, though, she grew more involved with the workings of the

14

farm and ceased to mind so much that there were countries she might never see; stopped dreaming of other places.

But God had not forgotten. When the phone call came from Richard Caffrey, Euan's theological college room-mate, saying he had given Euan's name as a possible replacement for him in Bahrain (there had been some accident; Ruth never fully understood the details, and he was coming home before his stint was up), she leapt at the idea: she knew it was meant to be. She had been more enthusiastic than Euan, at first: had persuaded him into it. Of course he had to go, she insisted, and of course she would go with him. And of course it would not be a problem having Anna with them. People had babies in the Middle East, didn't they? And the Church would arrange everything; it was not as if they were setting off with backpacks into the middle of nowhere. It was a Calling, she was convinced of it, straight from God, sending them in the footsteps of the first Christian apostles. It took longer for Euan to be convinced—this she did not understand—but after several days' prayer he decided that yes: they would go, they would do it.

People had asked her time and again if she was worried, or scared. Anna so young, the politicians nightly preaching war in the region. And Islam: was she not nervous of sharia law, of women stoned to death for adultery, of hands chopped off and public beheadings, of hostages? She laughed when her mother suggested the latter. It was Bahrain they were going to, she replied, not Iran or Iraq or Saudi Arabia; not Beirut in the eighties. There were cathedrals in Bahrain, Anglican and Catholic; there were malls that sold Marks & Spencer's clothing; you could buy alcohol in off-licences, just like home. She looked it all up on the internet and in the guidebooks. She read blogs written by expats, online editions of weekly English-language newspapers. She was disappointed, in fact—that became her joke, her punchline—that Bahrain seemed so normal, so ordinary.

The plane lurched suddenly and she was jolted out of her thoughts. It had been a turbulent flight from Doha; the plane, buffeted by high winds, lurched and fell often. More than once she had reached for her sick bag, felt the bile rushing to her throat. She swallowed, steadied herself. Anna had woken and started crying again, and Euan was staring out of the window, distant, lost in thought. He had been quiet all day. Gazing blankly out of the window or at the unturned pages of his book, unwilling to be drawn into conversation. She wondered if he was nervous: if both of them were more nervous than they cared to admit.

A voice came over the PA system, first in the strange, guttural sounds of Arabic and then in English. They were beginning their descent.

'Love,' she said, reaching out to squeeze Euan's hand, 'this is it, it's beginning.'

He turned and looked at her; blinked.

'Everything OK?' she said, softly.

'Sorry, Ruth,' he said. 'I was—' He stopped; took her hand in his; circled the palm with the pad of his thumb.

The plane juddered again, and she was forced to snatch her hand back, soothe Anna.

God would protect them, she reassured herself. This she knew. They were doing God's work: He would not fail them.

16

Euan's strange mood persisted. As they stood on the concourse waiting for Christopher, the man from the church who was coming to meet them, she clutched Anna to her and marvelled, taking in everything. The sweat and grime and cacophony of the night, the shoving, jostling, clamouring people, the muggy air thick with sand and cement dust, the curdled sounds of Arabic and shrilled sounds of Urdu. The men in long white *thobes* and red-and-white-checked *gutra* headdresses, the women gliding past in long black robes and veils—it really did look as if they were gliding. A chattering flock of Indian girls, like birds of paradise in their brightly coloured saris and jangling bangles and fluttering chiffon headscarves. She pointed things out: Look, look at that! but Euan was mute, impervious to her exclamations. When Christopher eventually arrived—he had been horribly delayed by the traffic, he said, pushing back a damp forelock with his wrist—Euan greeted him unsmilingly, and Ruth felt embarrassed. Christopher shook her hand—his was warm and limp—and made a joke about fresh blood and lambs to the slaughter. It was in poor taste, Ruth thought, but she laughed back, out of politeness. She felt Euan glance at her and frown. For goodness' sake, she wanted to say to him. Help me out, here! Usually he had the right smile and banter for everyone, and she stayed demure in the background. But now it fell to her to make conversation. In the Jeep, Christopher explained that it would take them longer than it should to drive back to the compound because Thursday

17

was the start of the Arabic weekend, when the highways jammed with Saudi boys who drove over the causeway to come to the nightclubs and hotel cabarets in Manama. As he spoke, she nodded eagerly, soaking in every detail, and encouraged him to tell them more about life in the Gulf. So he pointed out the monuments, and the notable buildings. There, lit up and proud in the centre of the big roundabout, was the great pearl clasped in the multi-pronged tower, a symbol of the island's past, of course, and the pearl-divers—but to him a reminder of the parable in Matthew, about the merchant-man seeking goodly pearls, and selling all he had for *the one pearl of great price*. That, in the distance, was the dome of the Al-Fatih Mosque, the largest building in Bahrain, gleaming green in the floodlights. They'd get used to the muezzins' calls to prayer, he said. Five times a day, through loudspeakers, from the Al-Fatih and all of the other mosques. The city didn't exactly grind to a standstill, as it did in other Muslim countries, and you could pretty much go about your normal business, but you couldn't ignore it. What he did was to lift up the name of Jesus each time he heard a muezzin; use it as a prompt to offer up his own, Christian prayer.

He caught her eye and winked, and laughed.

In that direction, he went on, was the King Faisal Causeway, stretching all the way to Saudi Arabia, and that highway took you into the desert, out to where they were building the new Formula One racetrack. It was a pity it was dark, that they arrived so late; tomorrow, he promised, he would drive them around Manama and show them the sights.

Even to this, Euan did not respond with more than a vague smile, and once more Ruth felt embarrassed for him, and for Christopher.

Finally, they arrived at the house. It was not what she had expected. It was in a compound of eight or so villas, single-storey, surrounded by a high concrete wall rimmed with barbed wire and stuck with broken glass. There was a sentry box, too, with a guard day and night, whose job was to keep watch of who went in or out, to raise or lower the barrier. Christopher saw her surprise at the security measures and told her not to be alarmed. It was not a dangerous area, he said, and Bahrain was not at all a dangerous country—the crime rate was, in fact, incredibly low. People just tended to live like this; the well-off or the expats, at any rate. Life out here in the Gulf, he added, was jolly good, all things considered.

They pulled up in front of the second villa on the left, and started to unload the bags from the boot. Ruth tried to catch Euan's eye, to ask, wordlessly, *What's wrong?* but he didn't meet hers. They walked up the little pathway to the veranda, where there was a small swinging bench and a stack of yellowing plastic chairs, a line of terracotta pots holding a sorry-looking jasmine and a few other wilting plants. Christopher knocked and a woman came out to greet them, grinning broadly. She was Indian, with very dark skin and masses of wavy hair, speckled with grey, plaited loosely back. She wore a bright red sari, and her nose was pierced with a gold ring. Christopher introduced her: she was his wife, Rosa. They made a funny-looking couple, Ruth thought, Christopher so lanky and English-looking, dressed in scruffy chinos and a Grateful Dead T-shirt, and his wife so tiny and exotic, and evidently older than him. Christopher must be in his early thirties, she guessed, around Euan's age, and Rosa would be late forties, at least. Oh well, she thought: she would meet other people her own age, make other friends.

She let Rosa kiss her, and bend to kiss Anna's cheek. 'We are honoured that you have come all this way to be with us,' Rosa said. 'By the grace of God your time here will be gainful for ourselves and for you.' Her voice was lilting, sing-song.

'Thank you,' Ruth said. 'Let us hope "his grace to us is not without effect".' It was Euan's line; she had heard him use it before. Rosa smiled broadly, added an Amen! and Ruth smiled back. But when Rosa greeted Euan, she noticed, it was altogether more gravely, meaningfully, with no trace of laughter.

'Reverend Deacon Armstrong,' she said, 'thank you,' and Euan kept hold of her hands a moment too long, and nodded, as if he understood.

Euan? she thought. Her exasperation at him was starting to tip into something else entirely: worry, almost fear. The bud twitched in her stomach.

But Rosa was leading them inside, now, keen to show them their house. The lights were switched on, so it was bright, but Ruth noted that there were very few windows, and they were little more than narrow slits set high in thick walls. The floors were laid with marble tiles, white, with thick veins of blue and grey running through them; the walls too were smooth and white. At the heart of the house was a large, square room with no windows at all: which kept it, Rosa explained, the coolest room in the

20

house. Its glossy floor was strewn with Persian rugs, midnight blue and gold, scarlet and orange, green and peach and violet, and it was furnished with an odd array of pieces, including a settee and matching divan upholstered in a maroon fabric embroidered with vines and satyrs and leaping goats. They were the ugliest pieces of furniture Ruth had ever seen. Rosa saw her staring at them and laughed.

'A lady from church donated them,' she said. 'I say "donated" but if you ask me, she was glad to get rid of them. If you want to replace them, please do, please feel free to do anything you want. I can show you around the souk, if you like? You can buy anything you could possibly want in the souk.'

'Oh yes,' Ruth said, her anxieties momentarily forgotten, 'yes, please!' She had read about the souk, and she could just picture it: the narrow streets and billowing silken roofs, blazing with colour and quick with people: hawkers and vendors, street musicians and snake-charmers, the cluster and the clamour of it! There would be music, and the scents of mingled spices, piled high in wicker baskets alongside mountains of fruit, gold, oil lamps. A thrumming, bustling scene straight from the *Arabian Nights*. She could not wait to experience the souk. She felt the rush of excitement at being here all over again.

Rosa wanted to show them the rest of the villa. Their bedroom, and directly opposite a boxroom for Anna to sleep in, just big enough for a cot and a changing table. A second bedroom, which they could use as a storage room, or a study for Euan, empty but for a folded-up campbed. A bathroom (no bath, but of course they wanted to conserve water, in the desert), the kitchen, pantry, and a little back room where the maid would do the washing and ironing.

'The maid?' Ruth said, surprised, and Rosa explained that everyone had a maid in Bahrain. The church had engaged two for her and Euan. Liweiwei would do the cooking, and Maria was to come three or four mornings a week to wash and clean. Rosa held up a palm to silence Ruth's objections. 'You are providing employment,' she said. 'You are doing them a favour. They come here, from the Philippines or the subcontinent, and they have nothing—no social security, no medical insurance, no education, nothing. It is a form of charity to give them work.'

Ruth shook her head, smiled, gave in. She could just hear her mother: Two maids, her mother would say. Two! Life of Riley you'll be leading.

When Rosa and Christopher were satisfied they were settled, and had everything they needed for the night—water in the dispenser, cartons of milk and orange juice and even a bottle of wine in the fridge, Tupperware boxes of food ready to be heated in the microwave—they took their leave. Ruth laid Anna in the cot and managed to undress and change her nappy without waking her—the child had fallen asleep in the Jeep, and it was a blessing she had not woken since—then went to find Euan. He was standing on the veranda, gazing at the sky. The air was hot and thick, even at that time of the night. If you breathed too deeply, the particles of dust caught in the back of your throat. She coughed; wondered if they would learn to breathe the air without noticing the taste and the feel of the sand. Euan did not acknowledge her.

'Sweetheart?' she said.

He did not move. 'Look, Euan—' she began again, angry now, but this time he turned and cut her off.

'We have to talk,' he said. His face was grey.

'What?' she said.

'But not here; inside.'

So they went back inside, and in the windowless central room, where he could be sure they would not be overheard, he told her the real reason he had come to Bahrain.

2

'I hate you,' Noor screamed at her father's back. 'I hate you so much.'

He walked calmly down the path, pretending he had not heard her. The hem of his fresh white *thobe* skimmed the dusty ground: already it was soiling at the edges, and his *agal*, the black cord wound round his head to hold the *gutra* in place, was lopsided, for all his careful twisting of it and his craning to check the back in the bathroom mirror. In all the time he had been married to her mother, she had never seen him in Arab dress, not once. It had been a shock to see him at the airport, wearing—as her mother would put it—a tea towel and a sheet.

She had known then that it was the wrong decision to come to Bahrain. But what else could she have done? There was nowhere else for her, anywhere.

It gave her a strange, bitter satisfaction to see the trailing hem and the clumsy *agal*.

'You look stupid, you know,' she shouted. Still

her father ignored her. He was opening the car door now, gathering up his robes as he climbed in.

'Really stupid!'

He looked like he was dressing up. He *was* dressing up. He was reinventing himself here, after all the years of apostasy and almost-estrangement from his Bahraini family.

'It's so pathetic, you know'—her voice was cracking now, and she had to make an effort to get the words out—'pretending you can't hear me. You'll be sorry. One of these days, you'll be sorry.'

But he had started up the engine and her words were lost. She watched as the sleek black car swept around the compound and out of the gate. Her legs were shaking and she felt sick. An Indian woman, carrying Tupperware containers into No. 2, turned to look at her and quickly looked away. Noor was suddenly conscious of what a sight she must be: barefoot and red-faced, screeching at a car. She turned and slunk back inside, trembling and ashamed.

*　　　*　　　*

She did not know how the fight had started. It had seemed to erupt out of nowhere, and before she knew it she was howling at her father and trying to hit him, so enraged she was hardly in control of her limbs, let alone her words, which came out in incoherent gulps. Dr Badawi had told her to picture her anger and despair as two black dogs, with red eyes and snarling, dripping mouths. When they started rearing up within her, she was to be stern with them, and send them back to their kennels. Noor thought Dr Badawi was stupid. It was the sort

24

of thing you might say to a child. Anger wasn't a dog, and you didn't tame it down to a manageable, chihuahua size.

She leaned against the marble wall to steady herself. It was cool under her hand. She pressed one cheek to it, and then the other. She could feel the thrumming of her blood, and the unsteady skittering of her heart. Her legs were wobbling so much now she thought they might collapse under her. She slid down to the floor. Her thighs strained against the hem of her shorts, and her stomach bulged over the waistband. That was how the fight had started: her shorts. Her father had ordered her to wear something more modest, and she had let rip at him. It wasn't really about modesty, she knew that. It was that she disgusted him. The way he had looked at her in the airport, the first moment he saw her: he had tried to hide it, but beneath the polite veneer she knew he was utterly disgusted with her, with what she had done. And over the past three weeks there had been nothing to do but lounge about the villa and eat. Seconds, and thirds, of the meals that Sampaguita cooked; boxes of cookies; whole cartons of grape juice. Sometimes at night she would creep out and eat whatever was in the fridge: chunks of cheese, slices of bread, just cramming them into her mouth, hating herself, able briefly to forget that she hated herself in the physical, mechanical, desperate act of chewing, swallowing. She had been plump before she came, but now she was grotesque: she knew that she was, without even needing to look in a mirror. A monster on the outside, to match the monster within.

When her legs had steadied, she went down to the basement. It was a low-ceilinged room with walls of raw concrete breezeblocks; sunless and airless. Large brown cockroaches stalked boldly across the damp floor, and you could sometimes hear the skiffling and squeaking of rats behind the shipping crates. But it was the only place that Noor could be alone: the only place in the villa that was safe from the prying eyes and hands of the maids or the various al-Husayns who had taken to dropping by, sometimes with dishes of food, sometimes not even bothering with a pretext, curious to see the prodigal daughter.

No: 'prodigal' was wrong. She was not a stray sheep, welcome back into the fold. She was a pig, an abhorrence, an embarrassment. They came to see her not out of kindness or compassion, for her or her father, but as you might go to see a freak in a travelling sideshow. She belonged down here, with the scuttling cockroaches and the rats.

She felt for the cord to turn on the light. It was a single, naked bulb, hanging from a flex taped to the ceiling. It cast a dim, watery pool of light over one end of the room, where Noor had tugged the dust sheets back from their old mahogany dining table and one of the Louis XV-style chairs—her father used the basement to store his share of the furniture from the old Surrey house—and here she sat, undisturbed. It was possible to wedge a plank of wood wrenched from one of the crates under the handle of the trapdoor leading down from the hallway, so that if anyone did try to come in, or came in search of her, she would have time to hide whatever she was doing. What she was doing was mainly writing. She had started to attempt a few poems—another Dr Badawi suggestion—but mainly she was writing a truthful account of what had really happened, so that one day everyone— her parents, teachers, all of them—would know what really happened. Only by then it would be too late, and they would be sorry.

She took out her exercise book, unwound the string and the elastic bands that sealed it, and flipped to find her place. From the hallway above, she heard the shrill, distorted sound of the telephone ringing. She waited. It stopped. It would be her mother. Her mother was the only person who ever called—apart from once, excruciatingly, her English teacher. Noor had liked her English teacher, a lot, and had been so surprised to hear her voice on the other end of the phone that she had mumbled, been rude, unable to think of anything to say. She had nothing to say to her mother, either. In a sudden fit she seized her pen and scrawled a list of the things her mother would say:

How are you darling?
Are you all right?
And how is Hisham?

Her mother never said anything else, was careful to keep the conversation light. She had probably been advised to do that. Anything that mattered, she emailed or talked about with Noor's father: who she never even called *your father* any more, simply 'Hisham'. Noor would see him take the phone from the maid and get up with a sigh, go into his bedroom and close the door. Sometimes she listened outside, but mostly she did not bother. It was usually her mother who did all of the talking, anyhow. Her father was a morose, taciturn man. He was happiest at work: the strict hierarchy that put him on top of the pyramid, above the polite, respectful doctors and deferential nurses who would never dream of questioning or talking back to him.

She ripped the page of platitudes from her jotter—just looking at them was making her angry—and crumpled it into a ball, threw it into a corner to be shredded and used as bedding by the roaches. Then she turned to the back of the book, where she was keeping a diary of her time in Bahrain.

The Diary of Noor Hussain

Thursday, 6th March 2003

1. Sleeping tablets
2. Razor
3. Hanging
4a. Drowning
4b. Being run over

1. <u>Sleeping tablets</u>
Advantages: Painless?? Like drifting off to a gentle sleep??
Disadvantages: Vomiting them up or someone (Baba, Samp.) finding you too soon. Getting hold of them. a) the pharmacist won't sell you any b) Baba locks spare drugs in cupboard (could get hold of key??)
N.B. Tylenol won't do because you have to take hundreds and hundreds of it and might just end up

with liver failure like in Biology video.

2. <u>Razor</u>
Advantages: Quick?? (is it?) so long as you cut the right way (find out which is right way) and get artery not vein
Disadvantages: <u>Painful</u>. Messy. No bath. Blood makes you faint. <u>Don't have a razor</u> and Baba won't buy one because girls shaving legs is sluttish. And Baba uses electric shaver.
N.B. Maybe you could use scissors? Ugh ugh ugh. Not razor.

3. <s>Hanging</s>
<s>Advantages:</s>
<s>Disadvantages:</s>

4a. <u>Drowning</u> and 4b. <u>Being run over</u>
Advantages: They both look like accidents (or is this disadvantage??)
Disadvantages: OK at swimming and sea too salty to sink well in. Swimming pool drained. Car might stop in time or might just end up paralysed not dead.

THINK NOOR THINK!

As soon as her Account was finished, she had decided, she was going to do it. That much was certain. Even if she did go to hell—and she wasn't sure if she even believed in such a thing, anyway—it couldn't be worse than this, here, now.
Maybe, she wrote, gouging blank despair through the previous pages, *this is hell and I'm in it already.*

She put her head down on the scratched, dusty table and wept.

3

He has come to Bahrain to smuggle Bibles into Saudi Arabia.

'Not "smuggle",' Euan objects, 'that makes it sound like drug-running.'

What, then?

'Introduce. Bring in. Please, Ruth'—he is close to tears—'don't get hung up on the word. It's not alcohol or drugs or illicit substances or what have you. It's bringing the Word of God to those who are dying of thirst for it.'

He shows her the gospel—it is the Gospel of Matthew, with the Sermon on the Mount—printed in a tiny font on rice paper, fragile and flimsy as the veined skeleton of a fallen leaf. The paper is rolled up into a tight tube, thinner than a pencil, and inserted into the body of a cheap biro, branded with the logo of a construction company or engineering firm. He has a whole box of the pens, one hundred of them. He carried them over in his suitcase, along with a carton of cheap pamphlets about the fictional Northern Irish business.

'You what?' She can barely form the words. 'Euan, you—' she tries again. Words fail her. She gapes at him. The whole way—in their luggage—alongside their books and clothes and Anna's toys—the whole time?

He tries to take her arm and she pushes him

away, so violently she almost topples over.

'Please, Ruth,' he says, 'I'm begging you. Please hear me out.' He kneels on the floor in front of her—he actually kneels—and she feels too sick and stunned to stop him.

He will make the trip across the causeway to Saudi Arabia, he says, along with another man, or men, ostensibly for the purpose of meeting with Saudi-based companies. There are networks in place to distribute the gospels. It must be done before Easter.

'"He led you through the vast and dreadful desert,"' Euan recites, '"that thirsty and waterless land, with its venomous snakes and scorpions."'

'Euan—' she interrupts, but he continues. His voice is thin. '"He brought you water out of hard rock. He gave you manna to eat in the desert, something your fathers had never known, to humble and to test you so that in the end it might go well with you." We must pour water on the thirsty land, Ruth.'

'But—' Her mind is starting to whirl with questions. 'You need a visa to get into Saudi Arabia. You can't just cross the border. It's the strictest place in the Middle East, you need a company to sponsor you, and a visa from the state, even I know that. And what about the fake company you're supposed to be representing, surely all it takes is a couple of phone calls or a Google search to see that they don't exist?'

He tells her that he cannot go into the details: that even he does not know all the details. They keep them secret until the last minute, even from him, until the last possible moment, in case the plan is discovered.

'They?' she says. She is almost shouting now. 'They? Who are "they", Euan?'

He does not know their names; not all of them. 'But trust me, Ruth, these people, they're not amateurs.'

'But you are!'

That's different, he tells her. They always need new people, new faces. You cannot make more than one or two crossings, your face becomes known. And it cannot be people who have lived out in the Gulf long; they become known, too.

'One or two crossings?' she yells at him. 'Are you out of your mind? It's illegal, Euan! It's worse than illegal—it's against Islam, it's blasphemy, it's the worst crime possible! They still cut off people's hands in Saudi for stealing a loaf of bread from a market stall, they stone people to death, they cut off people's heads! What if they catch you? What if it goes wrong? And what if it had gone wrong on the way over here, and they'd found the, the'—she casts about for a word—'the material on us? Us, Euan. Your wife and baby daughter. Us.'

'Please, Ruth,' he begs again. 'Please.' But she moves away from him, puts the divan between them.

'You brought us,' she says, struggling to keep her voice level, 'you brought your wife and your daughter into this country knowing that's what you were going to do?'

With all the talk of war, he counters, and hostilities to the Western world and Christianity running high, it is more important than ever that they support the struggle of their underground brethren in places suddenly more unsafe and unstable than ever.

' "Support"?' she says. 'It's not just "support",
Euan, it's not the same as coming to Bahrain to
help with the church—it's an illegal act that could
get us all thrown in jail, that could get you killed.
All this time,' she says, feeling her voice start to
crack, 'you've been—been—playing fast and loose
not just with your own life, but with ours, too?'

But it's not just our lives, he says. That's the
thing. It's far, far bigger than that. It's the eternal
lives of tens of people, hundreds of people, who will
otherwise burn in hell. It is far more than a matter
of life and death.

She does not know what to say when he says this.
She stares at him. His face is pale and set, like a
death mask of itself, and his eyes are gleaming.

'Ruth,' he says.

'Get away from me.'

Anna is crying. Ruth slowly registers the sound
of the child's voice, and realises that she has been
sobbing for some time.

' "For we who are alive are always being given
over to death for Jesus' sake, so that his life may be
revealed in his mortal body",' Euan quotes. 'Second
Corinthians, chapter 4, verse 11. Romans chapter 8,
verse 39: "Neither death nor life, neither angels nor
demons, neither the present nor the future, nor any
powers, neither height nor depth, nor anything else
in all creation will be able to separate us from the
love of God that is in Christ Jesus our Lord." ' It is
these verses, he says, that he kept being drawn to,
after Richard Caffrey's phone call, when he did not
know if he could, or should, accept the calling.

'Why didn't you tell me?' she wants to know now.
'Why didn't you tell me, at the start?'

He couldn't, he says. How could he? People's

33

lives were at risk, he was sworn to secrecy. He shouldn't have told her now, even. He wasn't meant to tell her. The fewer people who knew, the better, even her, even his wife. He had been planning on not telling her. Until he realised tonight that he couldn't not tell her, it was too big a secret, and they had never had secrets before. It was too much of a betrayal.

A betrayal. She almost laughs. Not telling her was the betrayal?

He begins to plead with her. Does she not see how torn he has been? How torn between himself, his family, and the Word? He waves the cheap biro at her, right in her face.

'This is what we believe,' he says. 'This is what makes us who we are. I understand you are shocked, and scared. I understand that. But I know you, Ruth, and I know you'll agree, once you've had time to think about it. I know—'

She marches into Anna's boxroom and slams the corkboard door behind her.

*   *   *

She does not sleep that night. Of course she does not sleep. She feels Euan not sleeping beside her, too. Once, he reaches for her. But she keeps her back to him and makes her body rigid. They have never fought before, never, not in two years of marriage, nor all the years before that. Petty arguments, sure, or angry words, but nothing that has not been settled and forgotten before they go to bed.

She knows there is nothing more to say. She knows that Euan will do it. He will: she knows him, knows his determination, once he has set his mind on something. There is nothing she can do: she can be as furious as she likes; she can beg and plead; it will not change anything. His course is set; hers with it.

But now that the initial shock is subsiding, she cannot stop going over things in her mind, piecing together what was really happening, what was really going on, when all the while she was ignorant of it. The airy assertions to her mother that everything would be fine; the way she jabbered at Christopher in the car. The way she had thanked Euan, thought him so considerate, when he insisted he finish packing the cases so she could walk over to the farmhouse to be with her mother. The way she misunderstood his doubts, and set about convincing him that they should go. She feels a fool.

She does not sleep at all. Euan falls asleep. She feels his breathing soften and lengthen behind her. Finally, an hour or so before dawn, she gets up, goes into the kitchen. The dark, and the noises in the dark—the rattle of the air-conditioning unit, the gurgle of the electric water dispenser—are unfamiliar, foreboding. When she flips on the fluorescent light, even the shadows seem to have a different texture, a different quality. She feels a long way from home. She sits at the breakfast bar with a mug of instant coffee and flicks uselessly through her Arabic phrase book. She had been so excited about coming here, so excited. She had learned to say *Murhuba*, and *Kayf haalak?*—*Kayf haalik* to a woman—and the reply, *Al-humdoolillah bikhair*, thanks be to God. She has practised *As-salaam alaykum* and *Wa alaykum as-salaam*,

35

twisting her mouth around the unfamiliar patterns. She has learned the etiquette—how Arabs may keep hold of your hands when they talk to you, after they have greeted you; how you must never ask directly about a man's wife, or sit so the soles of your feet point at someone. Your right hand only is used for eating, and you must never admire something, or your host will be obliged to give it to you. And all the while Euan listened to her, let her test her phrases on him, let her believe that they really were coming to strengthen Christian ties in a Muslim country. It had seemed a game to her; an adventure.

At the back of the phrase book, amid the dense explanations of grammar that she has not yet read, her eye falls on a short paragraph, separated from the rest of the text. *In Arabic*, it says, *there is no future tense. The present tense is also used to cover the future. The verb 'to be' does not exist in the present tense.* She rereads the paragraph a couple of times, trying to get her head around it. There is no future, only the present. When she rests her aching head in her arms, pressing her forehead against the cool black granite of the breakfast bar, the words purl and reverberate around and around in her mind.

4

On Fridays, the second day of the Arab weekend, Noor's father went to *jum'ah* prayers at the central mosque. He met his brother, sisters and their families there; afterwards, they all went back to the al-Husayn compound for a big, communal lunch:

up to thirty people sitting on cushions around the edges of the central living room and eating from dishes that the older women had spent the past two days preparing. Noor was shy of these family gatherings. The cousins were too numerous and too clamorous; she felt they all looked at her askance, and giggled or gossiped behind her back. Her Arabic was not good enough to follow when they talked fast; and sometimes they lapsed into Farsi, which she did not speak at all. Each Friday morning for the past two weeks her father had asked her if she wished to accompany him to *jum'ah*, and both times she had declined. Her mother, she thought, would be shocked if she knew how changed Hisham was since the divorce. Only a year ago, he had worn designer jeans and expensive loafers, belonged to the Wine Society and joked about his pious family. These days, he woke before dawn to perform *fajr*, the first of the *salah* prayers. From her bedroom, Noor would hear the shrill beeping of his alarm, the splashing of water in the bathroom, and the scrapes and bumps as he heaved furniture out of the way in the living room and arranged his prayer rug and *turbah* in the right direction. He was new to this. His own parents had not been zealous, and he had grown up mostly in Europe, and England. His spoken Arabic was fluent, but his voice when he recited the prayers wavered: the intonations and the gestures were a new language for him. She had found leaflets in his bedroom detailing the prayers step by step and explaining the etiquette surrounding them. To Noor, it seemed rigid, incomprehensible, impenetrable. The way to wash your face was using the right hand to wipe the face from top to bottom, in such a way that the water

37

reached all parts vertically from the hairline to the chin, the section on *wudu* said. It scared, and fascinated Noor, these strange, inexplicable rituals; this strange, unpredictable new father.

After her outburst the night before, Noor was not expecting her father to make his usual offer. When he did, politely and distantly as ever, she wondered if it was a test, or a trap.

'No, thank you, Baba,' she said, and he looked at her for a moment, then nodded curtly and set off.

*   *   *

So she was left alone. Sampaguita was mopping the floors, which meant that she could not get to her basement. Sampaguita was Filipino, and the weekends meant nothing to her: she worked her own hours. She had worked in Noor's father's household when he was a boy, and when he moved back to Bahrain, she came to work for him. She was a wily old woman, Noor thought; bony, with a hollow, inscrutable face and beady, darting eyes. Neither her English nor her Arabic were any good. At least, she pretended they weren't. Noor had started to suspect that it quite often suited her to feign ignorance or incomprehension. For the first few bewildering days, alone in the villa while her father was at work, Noor had tried to befriend her. She had asked what part of the Philippines Sampaguita came from, and if she had any family, and why she had never gone home. Most of the Filipinos and Indians came over to labour as maids or on building sites for a few years in the hope of earning enough money to get married, or send children to school, or buy a refrigerator or build a new house back home. They worked long hours, slept in outhouses or shanty towns on the outskirts of Manama or Isa Town, paid off their tickets and agent fees in monthly instalments and wired the rest of their wages back to Malolos or Dhaka or Cochin or wherever else they had relatives. But Sampaguita had brushed away or chosen not to understand Noor's questions. Noor had persisted for a while, out of exasperation as much as interest, following the old woman around the kitchen. But she had not been able to wear the maid down. It was as if, she decided, Sampaguita was showing that even though Noor was the master's daughter, she, Sampaguita, held the power. She liked to tease you with information, Noor was beginning to realise, dispensing it in short, sharp bursts and stopping suddenly, watching you with glittering eyes, waiting for you to ask more, enjoying the hold she had over you. Noor wondered if she knew about the basement hideout, and was taking pleasure out of mopping the floor so thoroughly, knowing that Noor wanted to go down there but could not.

The radio was on, tuned to a station that alternated Arab songs with American hits. Sampaguita was wailing along, singing vowels rather than words, and the noise was getting on Noor's nerves. She went outside, and slumped listlessly on the veranda. The compound was dead, as usual. But she remembered the Indian woman, and the Tupperware containers of food, and wondered if the new people had arrived. A week ago, someone had come to paint the walls, and for the last few days the Indian woman and white man had been coming and going, carrying pieces of furniture in and out, washing down the terrace, putting plants by the door. Sampaguita had been dropping hints, too, in her usual, cryptic way. The new people were God Squad, she had said—laughing to herself at the term—come to save wicked souls. Noor had not known whether to believe her. Now, with nothing else to do with her day, she decided to watch the villa until the new people came out. She hunkered down and took a cigarette from her secret tin stashed under the veranda. They were mostly Marlboro Reds, sneaked from her father's packet, with a handful of Camels that one of her cousins had given her. She could not inhale properly yet—the smoke made her cough and feel dizzy—but she was practising. Why, she did not really know. She had never been one of the girls who smoked at school, making a big deal of sneaking off behind the sports hall, or up to the common-room fire escape, so they could be sure that everyone nearby knew what they were doing. But since coming to Bahrain it had given her a stab of pleasure each time she stole a cigarette from her father, and smoked it when he was out: as if it was a victory over him.

She waited, smoking her stolen cigarettes, until the new people appeared on their veranda. They were not what she had expected. She did not know quite what she had expected: but whatever it was, it was not this couple. They were much younger than she had imagined, for a start, and good-looking: they could have come out of a magazine, Noor thought. Sampaguita had said they were Irish. They looked it: they looked romantic. The man was tall with curly red hair and the woman was slim and willowy with light brown hair cut straight across her shoulders and a pretty, heart-shaped face. They had a baby girl, too, with masses of golden curls and fat little legs. They walked the length of the compound, each holding one of the baby's hands and jumping it in the air, and it shrieked with laughter. Noor had a strange, churning feeling in her stomach as she watched them. She tried to imagine her mother and father doing that to her, and she could not. She watched the couple and the baby until they disappeared out of sight behind the furthest villa—where the bad joke of a tennis court was, and the disused swimming pool—and then she waited for them to walk past her again, on their way back in. In the morning light, with the sun behind them, they were haloed, golden. The sudden, irrational idea that they were angels, come to save her, flashed through her mind, and she had a vision of running to them, falling at their feet and telling them what she had done.

They went back inside their villa and shut the door. There were no outer windows to any of the villas, so you could not see what was going on inside. Noor waited a while, but they did not come out again. Her heart was beating inexplicably fast. She went inside, seized with the notion that something had happened which needed to be written down, recorded, made sense of. Sampaguita was in the kitchen, preparing that evening's meal, but for once Noor went straight down to the basement without heeding her own precautions.

She did her best to put into words the strange feeling—how it had been to watch the golden couple, in the light and the heat—but it was no use, and every attempt just made her crosser and more frustrated. Eventually, she gave up, and crept back upstairs.

41

There was nothing to do. She poured herself a beaker of grape juice and took a box of *koloocheh*, her father's favourite walnut-stuffed cookies, and sat down in front of the television to channel-surf. There was nothing on: only the rolling news on CNN, covering a four-day walk-out of musicians on Broadway who feared they were to be replaced with a synthesised orchestra, and the daily instalments of interminably melodramatic Arabic soap operas. She flicked between the music channels for a while, then watched cartoons on Nickelodeon. This was how most of her days so far had been spent. She was allowed to use the computer in her father's room, but she had not logged in to her email account since leaving school, six weeks before, and she had no intention of doing so now. She had signed in to MSN Messenger once, just to see who was there and what they were saying, but as soon as people saw she was online they started bombarding her with hate mail. She signed off almost immediately and was too shaken to try it again, even invisibly or under a pseudonym.

She ate through the biscuits one after another until the box was finished, and immediately loathed herself for it. She had not even been particularly hungry. She slid the carton under the settee, for Sampaguita to find later, and skulked into the kitchen. Sampaguita was frying spices for *kare-kare* stew. The kitchen smelt earthy and pungent. The bony, gelatinous oxtails sat in a heap on the counter, oozing thick dark blood into their paper packaging.

'I hate *kare-kare*,' she said. Sampaguita did not reply, just carried on stirring, tossing, shaking the frying pan. Noor poked the spongy meat with her forefinger. 'I said I *hate kare-kare*.'

Sampaguita turned and fired a sudden burst of staccato Tagalog at her. '*Umalis ka!*' she finished up. '*Umalis ka!*'

Noor knew what that meant. 'OK, OK,' she muttered, 'I'm *umaliska*-ing,' and she slunk from the kitchen and out onto the veranda: just in time, it turned out, to see the blonde American from number four walking across the compound to the Irish couple's house, carrying something wrapped in a cloth. The pretty woman opened the door, admired whatever was under the cloth, and welcomed her in. Noor squatted in the shade of the stunted date palm beside the villa and smoked a cigarette. Then she sat on the steps of the veranda and drew patterns in the dirt with a dead twig, trying to look as if she was just sitting there, not watching the house. The American left and a few minutes later Anjali from number five, Dr Maarlen's wife, came out of their villa and walked to number two, also carrying a tray of food. The Irishwoman came out again, with the baby this time, and talked with Anjali for a few minutes. The baby was tangling its hands in its mother's hair and babbling to itself, and when Anjali turned to go it waved at her and beamed a dimpled smile.

Noor got up abruptly and went inside.

'Sampaguita,' she said, 'is the *kare-kare* ready?'

'Ay, is it ready!' Sampaguita laughed a brown, gap-toothed smile at her. 'Is ready tonight, for Doctor. Now shoo!'

'I need some food, Sampaguita.'

'What a fat girl like you need food for?'

'Sampaguita,' Noor said, feeling her cheeks grow hot but standing her ground, drawing herself up to

43

her full height, 'I need some food, and I need a dish to put it in.'

Sampaguita just laughed this time and turned back to her pot of stew. Noor stood for a moment, then yanked open the door of the refrigerator and took stock of what was inside. The only things she knew how to make were marmalade sandwiches and baked beans with chopped ham and cheese. There was a half-open packet of crabsticks on the top shelf and she suddenly remembered a salad she had eaten once at the American Club, of soft shredded crab on a bed of lemony lettuce. She took out the crabsticks, and the remains of a sliced tomato. There was most of an iceberg lettuce and a bottle of mayonnaise, and she lined them up, too. She could not remember what else went in the salad. Cucumber—but there was no cucumber. Avocado? There were no avocados, either. She found a tin of sweetcorn in the cupboard: that would do. Ignoring Sampaguita's muttering, she carefully cut the crabsticks into cubes, sliced the lettuce into strips, drained the can of corn and mixed it all together, squirting mayonnaise liberally on top. It did not look very pretty. Then she thought of a trick of Sampaguita's, sprinkling red pepper on top of prawn cocktails to brighten them up. She found the tub and shook it over the salad. She eased the mixture into a plastic container and tapped some more red pepper on top, wiping away the smears around the edges. And then, before she could change her mind, she slipped her feet into her outdoor flip-flops and ran across the street.

When the woman and baby answered the door, she suddenly found that she did not know what to say, and all she could manage to do was to proffer the lunchbox. The woman took it, her grey eyes widening and her cupid's bow of a mouth forming an 'o', but before she could speak Noor turned and ran back home. Her heart was pounding and her palms were greased with sweat. She wanted a cigarette, but did not dare go out in case the Irishwoman was still standing there. The thought occurred to her that the woman might come over to the house, to say thank you: she had seen where Noor lived.

For the rest of the afternoon, Noor sat restlessly in front of the television, half-watching sitcom reruns on the Comedy Channel; waiting, but not quite knowing what it was that she was waiting for.

5

When she looks back over it, the day seems to have happened without her: or rather, regardless of her. She has never before had such a sense of not existing, not mattering. She is heavy and slow, and yet light with tiredness: her limbs too cumbersome to do her bidding, and yet the slightest puff of wind, it seems, could blow her away. He would sacrifice her, she knows that; he would sacrifice both her and Anna. Just like Abraham and Isaac: she has never thought of the story in that way before, as anything more than a story. *Father? Yes, my son? Abraham replied. The fire and wood are here, Isaac said, but where is the lamb for the burnt offering? Abraham answered, God Himself will provide the lamb for the burnt offering, my son. And the two of them went on together.* Never before has it been more than an allegory: about what God asks of us, about how hard it can be to do and understand his bidding. But now she hears the creak of the rope and the screams of the bound boy, his pleas and tears. Did Abraham stuff his mouth with rags to stop the cries? Turn him face-down to avoid looking him in the eye? *Then he reached out his hand and took the knife to slay his son.* He was right to do it, of course. In the eyes of God, he was right, and he was blessed. She has heard the story explained before, in sermons, countless times. And God, too, gave up His only son.

But yet. Something in her has cracked. A hairline fissure, invisible to the eye. But cracked, nonetheless.

*   *   *

She dozed off at the breakfast bar and woke with a shock to Anna's chatter: Euan had got her up and was bringing her in for breakfast. It was just after seven. The kitchen felt dingy: the narrow windows let in only a suggestion of light. Euan looked haggard, his skin greasy with the sweat of a restless night, his eyes puffy with blooming mauve bruises. From the way he looked at her, she knew she looked just as bad. She went to get up, and stumbled, her legs thick and torpid. She knocked the mug, which went spinning to the floor and shattered, shards of cheap china quivering. She stood looking at it, dumbly. Her vision was tight and grainy, as if her eyes had been sandpapered. She watched—felt herself watching—as Euan put Anna into the high chair and bent to pick up the pieces, daubed at the slick of coffee dregs. She thought of how he had kneeled before her last night, begging her to listen, to understand, and she felt weary with a strange, distant sort of sorrow; like remembering something from long ago. Euan straightened up with an involuntary groan, placed the pieces of cup on the counter. They looked at each other, and something, some movement he made, some tremor of his jaw or pulsing of his temple, sparked the habit of love and her hand reached out to pick a crumb of sleep from the corner of his eye. His eyes closed, eyelids fluttering, and he took her wrist and held it there, her hand against his face. His grip was strong and warm.

'I love you, Ruthie,' he said into the base of her palm. 'I love you.' She felt a slow, tight ache start to spread through her chest. Her tongue was swollen and dry in her mouth. She swallowed, started to speak. But Euan went on: 'We must remember, Ruth. God does not allow us to be tested beyond what we can bear. And when we are tested, He always provides a way out, so that we can withstand it.'

She closed her eyes. They smarted so badly when she shut them it was almost less painful to keep them open. She felt wetness start to seep through her eyelashes and she knew Euan would think she was crying: but she was not, not quite, not exactly.

Anna was banging her fists on the tray of her high chair.

'OK, Anna,' Euan said. 'OK, hang on.'

'You can't just tell her to "hang on",' Ruth said. 'She's a baby, she doesn't understand "hang on".'

Euan looked at her. And then, out of nowhere, she heard herself saying: 'And what would have happened to her if we'd been arrested at Bahrain

47

airport, then? Did you think of that?'

Euan turned away, bowed his head, and she suddenly wanted to hit him, hurt him.

'I said, did you think of that?' Her voice came out distorted, harsh. Her chest was so tight, now, it hurt to breathe.

'Christopher's not coming till ten,' Euan said. 'If you want to get an hour's sleep, you can. I'll deal with Anna.'

Before she could speak, before she could formulate a reply, there was a noise in the hallway. The maids had arrived. They rapped perfunctorily at the door, but from the inside: they had their own keys and they had let themselves in, were already exchanging outside shoes for flip-flops, putting down their bags. They introduced themselves in their stop-start, fluting language, then set about their work, completely at ease. Ruth felt horribly awkward, standing there bare-legged in the faded old T-shirt she slept in. Euan was embarrassed, too: he ran his hand several times through his hair until it was sticking up in all directions, messier than ever, and he tried to joke with the maids. After a minute or so, they retreated to the bedroom. Sleeping, now, was out of the question. They took turns to shower and dress, then had breakfast on the veranda. It was thick with dust: Ruth felt the dust settling on her damp hair and skin, and each mouthful of yogurt tasted of grit. They barely spoke, just took it in turns to steady Anna's hand and spoon more yogurt into her bowl. Outside the villa directly opposite, a teenage Arab girl slouched, smoking. She stared at them. She was sullen-looking, and fat, wearing tight blue jeans and a pink T-shirt a size too small for her. Ruth met her hostile stare for a moment then looked away. The day felt wrong, somehow. The maids, the dust, the Arab girl—it should not have happened like this; this should not have been their first day in Bahrain.

They killed the time waiting for Christopher by walking around the compound. They each held one of Anna's hands, playing one-two-three-*jump* whenever they came to a pothole: the dusty road was riddled with them. The compound was small, each squat bungalow the same as its neighbour, with its covered veranda and little garden. Two of the villas looked empty and run-down, paint flaking in saucer-sized scales from the walls, heaps of dust and dead leaves on their terraces, their gardens little more than scorched squares of grey scrub. But a few of their neighbours had made a real effort with their garden: little flower beds and pebbled pathways and plants arranged in pots. One even had roses: huge, crimson, overblown blossoms twined up in an immaculately whitewashed terrace. It would be hard, Ruth thought, to cultivate things here, in a city wrested from the desert. Things must very quickly disintegrate, in the dust and the heat. A few days without water, and the plants would shrivel and die; a few days without cleaning, and the sands would start to reassert their rightful claim. It must take constant vigilance, constant attention, to stay ahead of the desert.

At the bottom of the compound was a small swimming pool. The water level was low and there was a dirty brown tidemark around the sides. Several of the tiles were cracked, or dropping away from the sides. A strip of fake grass, bleached yellow by the sun, ran around the edge of the pool, and a couple of plastic sunloungers were stacked

49

along the wall beside a concrete changing hut and a rudimentary metal shower. Euan picked up a hollow metal pole and stirred at the water.

'Nobody must use it,' he said. 'Pity. I wonder why.'

She did not reply.

They walked around the swimming pool and through the metal fence onto the compound's tennis court. Its surface was cracked and faded, its net ripped and sagging in the middle. They sat for a few minutes on the bench. Its green paint was coated with a layer of grey sand. Ruth picked with a fingernail at the edges where the paint had bubbled and chipped, and Anna squatted down and scratched at the tarmac.

'Come on,' she said, hauling her daughter onto her lap. 'You'll get your dress all dirty.' Anna squirmed and started to cry.

'Well,' said Euan, 'neither of us even plays tennis. And it's not as if we'll have much time to be idling around swimming, anyhow.'

'No,' she said, keeping her voice calm. 'You certainly won't.'

'Ruth . . .' he said. But he did not say anything more.

The sky above them was white and hazy. From somewhere nearby came the dull, clattering noise of piledrivers and the whine of stone-cutting.

It wasn't meant to be like this, Ruth wanted to say.

They walked back in silence.

*   *   *

When Christopher arrived, they seemed to slip into

50

their roles: the Reverend, and the Reverend's Wife. Christopher couldn't know, Euan had said, that she knew about the Bible-smuggling. It gave her a mean, savage pleasure greeting him, asking about his T-shirt (it was another Grateful Dead one; his private joke, he explained, because a 'Jesus Saves' one would be out of the question), and answering his questions about the villa, were they comfortable, had the maids arrived, all the while knowing that he didn't know she knew. It surprised her, how easy it was to prevaricate, dissemble. She felt Euan watching her, and wondered if she was overdoing it. But even this gave her a bitter satisfaction.

They drove around Manama, Christopher keeping up a stream of commentary. The highways, even at this time of the morning, were chock-a-block: a mass of oversized cars jammed nose-to-tail, blasting their horns at the slightest provocation, real or imagined. They moved in fits and starts. Downtown Manama, so far as Ruth seemed to see, was a sprawl of low-rise buildings, most of them white but many of them discoloured with exhaust fumes and dust. New blocks stood side by side with others in various states of dereliction or decrepitude, and yet others in varying stages of construction. There seemed no rhyme or reason to it. Stray cats slunk in towers of tyres on patches of wasteland. Indian migrant workers, thin men with deeply lined faces and dirt-streaked cloths wound around their heads and mouths, wheeled breezeblocks balanced on rusty barrows. There were few other pedestrians on the pavements. As they drove round, she and Euan took turns to answer Christopher's questions, and to ask further questions of their own. They were all equivocating,

51

she realised. Pretending an interest where there was none, paying lip-service to sculptures or feats of engineering, puffed up with airy lies—like the Pharisees' bread. That was what they were: the yeast of the Pharisees, hypocrisy itself.

*   *   *

It was like that at church, too. The Cathedral of St Thomas was smaller than she had imagined; no bigger or grander than a modern parish church. She expressed her surprise at this, and Euan pointed out that 'cathedra' simply meant 'the seat of the bishop', and bore no relation to the size or style of the church. That he knew this, and the way he told her—civil, jocular—made her furious with him. He was the Reverend, he was saying. He knew what was right. This was a foolish thought, she knew, petty: but yet she could not shake it. It was the way he had been behaving all morning, like a martyr; not rising to her gibes, turning the other cheek. He knew he was in the right—even if he was wrong, he knew he was right—he knew he was doing the right thing. He would be praying for her to come round, to understand; this, somehow, made things worse.

They had a tour of the building—the bright white nave with its rows of blue-cushioned stackable chairs; the modest chancel with its simple pine altar and lectern and an unadorned wooden cross suspended from the ceiling; the east-facing apse inset with three modest stained-glass windows; the little cupboard of a sacristy—and the satellite rooms used for Sunday school, Bible study, meetings and other church functions, then met the Archdeacon. He was a mild, bespectacled Englishman called

Graham Day, who greeted them politely, and started talking about the help they could give him with study groups and community outreach. It was a sensitive subject, he explained, because although freedom of conscience was enshrined in the Bahraini constitution, Islam was the official state religion, and for Bahraini nationals, conversion to Christianity was a grave offence. Tales circulated, he said, of the confiscation of passports, the denial of medical treatment, the loss of employment: and not just for the convert. Friends and family of a convert were liable to be ostracised and treated as second-class citizens, too.

'"I came to set a man against his father,"' Christopher interjected, '"and a daughter against her mother, and a daughter-in-law against her mother-in-law; and a man's enemies will be the members of his household."'

Ruth looked at Euan. She willed him, dared him to look at her. But he kept his gaze on the Reverend, and did not flinch. She wondered if the Reverend Day was in on the plot, too. If all of the polite talk was for her benefit, and if once she left, as soon as she left, they would start discussing the real matters. Or if the Reverend, like her, was meant to be innocent of what was going on. Christopher certainly looked on edge. His eyes kept flitting from Euan to the Reverend, and he was too eager to jump into the conversation, to agree with what the Reverend said or quote from an appropriate verse. He was behaving like a man who had something to hide. Euan, on the other hand, looked perfectly calm. He had slipped into his professional mode: easy, assured, with a ready, confident smile. Watching him, if she did not

53

already know, she would not know that he was concealing something. She had not thought that possible. But when the conversation turned to her, and to Anna, she felt herself too slip into a familiar version of herself, one who could talk about the church at Kircubbin with a smile, even sketch an amusing picture of the grey stone walls huddled defensively against the squally winds blowing in from the Irish Sea and the creeping damp of the vestry beyond the reach of the fan heaters. She had not been conscious, before, of these capacities within herself.

*　　　*　　　*

And the afternoon, too. Christopher left her and Anna back at the compound, then drove off with Euan. 'To discuss a new study group,' Christopher lied, looking her straight in the eye and not even blinking.

'A new study group?' she said, making her voice bright. 'Well, have fun. You're right to drop us back here, Anna would only get in your way.'

Euan leaned in to kiss her, but she turned her head so he only brushed her cheek.

*　　　*　　　*

She tried to sleep, but Anna would not sleep; and the hard floors were too dangerous to let her run about on, unobserved. In the end, they sat in front of the television, in the lightless central room, and watched a series of mindless children's programmes. Visitors came by, her new neighbours, each bearing a dish of some sort. A doll-like

54

American, with fluffy blonde hair and round blue eyes, who brought banana bread—golden, perfectly risen, still warm—and said things like 'oh my' and 'golly'. Ruth invited her in, and they sat on the divan and made conversation. Trudy was only twenty-two, even younger than Ruth. Her husband was a construction worker; he had been posted out to the Middle East three years ago. They had got married, she said, the week before they came, in order that she could come with him. They had lived in Dubai for a while, and now Bahrain. They were trying to save enough money to build their own house back in Ohio, and start a family. They had only meant to come for a year, at first, and she missed home something shocking. She gazed at Anna greedily. If she got pregnant, she said, they would have to go home: they had agreed on it. She talked non-stop for at least twenty minutes. Then she asked Ruth what she was doing—she had heard Ruth's husband was a minister?—what church they were based at, how long they were staying. And once more Ruth dissembled, answering the questions smoothly, inventing schemes they would be running at church and projects they would be involved in; answers that could have been true, that should have been true. After Trudy came Anjali, a plump, pretty Indian woman who brought a dish of samosas and a tub of yogurt sauce. They had the same conversation, a variation of it, and Ruth tried to stick to the same answers. As she left, Anjali pointed out her house— it was the one with the roses—and invited Ruth to come over some time, any time. After she had gone, Ruth felt suddenly lonely. She had imagined herself and Euan throwing themselves into the social life out here, into the church. She had wondered about the people she would meet, the friends she would make. But now, she was sure that they would have to keep a low profile, hold themselves somehow aloof from everyone else, in case they slipped, or gave something away. She had not enjoyed the conversations with either Trudy or Anjali. They had seemed too much like a test, as if she could be caught out; her voice to her ears sounded hollow, insincere.

She imagined how different it would be if she didn't know, and wondered if she would rather not know: if it would be better if Euan had never told her. Or if she would have worked it out for herself, anyway: *There is nothing concealed that will not be disclosed, or hidden that will not be made known.*

She phoned home, and that too was a dissimulation: feigning excitement at the place and the people; telling her mother about the maids and the neighbours with as much enthusiasm as she could muster. When she put down the phone, she felt further from home, and more alone, than ever.

Another knock came at the door.

'Let's not answer it,' Ruth said to Anna. 'Let's pretend we're sleeping, or dead.' But of course she went to see who was there. It was the teenager from the villa opposite, the one Ruth had seen smoking that morning. She stood, mute, then thrust a Tupperware container out in front of her, muttered something, then turned and ran back to her house.

'Thank you,' Ruth called after her, but she did not reply. 'Well,' Ruth said, aloud, to Anna, to nobody. 'What an odd girl.' She took the Tupperware into the kitchen and prised it open. It was a sorry-looking salad made of limp lettuce, tinned sweetcorn, chunks of tomato and some

56

sort of pink cubes, smothered in mayonnaise and paprika. Ruth poked at a lump with her finger: it was jellied crabstick. She shuddered and scraped the mess into the bin, and rinsed the container in the sink.

There was nothing more to do. The maids had cleaned the house, unpacked the clothes and left food for the evening in a pot on the hob.

She went back into the living room and wondered what she was going to do. This was not supposed to be what her first day in Bahrain was like, she thought, once more. This was not how it was supposed to be.

6

Saturday morning should have been Noor's next appointment with Dr Badawi. She had been seeing the therapist twice a week since arriving in Bahrain. But after the last time, there had been a showdown with her father. Dr Badawi had instructed Noor to make a list of things she liked about herself and things other people liked about her. When Noor started to get into a downward spiral, she was to take a deep breath, count to twenty, and remember her list. Noor had tried to make the list that evening—she really had—but she had not been able to come up with a single thing to write down.

'I hate Dr Badawi,' she had announced to her father. 'I hate her and I'm not going back. And if you try to make me go back—'

'*Aiwa,*' her father had interrupted her. '*Mafi mushkila.* You don't want to go back, you don't go back, *tayib*, problem over.'

She was taken aback at that. Her mother would have argued, threatened, cajoled. But her father was losing his patience with her, she could see that: he was regretting having agreed that she could move to live with him, already, after less than a month. Noor had quite liked the clinic at Riffa: the cool blue walls and antique wooden ceiling fans, the manicured gardens and miniature fountains. Dr Badawi, an Egyptian doctor in her mid-fifties with a black hennaed bob and rimless glasses, a smooth, low voice and steady gaze, had not been so bad, either. But once Noor had declared so vehemently, so confrontationally, that she was never going there again, there was no way of backing down.

She spent the morning slumped on her bed, staring at the ceiling, lacking the energy to go to the basement and work on her writing, or even to sit outside and watch for the missionaries. For a while, she tried to count the cracks on the plaster ceiling. But each crack branched out into so many smaller subsidiaries that it was impossible to tell for certain where one began and another ended.

*   *   *

Dr al-Husayn came back at lunchtime, and after eating the reheated leftovers of the *kare-kare*, they set off for an interview with the headmistress of Noor's prospective new school. Noor's mother had insisted that if Noor really did go to school in Bahrain she should attend an institution where the British curriculum was taught. Of the two possibilities, the British School and St Jude's, the latter was the biggest and the best endowed, with the glossier prospectus. *In our school we encourage the notion that personal improvement and development is always possible. We seek to promote an environment in which it is considered natural to help and support others within the school. We take a tough, zero-tolerance approach to bullying.* The spine of the prospectus was broken at that page, and Noor imagined her father poring over it, grimly, meaningfully. She tossed the prospectus into the back of the car. Her father glanced at her, but said nothing. Dr al-Husayn did not quite know how he had ended up with custody of the problem child, rather than her mother. Noor saw the thought on his face as plainly as if he had spoken it.

They skirted the traffic snarl of downtown Manama and joined the highway to Madinat'Isa, or Isa Town, the middle-class suburb where most of Bahrain's private schools were situated. They drove in silence. Noor was wearing a long, shapeless brown skirt that made her feel like she was dressed in a hessian sack, and she had plaited her hair back neatly. Her father, for once, was not in *thobe* and *gutra* but one of his old suits, from his previous life. It was slightly too small for him, now; Noor could see the creases in the jacket and the buttons straining. He looked as ill at ease in it as he did in his Arab robes.

They drove into the school complex past the playing fields, which in the heat of the afternoon were yellow and empty. On the edge of the school grounds was an impressive-looking building housing the sports hall and indoor tennis courts. Workmen were toiling on what was to be an eight-lane swimming pool, due for completion in time for the new school year. It was to be four metres at the deep end, so that students could dive and learn scuba techniques. Dr al-Husayn had been impressed by this. But Noor hated sports, especially swimming. The thought of group swimming lessons and galas, of struggling to change into a too-tight costume behind a towel, of having to parade practically naked in front of other girls, not to mention the shame of communal showers— didn't her father see this, couldn't he understand? She hunched lower in her seat and scowled when he pointed out the swimming pool, feeling more utterly miserable than she had known it was possible to feel. The only thing that made her able to get out of the car was the thought that by the time the swimming pool was finished, she wouldn't be here any more, anyway.

A smiling prefect was waiting for them in reception, to escort them to the headmistress's study. She chatted about the school and her experiences there as they walked through the corridors and up the stairs, never once losing her smile. She addressed one or two questions to Noor, but did not ask anything directly about Noor's last school, or why she had left in the middle of a school year—the middle of a school term—to come to Bahrain. Noor wondered if she had been warned, or how much she knew. She mumbled her answers, could not meet the older girl's eye, felt her father's silent disapproval. Then she tripped on the hem of her stupid sack-skirt and almost fell. Her father caught her arm in time, and there was not a trace of laughter in the prefect's expression of concern, but even so Noor felt herself burning up with humiliation. It would be as bad here as it was in England, she suddenly knew that. You could never make a truly new start, ever. No matter how far you went, you could never leave your old self behind. She felt another wave of pure misery wash over her.

She sat silent, eyes downcast, while the headmistress conversed with her father. The headmistress, a tall, broad-shouldered Englishwoman of about fifty, had a brisk, no-nonsense way of speaking. They talked about the school, about the curriculum; about how good Noor's academic record had been until the divorce and the problems in school. Noor glanced at her father as he mentioned *the problems in school*, worried that he would say too much, give something away. But he simply emphasised his desire for a school with a strong pastoral care network and systems in place to identify and combat sources of bullying. *We take a tough, zero-tolerance approach.*

Then it was Noor's turn. She spoke haltingly about the books she liked in English, the subjects they had studied in history, a biology field trip she had enjoyed. Her mother had warned her to prepare something about extra-curricular activities, so she said she liked writing poetry, and would be interested in editing the school magazine. She stumbled as she said it. The school magazine had been her mother's idea, not hers. But the headmistress nodded smoothly, did not bat an eyelid. She turned back to Noor's father and they began discussing whether it would be better for Noor to start in the coming summer term, or, given the disruption to this academic year, to wait until the autumn and repeat the year.

Relieved that her part was played, Noor sat back and gazed at the paintings behind the headmistress's head: watercolour scenes of

English country life through the seasons. They showed golden harvest fields and boys sleeping on haystacks, bare black trees on a starlit night and fields of bluebells in spring. They were all lies, Noor thought. Everything was lies. A haystack was prickly and full of insects; trees in winter were dead and slimy. Nothing was ever as good as it looked on the surface, as it was in pictures—or words. You read a book where children set off on a train journey and shared segments of an orange, and it sounded so romantic. But if you did it yourself it was just a smelly, juddering train and the orange was dry and sour-tasting and made your fingers sticky. Words were lies, pictures were lies, a pretence that the thing they showed was better than it actually was.

The headmistress was standing up, extending her hand. Noor scrambled to her feet and took the outstretched hand. It was dry and firm. Her own hand, she was all too aware, was limp and clammy.

'Congratulations,' the headmistress was saying. 'We would be happy to welcome you as a student. We just have to decide on the best time for you to start. Let's have a think about this over the next week or so.'

Noor's father thanked the headmistress, profusely: so profusely she felt embarrassed for him. He whistled as they walked back to the car. His troublesome daughter would soon be back in school and life would settle down again. She watched him thinking it.

*   *   *

Dr al-Husayn had to go back into work after that. He left Noor back at the compound and said, 'Don't worry, when you start school you'll soon make friends.' Noor could not even summon the strength to scoff at him. She spoke to her mother, who was keen to hear about how the interview had gone. When her mother heard the news, she said she was thrilled: that Noor would be able to put everything behind her now, and make a fresh start. Noor did not bother to contradict her, either. It took less energy just to agree. She let her mother chat on about inconsequential things—Noor's brother Jamal and his new girlfriend, how she was ever so pretty, how good she was at tennis. That would have been her mother's dream, Noor knew: to have a daughter who was slim and pretty, like her, and fabulous at tennis, and the two of them could go arm in arm together and the shop assistants would say, My, you'd think the two of you were sisters! When her mother had heard what had happened, the first thing she had said was: What did I do to deserve you as a daughter? Tell me—what did I do wrong?

When the phone call ended, Noor wandered out onto the veranda. The sun was setting and the evening breeze was picking up. It whirled the grey dust of the compound into a cloud, a miasma, so that you couldn't see the bottoms of things: villas, cars, walls, everything looked as if it was floating, suspended. Noor sat for almost two hours, and in all of that time there was not a single indication that even one of the villas was inhabited. The lack of windows meant that even if someone was having a party, there was no sign from the outside. It meant, too, that you caught no more than glimpses of people: as they parked their cars and carried their paper sacks of groceries up their little pathways, or as they walked down to their cars, dressed up and heading out somewhere, to one of the big hotel bars or private clubs. Tonight, there was not even that. Noor had not known such loneliness was possible.

When she had insisted, day in, day out until her parents caved in and agreed, that she did not want to go to another school in England, her visions had been of the Bahrain they visited when she and Jamal were little. The heat, the swimming pool at the American Club, the waiters bringing unlimited supplies of Coca-Cola and fruit cocktails, elaborate concoctions with paper umbrellas and straws. The Aladdin's cave of the souk, packed with sweets and stuffed toys, the camel farm in the desert and the salty sea at Al-Jayazir, the waters so saline that you couldn't stay under, even if you tried: that you could lie back and read a newspaper on. The picnic trips out to Dar Island with their hordes of cousins, cool boxes full of grape juice and *khubz* flatbreads, Tupperware cartons of sliced *qoozi*, legs of lamb stuffed with spices, onion, boiled eggs and rice. And the delicious Persian pancakes her aunt Azar used to make, thick and greasy and salty and sprinkled with chopped herbs. They had been some of the best days of her life, those weeks when she was part of a ready-made gang. Racing bicycles up and down the dusty avenue of the cousins' compound or playing on the roof of a downtown apartment building, games of chase in the stairwells and dressing up in headscarves and lipstick like the aunts. Even Noor's mother, much as she moaned about her husband's family not liking her, had been happy then, escaping the cold and drizzle of England for the sun. But now the cousins had grown up and moved away: they were studying in America

64

or working in Dubai; and those who remained were married with young children and wore the *hijab* for real. Noor felt as different from them as she did from the English girls at boarding school.

She watched the sentry climb out of his hut to take a piss behind the empty villa. He walked bow-legged, as if he had been riding a horse too long. She supposed his legs got terribly cramped, sitting in the little brick box for hour after hour. She wondered what he did to pass the time in the long, lonely hours of the night, other than listen to his Urdu radio stations and read his newspaper by the light of his lamp.

She stood up. The missionaries were not going to appear. She had a strange longing to see them again; she did not know why. But she could not even tell if they were in or out, because they had no car of their own. She supposed they were out: everyone seemed to have somewhere to be. Everyone but her.

She went back inside and resumed her Account. She was almost finished, now. Just a few more pages, a few more days, to go.

7

Euan was invited to speak at the Sunday morning service. They got there early, left Anna in the crèche and joined the Reverend Day and his wife as they greeted parishioners. Everyone was keen to meet the new Irish deacon and his young wife. Euan, meeting people, shaking hands, sharing jokes, was in his element; and she felt a sudden pang: of love for him, of missing him, of sorrow. His years at Braemore Park had been tough: a lot of introspection and self-study. Ordinands were made to understand and confront their own weaknesses and failings, undergo an intense examination of their faith. There were times, at the rare weekends they had together, when he had collapsed in her arms in tears, had been (she feared) on the verge of some sort of breakdown. He had often considered dropping out. But he had come through, and become stronger for it, both in himself and in his faith. And increasingly, as his confidence and experience grew, Ruth was watching him visibly blossom in his calling. By September, he would be officially ordained, able not just to take services and preach, but to preside over Communion. He would be assigned a small congregation of his own—a rural parish, most likely, or several small churches. And she could see he was ready for it: he was restless in Kirkskeagh, living in the farm cottage and assisting with their own congregation.

She stood beside him and smiled, shook hands, answered questions about Ireland and about Bahrain. Yes, it is a long way. Oh, very much, so far, everyone is really so friendly.

St Thomas's had a healthy-sized congregation and a good mix of people. Rawly shaven young men and fresh-cheeked young women, families with babies, a few with teenage children. About half of them were British expats and the rest were Indian or Filipino: none were Arab. The Indian women were dressed in a shimmer of saris, their husbands in dark suits and gleaming shoes. The Filipinos wore high heels and hats and handbags, button-down shirts and cuff links. Little girls were in party dresses, froths of white frills and sashes, and ribbons in their hair, and many of the little boys were in sailor suits. It was like going back half a century. There was a buzz of anticipation in the air, too, an atmosphere you rarely felt before an ordinary service at home. Anglican congregations were diminishing by the year; or by the week, it sometimes felt. Roman Catholic churches were seeing an increase in numbers, mostly from the Poles and Eastern European immigrants who wanted to attend High Mass, and at the Baptist churches American-style evangelical worship was growing in popularity. She had been to a few evangelical services. She found it all a bit embarrassing, too earnest and flamboyant, the shouting and tears and speaking in tongues. But Euan insisted that church had to be more accessible and he was encouraging young people in Kirkskeagh and Kircubbin to form music groups and play in services. At Christmas there had been a heated debate among the elders about whether or not a boy should be allowed to play his electric guitar. This had infuriated Euan. In his study there was a red and black poster of Jesus in the style of the iconic Che Guevara images, with the slogan: *Meek. Mild. As If.* He liked to give copies of the poster to his youth group to remind them that Jesus was not a long-suffering wimp in a nightie— that was the phrase he used: 'wimp in a nightie'— but a passionate, revolutionary radical. *I did not come to bring peace, but a sword.* If Jesus was alive today, Euan said, He would not have sung soft, gentle songs about sparrows and sunlight. He would have rocked out. Young people needed to know that Christianity was not about suppressing or

67

repressing yourself. It was quite the opposite: it let you express yourself as fully and exuberantly as you possibly could. Euan had also got himself into hot water over his proposals to conduct informal Q&A sessions for non-believers: because he was emphatic that he did not want to hold them in the vicinity of the church.

'Think about it,' he'd said to her, over a barely touched dinner, 'these people will be unsure of themselves, awkward, vulnerable and feeling unbelievably exposed. We don't want to meet in the crypt, or in an anonymous, echoey village hall. Why not meet in the pub, casually, and we can discuss whatever matters might arise over a drink? I'm not saying we get ourselves stocious, far from it. I just think we need to meet people on their own ground. And we need to do it sooner rather than later.' There were more Muslims, he was fond of saying, than Anglicans in Ireland. More Muslims than Anglicans!

The final few stragglers arrived, the final smiles were exchanged and hands shaken and the service began. After the Collect, the Reverend called upon the Reverend Deacon Armstrong to speak. She felt the eyes of the congregation upon them. They were sitting at the front, and she could feel the gaze, as if it was a weight. She sat up straighter. She felt Euan take a breath and say a quick, silent prayer. Then he stood up, walked to the lectern. He paused before speaking, ran his fingers through his hair. He had spent ten minutes that morning damping it down, and now he was yanking it back into wild tufts. He looked up and out at the congregation, taking in as many of them as possible—that was the technique, that was what you were taught to do—and began to speak. He spoke of his own personal journey to Christ: the moment when, aged fifteen and on a Boys' Brigade camping trip, he had asked Jesus into his heart. The dismay of his well-to-do parents and the derision of so many 'friends' when he started attending church on Sundays and worship groups after school. He spoke of the doubts and fears, the struggles and setbacks, that were an inevitable and necessary part of any Christian's journey. He spoke of the Mission to Seafarers, the reason he was here in Manama. He recited the Mission's motto, and the perils that seafarers face: loneliness, danger, separation from loved ones. And then, walking out from behind the lectern and into the aisle he declared that these were problems that faced us all: that in many ways we all were seafarers, trying to navigate stormy waters in tempestuous times, seeking the sanctuary that only God could provide.

He was a compelling speaker. She could feel the audience listening, swelling, following where he led. But for the first time—the first time ever, and she had heard him speak many times—what he said did not feel real. She could see what he was doing, and how he was doing it: the making of eye contact, the dramatic pauses, the raising and lowering of his voice, the stepping forward into the aisle. All of it was choreographed, meticulously practised. She thought of how, in the early days of his training, he and his fellow students were told to go to comedy nights at the Capital Club and the Ha'penny Bridge, to study the comedians and learn how to hold an audience, how to work an audience, how to pace yourself and how to perform. Ruth had gone along with them, once or twice, and thought they made a comic group themselves, sitting in a pale-faced huddle nursing their pint or their lime-and-sodas, concentrating too hard on the comedians, frantically scribbling down notes between sets and conferring with each other over a particular technique or method of delivery. Euan was among the best of them: he was a natural performer. And it was performing, she suddenly saw, that he was doing. The words were shells; hollow, essentially meaningless. It was how he strung them together, the pace of them, the rhythms. What he said was unimportant: it was the way he said it. He could have been preaching Islam, or the merits of batch-calving: the audience would have listened and believed in exactly the same way. She wondered why this had never occurred to her before.

When he sat down beside her, she whispered, Well done, but she did not look at him. She could feel the heat coming from him, hear how fast his heart was beating. He was fired up, alive. He was someone else, no longer the man she woke up with, no longer the man she prayed with last night (Paul's journey to Italy, in Acts 27: *When neither sun nor stars appeared for many days and the storm continued raging, we finally gave up all hope of being saved*; chosen by Euan, of course, as a message to her). Precisely because she knew him so well, knew what he was doing, and how he was doing it, why, he was become almost a stranger.

The service continued.

The reading was from chapter 11 of Mark's gospel, and the sermon was an exposition of the same passage, where Jesus curses the fig tree for not bearing any fruit, even though it is not the

70

season for figs.

'People often worry that Jesus is being petulant, or arbitrary, or cruel,' the Reverend Day said in his dry, scholarly voice. 'The tree isn't being offered any *choice* as to whether or not it bears fruit, unlike Luke's parable where the withered fig tree is given a year's grace. But, you see, if you read Mark's account *in context*, then you understand that it is deliberately bookended with the descriptions of Jesus cleansing the Temple . . .'

She glanced up at Euan. He was frowning, nodding, fully engaged. She turned her attention back to the Reverend.

'. . . and so you see,' he was saying, his voice growing louder as he slipped into declamatory mode, 'at first you have the *appearance* of fruitfulness, i.e. the leaves on the tree *and* the rituals of religion. But up close, there is nothing of sustenance: it is a religion without substance. This lesson is one of the most important lessons in the Gospels about faith. It *is* a matter of life and death.'

Again, those words. *But, Ruth, it's far more than a matter of life and death.* The pallor of his face and the intensity of his eyes. It had scared her, seeing him like that. Now, he was nodding so vigorously his chair was quivering. She inched her chair away from his, but it still shook with the reverberations.

For the rest of the service, the Creed and the prayers, the penitence and benediction and receiving of Communion—especially the receiving of Communion—she tried to force her mind to stay focused and reverent. She recited the Lord's Prayer loudly, matching her voice and her rhythms to Euan's, feeling her words blend with his, and their words with those of the people around them. *Now*

71

and for ever, Amen. But she felt like a fraud. She felt, for the first time ever, that the words she was saying were lip-service only; meaningless.

*   *   *

After the service, there was tea and coffee and baklava: yet more small talk to be made while people milled around praising Euan's speech. Names and faces jockeying to be closer, to be closest, to be the one who refilled his coffee cup or brought him another tooth-numbing bite of baklava—and they pressed around Ruth, too, as if she was part of him, could reflect the same glory.

It was a relief to get home. Euan was going back to church after lunch to take the afternoon youth group and to speak again at the evening service. At least, that is what he said. She did not bother to question him: she suddenly realised that she did not care even if he was lying to her.

While Anna had her nap, she lay in the dim bedroom with a cold towel over her eyes. There was an aching, throbbing behind her temples, a buzzing in her head. But she could not sleep. She got up after only ten minutes, and busied herself baking barmbrack for the neighbours, in return for their gifts of food. It was the wrong time of year for barmbrack. Her mother made it every Hallowe'en, baking trinkets inside it. A dried pea, a twig, a silver coin, all wrapped in foil. Finding the coin meant riches for the forthcoming year but the stick meant marital dispute and the dried pea, bad luck in love. It was an occasion of much hilarity, sitting around the kitchen table with her father and the farmhands while her mother cut the still-warm loaf and handed

72

around the slices. She always got a silver coin, as did the farmhands. Her father always ended up with the twig and no one ever found the dried pea. They joked that it was in the crust given to Trooper, the Border collie, or later her pup, Rosie.

Anna sat in the high chair and played with a handful of raisins while Ruth warmed the milk and measured out the yeast and sugar, sifted the spices and weighed the tea-soaked fruit. They had gone shopping, yesterday, to one of the big malls, to buy everything she needed. The mall was massive, big beyond imagining. It looked from the outside like a fairy-tale Oriental palace, its rose-blush façade decorated with midnight-blue tiles and painted stars, its dome made of thousands of sheets of curved glass. Inside, the escalators were flanked by forty-foot palms. There were more shops, in that single mall, than in the whole of Belfast— the whole of Northern Ireland, probably. After they had wandered round, and stocked up on groceries, they sat in the forecourt of Starbucks and had cappuccinos and muffins. It was evidently the place to be seen. It was packed with people, mainly Arabs, and there were signs up everywhere saying that each coffee bought you twenty minutes' sitting time, after which you had to buy another or go. It was strange watching dignified-looking men in headdresses and white robes slurping iced coffees through straws. And the women did not eat or drink at all—they couldn't, without taking their veils off, and many of them had grilles of mesh over their eyes, so even their eyes and foreheads were covered up. Instead they sat silently waiting for their menfolk to eat and drink, or feeding their children. It had made Ruth feel uneasy: she had been glad when their twenty minutes were up and they left.

Her mother's recipe was complicated, calling for lots of kneading and mixing, beating and sifting, waiting and testing. On a farm, the day revolved around mealtimes. Ruth's mother was constantly at the Aga, making cooked breakfasts for Ruth's father and the farmhands after morning milking, a hot dinner for whoever happened to be there at midday, soda bread or scones for tea, then supper for the three of them, cakes and a tureen of soup on standby for the vet or the neighbours or whoever else might drop by. But although Ruth had frequently been conscripted into chopping or mixing or stirring, she never particularly took to it. She was not a natural baker, like her mother; her dough was sticky and her loaves leaden, her stew too watery or not salty enough. No matter how many times she did it, she could never remember offhand the ratio of eggs to sugar to flour in a Victoria sponge, or whether you used baking soda with buttermilk, or baking powder. She was much happier outside, with her father, walking the cattle out to pasture, or bringing them in during the warmer months for milking; forking silage into their food troughs during winter, even scraping and hosing down the loafing area. She knew the signs of milk fever and of bloat, she knew how to check a field for excess clover. Once, she had helped her father save a heifer's life by piercing her side and rumen with a screwdriver, a sort of makeshift trochar and cannula, for fear the animal would die before the vet could get there or a stomach tube could take effect. That had been frightening: the bellowing animal, terrified, snorting foam from its nose and rolling its eyes, its stomachs swollen to four or five

74

times their usual size. She had had to help steady it while her father raised his arm and stabbed, with as much force as he could, to break through the tough hide and into the rumen wall and release the built-up gas, which came out in a rush, with blood, and the animal screaming. But she had not flinched. Just as she did not flinch when rabbits had to be shot, or young male calves put down, or else sold for veal. She should have been born a boy, her father sometimes joked, and then she could have inherited the farm from him. And she had considered it, anyhow: it had been at the back of her mind when she started her degree at agricultural college. But by then there was Euan. And besides, it was not an easy job, running a farm. It was lonely, hard, back-breaking work. Perhaps, even if it had been a real option, she would have decided against it, anyway.

She made three batches of barmbrack, six oblong, slightly lumpy loaves. While the last pair were cooling in their tins she showered and dressed in fresh clothes, washed Anna's face and tied a ribbon in her hair. They set off for the neighbours'. The first villa in the compound, to the right of hers, was empty. The third was occupied (Trudy had told her) by a middle-aged Englishman. She knocked, but there was no answer. The fourth was Trudy's: but there was no answer from her, either. Across from Trudy's, past the run-down swimming pool and tennis court, was Anjali's villa, with the blowsy roses. A man answered the door, thin-faced with a balding head and thick grey moustache. He must be Anjali's father, was Ruth's immediate thought, but then he introduced himself as Maarlen, her husband. Anjali appeared, wearing turquoise *salwar kameez* and a shimmering golden scarf. She was plaiting her hair as she walked, her fingers moving fast. The rope of hair hung thick and fat almost to her waist. When she greeted them, Ruth noticed a neat bump under her tunic. Anjali cast her eyes downward, modest.

'It is true,' she said. 'I am five months gone with child. It shall be our first.' She took the barmbrack and invited Ruth in to see their house, and the baby's room. It was strange being in a different villa, the mirror image of her own. Inside it was immaculate: thick cream wallpaper, printed with strawberries the size of Ruth's fist, mock-crystal chandeliers and rows of oil paintings, all in identical faux-antique gilt frames. In the centre of her living room was a massive cream sofa and matching chaise longue, both angled towards a huge flat-screen television. There were nests of wooden tables with onyx bowls of pot-pourri and other bric-a-brac, candles and censers and everywhere statuettes, large and small, bronze and polished wood, of Ganesh, the Elephant God. The second bedroom—Ruth's spare room—was to be the baby's. It had plush carpet and embossed wallpaper, and in pride of place stood a canopy-cot, cascading with lace and ribbons, like an illustration from a children's fairy tale. Ruth thought she had never seen anything so gaudy in her life.

Both Maarlen and Anjali were twinkling, waiting for her reaction.

'My goodness,' she said, 'it's quite something,' and they clapped their hands and laughed.

'I read about one hundred *Hello!* magazines to find inspiration,' Anjali said. 'Maarlen brings them home from the hospital, sometimes they are a little behind the date but it does not matter so much.'

'I bet Little Miss Princess has a beautiful

bedroom at home,' Maarlen said, bending down to ruffle Anna's hair.

Ruth laughed, thinking of Anna's battered cot—the cot that had been hers, when she was a baby—and scuffed plastic toy-box. 'Not quite,' she said. 'We've been living in one of the old cottages on my parents' farm, until we get our own place. It's only temporary, and full of their old furniture. We haven't been able to decorate it at all, really.'

'Your family has a farm?' Anjali said, her eyes round.

'A small dairy farm.'

'Dairy, this is milk-cows, yes?'

'That's right.'

'And you have pigs, and sheep, and ducks too?'

'No. Just cows.'

'I find this very interesting. Ireland is good for farms, very green, yes?'

'Very rainy.'

'That is why she has such a good complexion, Maarlen. The moisture in the air. I know Egyptian ladies who travel to Ireland for their complexions. This is true, Ruth! They go in the hope that Irish rain will make their skin soft. Maybe one day I come to visit you in your farm!'

Ruth had a sudden vision of Anjali holding up the gauzy ends of her sari and tiptoeing through the cow-clap and slurry of the farmyard. She suppressed a giggle. I must tell Euan this, she thought.

But the thought made her immediately sad. She wouldn't tell him, she realised. She couldn't. He would frown and think she was being uncharitable, mocking their neighbours. Or even if he didn't, even if he wasn't so judgemental, he wouldn't

77

understand. He would smile, and pretend to, but he wouldn't really understand. He was not too fond of the smell and muck of the farmyard, either. To him, the cattle were messy beasts with slubbery noses and fetid odours.

*   *   *

The villa beside Anjali's and Maarlen's was occupied by an English couple working as teachers at one of Bahrain's private schools. A swarthy Pakistani maid answered the door. She did not appear to speak any English. She stood blankly as Ruth pointed at her villa and at the barmbrack and tried to communicate with gestures that she wanted to greet her new neighbours. Finally, the maid took the loaf and closed the door.

Their final house call was to the last inhabited villa in the compound, where the Arab teenager lived. The girl herself answered the door. She pushed her glasses up her nose and stared at Ruth.

'Is your mother in?' Ruth said. 'This is for her, to thank her for the food she so kindly sent over.'

The girl's mouth opened, but still she said nothing.

'OK, then,' Ruth said. Maybe the girl's English was not good, she thought. She handed over the barmbrack and stepped back. 'OK,' she said, 'nice to meet you.' She was turning to go when the girl blurted out, 'What's the baby called, if you don't mind me asking?'

Ruth stopped, surprised. The girl had an impeccable, cut-glass English accent.

'This is Anna,' she said.

'Anna,' the girl said.

'Say hello, Anna,' Ruth said, prising Anna's fingers from her skirt. But Anna buried her face in Ruth's legs and squirmed.

'She's at a funny stage,' Ruth said.

'How old is she?'

'Twenty-two months. She'll be two in May.'

'Two in May,' the girl repeated in the precise, clipped accent. 'That's a lovely age. I like babies. I really, really like babies and your baby is beautiful.'

'Well, thank you,' Ruth said, taken aback.

A man called in Arabic from inside. The girl froze, then turned around and shouted something back. The man appeared. He was a tall, stoop-shouldered man of about fifty, Ruth guessed, dressed in a white robe and flip-flops but without a headdress. His greying hair was brushed upwards and greased back. He took off his glasses and peered at her.

'Who are you?'

His brusqueness was disconcerting. 'I'm—well, we, I mean my husband and daughter and I, we're your new neighbours, we're across in the third villa,' she floundered. 'My name's Mrs Armstrong, Ruth Armstrong, and this is my daughter, Anna.' She stopped. The man said nothing. 'Well, I'm sorry to disturb you,' Ruth said. 'I just wanted to give this, it's Irish, typically Irish, it's called "barmbrack", it's a sort of cake-bread. We eat it sliced, like a loaf, or toasted, with butter. It's to say thank you for the food your wife so kindly sent over.'

'My wife?' The man frowned. Then he looked at the girl and said something rapid in Arabic. She replied, her fat cheeks quivering. The man turned back to Ruth.

'I must apologise,' he said, in accented English.

'There seems to have been a misunderstanding. My wife is no longer with us, and I knew nothing of any neighbours, or food parcels. It appears that this is my daughter's doing.'

The girl was staring at her feet, flushed and miserable. Ruth felt a pang of pity for her.

'Well, it was very kind of your daughter,' she said. 'The salad she brought over was absolutely delicious, and it was a very thoughtful gesture.' She smiled, firmly. The girl's head had jerked up at Ruth's words, and she was staring wide-eyed at her. 'Very kind indeed,' Ruth repeated. 'What's your name?' she asked the girl.

The girl whispered something.

'Speak up,' her father barked.

The girl cleared her throat. 'Noor,' she said.

'Noor,' Ruth said, 'what a pretty name.'

The girl gaped. Then she collected herself, swallowed, and spoke a few words to her father. He sighed, then inclined his head to Ruth. 'My daughter reminds me,' he said, 'that I am a negligent host. This is most unforgivable. In the Arab world we pride ourselves on our hospitality. Will you please come in?'

He evidently did not mean it.

'Thank you,' said Ruth, 'but—'

'Oh please,' the girl burst out. 'Do come in and have a cup of coffee. I was just about to make some more, wasn't I, Baba? Oh please, Mrs Armstrong. Please come in.'

'Indeed,' the man said. 'And let us introduce ourselves properly. I am Hisham al-Husayn, Dr Hussain, if you prefer.' He inclined his head again. 'Please, after you. *Baytiy baytuka*: my house is yours.'

80

Ruth could not refuse. '*Shukran,*' she said, carefully; her first word of Arabic.

*   *   *

Inside, two more Arab men were drinking glasses of coffee and smoking.

'I'm afraid I have interrupted something,' Ruth said.

'Oh, no,' the girl—Noor—said. 'Don't think that. It's only my uncle, and my cousin. It's nothing special.'

The men stood, and introduced themselves. The older man, Sayyid al-Harun, was Dr Hussain's older brother; the younger, his son Farid. Farid was tall and slim, with pale skin and thick, shoulder-length black hair. His eyes were hooded, and the curve of his mouth made him look as if he was laughing privately to himself. He looked Ruth up and down. She felt a slow blush creep up the back of her neck and into her cheeks, and she turned slightly away, held Anna closer to her.

*   *   *

Unlike his brother, Sayyid al-Harun was expansive, charming. Within a few minutes he had invited Ruth and her husband to his house, offered the use of a car, his daughters as babysitters for Anna. But nonetheless, Ruth felt ill at ease. She had realised, suddenly, that she did not know them at all: they were Arabs, Muslims, and she must not slip up or give too much away. She answered even their simplest questions about her husband and Ireland evasively, and tried to speak about the Seafarers'

81

Mission as if it was a charity, only incidentally related to the church, hoping they would ask no further. She talked instead about Bahrain, about what she had seen and done so far—the Pearl Monument, the Marina Corniche, Seef Mall.

'But what else have you seen?' Sayyid al-Harun asked, in mock dismay. 'You cannot tell us that you come all the way to the Gulf of Arabia, and all you do is drive round downtown, and go to a mall? What about the beach at al-Jayazir, the wildlife park at al-Areen? The holy tombs at a'Ali, the Q'aalat Fort or the basket-weavers at Karbabad? *Yallah!*'

She wanted to see all of these things, she said, feeling a wave of sadness at the hopes she had had for Bahrain. She had wanted to see the Tree of Life, in particular. But, she shrugged. Her husband was very busy.

'But you must see these things!' Sayyid al-Harun exclaimed, slamming his palms on the coffee table. 'If you are so set on seeing them, my son Farid will be glad to drive you there.'

Farid inclined his head.

'Thank you,' she said, 'but—'

'It will do him good,' Sayyid al-Harun said. 'He should be studying, or working; he is doing neither. He will do this for me. You must not go back to Ireland, and say that the Bahraini people are not hospitable.'

'Thank you—' Ruth tried again, but this time Farid himself interrupted her.

'It is no trouble,' he said. His voice was low, softly accented, husky around the edges. He flicked the ash from the end of his cigarette. 'No trouble at all.'

'You decide on a time,' Sayyid al-Harun declared, 'and my son will take you there. What about tomorrow? There is no time like the present. Tomorrow morning, he comes for you and takes you both there. And my niece will go too,' he added, 'to help you with the baby. There, it is settled. Tomorrow, you go to the *Shajarat al-Hiya*, *inshallah*.'

'I have to ask my husband,' she said.

'Of course. I will speak to him myself, if he has any objections. Perhaps, if he is not too busy, he will go too.'

'Well,' Ruth said, helplessly, 'it is a very kind offer and I will pass it on to my husband.' She stood up. 'I must get my daughter to bed. Thank you for your hospitality.'

'You won't have one more cup of coffee?' Noor said. The girl had hardly spoken, the whole time, just crouched in a corner, watching them.

'No, thank you.'

'You're positively sure?'

'I am, thank you all the same.'

Noor scrambled to her feet. 'I'll see them out, Baba.'

They said their goodbyes. As she opened the door, Noor hesitated and said, 'What my uncle said—I mean about me going with you, to the *Shajarat*.' Her face was flooding scarlet.

'If we do go,' Ruth said, feeling sorry for the girl, so clumsy and awkward, 'if we do go, of course you can come. But we'll see. I do have to speak to my husband.'

'Thank you,' Noor said. 'Oh, thank you so much,' and her face was glowing.

As Ruth and Anna crossed the gritty road, the evening wind was setting in. Dust twisted, swirling in loose puffs and eddies, making whirlpools at her feet. She was suddenly exhausted. The buzzing was still inside her head, like a loose wire, or distant bells. She put Anna down and went straight to bed herself, without waiting up for Euan. But although she slept, her mind did not; it swirled like the dust clouds in the street, making shapes that she could not quite get a hold on, even in her dreams.

8

Ruth and Euan and Anna Armstrong, Noor wrote in her diary that night. *Ruth Armstrong*. Then, underneath, she copied down the things Ruth Armstrong had said. The salad was 'absolutely delicious', and Noor was 'a very pretty name'. Noor could not remember the last time someone had used the word *pretty* about her, or had complimented her on anything. But Ruth Armstrong had been charming, polite—*just like an angel*, Noor wrote. Her heart had stopped when she heard the knock on the door: because she had known (she did not know how, but she had *known*) that it would be the missionary's wife standing there. She had been almost too shy to look her in the eye, let alone talk to her. But the missionary's wife had come in for coffee, staying for almost twenty minutes, and Noor had played with the baby on the rug while she and Noor's father and uncle talked. *Baby Anna*, Noor wrote, *is adorable. She has pink-and-white skin that Mummy would say is peaches-and-cream. She has golden ringlets and the cutest little squashy cheeks and red lips and little pearly teeth. She is twenty-two months old and will be two this May—and Ruth Armstrong said I was very good with her, 'a natural' were her words.*

But best of all was the fact that Noor was invited on an excursion with the missionary's wife the following day! She did not quite know how it had happened. The conversation had been about the Tree of Life, the *Shajarat al-Hiya*, and before Noor knew it, her uncle volunteered his son Farid to drive the Armstrongs there, and Noor to accompany them. She had wanted the ground to open up and swallow her when he foisted her on them like that. But when Ruth Armstrong was leaving, she said, 'of course you can come', just like that, 'of course you can come', as if it wasn't even a question. *I think*, Noor finished off, *that she is the kindest person I have ever met.*

*   *   *

She hardly slept that night. She had hardly slept at all, since that day in January. When she closed her eyes she saw Hong's face, blank and accusing, the tongue lolling, the broken veins, the red eye crying a trail of bloody tears. And when she did drift off she had nightmares, wordless terrors from which she would wake too paralysed even to scream, the sheets soaked. Twice, to her utter shame, she had wet the bed, and been forced to lie there, squeezed to one side, as the urine cooled and dried beneath her. But tonight was different. Tonight's sleeplessness was in anticipation: of what, exactly, she did not know; only that it was the first time since arriving in Bahrain that she had something to look forward to.

She was wide awake as her father got up and performed the *fajr*. Afterwards, as he made coffee and studied his portion of the Qur'an, Noor went into the bathroom and locked the door. Since that awful January day, she had avoided all mirrors: keeping her eyes fixed down in the bathroom, turning rapidly away at any glimpse of a shiny or reflective surface. But now, she decided, she was ready to face herself. She could not quite meet her own eye in the mirror, and focused instead on the lower half of her face. In the strip light of the bathroom, her skin was pale and sallow, and the dark hairs on her upper lip, chin and the side of her face stood out. She had started bleaching them, a year or so ago, but she had not done them for several weeks. There was a packet of facial-hair bleach under her bed, somewhere, in the plastic bag into which she had swept the contents of her locker and bedside table, and not touched since. She found it: and it was still half-full. She stirred together the cream and powder, leaving the sharp, fizzy mixture on longer than the guidelines advised, to be sure of it working. When she wiped it off and dabbed her face with lukewarm water, the skin was mottled, coming up in a series of hard, itchy white lumps. She almost panicked, but then remembered the potted aloe vera on the veranda. She cut a stalk and smeared the meaty-smelling gel onto her face. It dried in sticky brown streaks, making her feel uglier than ever. But it was not yet seven o'clock; in an hour, her face would calm down.

86

Her father rattled the bathroom door. He was surprised to find her there. For the past few weeks, he had had to remind her to take showers: now, she was up early, and in the bathroom of her own volition.

'Open the door,' he ordered. 'Let me see what you're doing in there.'

'I'm taking a shower, Baba,' she called. 'I want to wash my hair.' She opened the door a crack, so that he could see her.

'What's that on your face?'

'A facemask, Baba. Now please let me have my shower.'

'What's got into you this morning?' he persisted.

'*Nothing!* I just want to wash my hair, for God's sake!'

He hovered. 'It must be a relief to know you're starting a new school.'

'Yes,' she said, to appease and get rid of him. 'That must be what it is.' Still he hovered. 'Baba!'

'You should probably have some new clothes,' he said. 'Next weekend, we can go to the mall, if you want. Or I can give you a card and you can go by yourself.'

That stopped her in her tracks. 'Really?' It wasn't the prospect of clothes—there was no way she would go shopping, looking like she did now—that startled her, but the offer itself. Her father was trying, she suddenly saw, and the attempt stirred something in her.

'You probably should,' her father said again, then he turned abruptly and walked away.

For a moment, Noor felt lighter than she had done in weeks. Perhaps there was another way, after all, she thought; and when the guilt and hopelessness came crashing back down, it was slightly less heavy than before.

And in just over an hour's time, she was to spend a whole morning with the missionaries. She did not know what their pull was, but she had felt it, from the moment she first saw them. She stepped into the shower and turned on the tap, and with the first shock of the icy water she allowed herself to pretend that everything—guilt, sin, memories—could somehow be washed away.

9

He came for her the next morning. She answered the door and there he was, dressed not in the jeans and polo shirt of the previous evening but in a crisp white *thobe* and a white *gutra* bound with black cord, tall and straight and proud.

He bowed slightly. *'As-salaam alaykum.'*

'Wa-alaykum-as-salaam,' she managed. She had mentioned last night that she was learning Arabic. Sayyid al-Harun had clapped his hands and said, Excellent, and she must practise.

'Kayf haalik?' Farid said, and she wondered if he was laughing at her.

'Al-hum-doo-lillah,' she mumbled, feeling ridiculous.

'Ruth?' Euan had come to the door. She felt her cheeks redden, as if she had been caught out in something. She had not had a chance to tell him about yesterday, about meeting the al-Husayns, or about the idea of a trip to the Tree of Life. He looked at Farid, and looked at her.

88

'Can we help you?'

'Euan, this is Farid,' she said. 'He is the son of one of our new neighbours. Farid, my husband, Euan.'

'*As-salaam alaykum.*'

'How d'you do?'

'You have not learned Arabic?'

'Pardon?' Euan frowned slightly, then smoothed it away. 'Ah. My wife puts me to shame.'

There was a moment, then, when none of them spoke. Ruth swallowed. The air already tasted of the white heat of the day to come. 'I had coffee with the al-Husayns last night,' she began, feeling like a child caught out in a lie. 'They offered to take us to see the Tree of Life today. I—' She broke off, awkward. 'I didn't realise the offer was in earnest.'

'Well,' said Euan. 'Well, that's exceedingly kind of them. But—'

'You are busy, we know,' Farid interjected. 'Your wife told us about your charity work. Perhaps we could arrange some other time, or perhaps'— he paused—'perhaps your wife would like to go, anyway.'

Euan looked at her.

'This was arranged?' His voice was level; too level. She could see a muscle pulsing in the corner of his jaw. He was trying to control his temper, to be reasonable.

'Well, yes,' she said. 'I mean—' She felt tongue-tied, flustered. 'I've been wanting to see the Tree of Life since we first decided to come here, you know that, and I just happened to mention it, that's all.'

'I see,' Euan said, and she knew he was preparing to make excuses on her behalf. He was not happy, she could see that, at the thought of her meeting people without him. But before he could begin to talk, Noor appeared, hurrying across the road towards them.

'Good morning!' she said, 'Good morning, Mrs Armstrong, and you must be Mr Armstrong, I mean Reverend, it's such a pleasure to meet you, it really is—will you be coming on the excursion with us, too?' She rushed on, without waiting for an answer. 'It was so kind of you to invite me along with you, I'm so excited about it. Baba says we should get going early, before the roads clog up. So I'm all ready, whenever you are.'

Euan hesitated.

Ruth could see him, fazed. Euan was rarely fazed. 'Well, then,' she said, 'in that case we really should get going, shouldn't we?'

'And you're bringing Anna?' Euan said.

'Yes, of course.'

'I borrowed a child seat from my sister,' Farid said, gesturing towards his car. It was a sleek silver Chevrolet Camaro that purred softly, its engine still running. 'So it will be perfectly safe.'

'Well, then,' Euan said. 'Ruth, a word?'

'I'll wait in the car,' Noor said, 'unless you need a hand with anything?'

'No, thank you,' Euan said, 'thanks all the same.'

They stepped back into the house.

'You're going?' he said. 'You're going on a trip, with these strangers?'

'They're not strangers,' she said. 'I told you, I met them, last night. They're our neighbours. It's a trip to see the Tree of Life, Euan. What harm can there be in that? Of course I won't'—lowering her voice—'give anything away—'

90

'Ruth—'

'And besides, if I don't go, I'll just be stuck in here all day, while you're out. And I can't relax with the maids here, I can't do anything, and there's nowhere to go with Anna. And it's not as if you were particularly keen on seeing the Tree of Life, in fact I seem to remember you laughing at me and calling me naive when I said I wanted to go there.' She felt her voice rising. She had not known she was so angry, so worked up. She took a breath. 'I want to go, Euan.'

Euan looked at her, exhaled. 'Fine,' he said.

'Fine?' She had been steeling herself for an argument.

'Fine,' he repeated. 'Go. Take some pictures for me. Now I have to get going. I'm late.'

He turned and went into the bedroom. Ruth felt suddenly limp. 'Fine,' she said. 'OK. Then I will go.'

*   *   *

Two of the main highways out of Manama were shut due to accidents, so they took a circuitous route, driving east towards the Marina Corniche. Farid drove smoothly and carefully. Noor even teased him, at one point, for letting too many cars cut in front of him. He was being careful, Ruth realised, to show her that she and Anna were safe with him. They had talked last night of the dangers of driving in Bahrain. As they drew parallel to the Corniche, Farid slowed down even more, gestured with pride towards the vast expanse of the Gulf, glittering for miles in all directions. Ruth wound down her window to look: and after a minute or so, she found that she could no longer tell what was sea and what

91

was sky, all was so white, so dazzling. The light in Bahrain was not crisp and bright and clear, as she had imagined. It was hazy and oblique, shifting and impenetrable. You could hardly see the sun for the dust clouds; just feel it pressing down on you.

Farid was quiet as he drove. Noor played games with Anna in the back. Anna seemed happy, squealing with laughter. Ruth wound up the window, pressed her cheek against the cool glass, gazed out. Now they had left the Corniche and were heading south. Palm trees lined the road, short and squat, with ragged, bulbous trunks. The ground to the sides of the road was covered with dirty, whitish sand, scattered with dense, grey, tough-looking clumps of grass. The desert here looked morose and insipid, a wasteland between settlements. They drove. Ruth gazed at the sentinel palm trees, marking their rhythm like telegraph poles seen from a train. Then suddenly the road beneath them changed: it felt smoother and newer and the palm trees were little more than baby stumps, some still encased in hessian sacking, with shy green shoots where the fronds should be.

'We are on the new road, now,' he said, 'the road to the Bahraini International Circuit. Formula One, you know? It will be finished by the end of this year. I would take you there, but there is not much to see, yet. It is better we go on to the *Shajarat al-Hiya*. It is not far, now.'

'Not far?' Ruth said, surprised. She had imagined it would take them hours to get there, right out into the middle of the desert.

'No,' Farid said. 'Half an hour, maybe less.'

They drove on. The new road ended, and they were back on the old. There were few other cars on the road. The landscape was becoming shabbier and dirtier by the minute. There were no more palm trees, just greying shrubs, most of which looked dead or dying. All along the roadside were piles of rubbish, old tyres and broken crates and bits of twisted, blackened metal; rusting tin cans and tatters of bin-bags and faded plastic drums. Big brown pipes criss-crossed the wasteland: oil pipes that ran the length of Bahrain, all the way from the refineries in the south and under the sea to Saudi Arabia.

'Can I ask you,' Farid said suddenly, 'why do you want to go to the Tree of Life?'

Ruth looked at him; looked away, back out of the window. 'I read about it in my guidebook,' she said.

That wasn't entirely a lie, but it wasn't true. *Now the Lord God had planted a garden in the East, in Eden,* the verses in Genesis went, *and He put there the men that He had formed. And the Lord God made all kinds of trees grow out of the ground, trees that were pleasing to the eye and good for food. In the middle of the garden were the tree of life and the tree of the knowledge of good and evil. A river watering the garden flowed from Eden; from there it was separated into four headwaters.*

She had studied the verses before they left for Bahrain. The first river was the Pishon, winding through the land of Havilah, *where there is gold*. The second was the Gihon, in the land of Cush. The third was the Tigris, running along the east of Asshur, and the fourth was the Euphrates. It was possible— just about possible—that all of those rivers had originated in Bahrain; that Bahrain was once Eden. The guidebook said this, and if you looked at a map

93

(she had taken down her parents' old *Reader's Digest* atlas once more) you could trace the Tigris and the Euphrates (scholarship was divided, the guide said, on the Pishon and the Gihon) and see how they started in the Persian Gulf.

Ruth was not a Bible literalist, and she was certainly not a Creationist—and you got plenty of those back home, tub-thumpers who gave Christianity a bad name, Euan said—but still, she knew, she just knew, that the Garden of Eden must have existed, once. Euan had laughed at her for this—that was when he called her *naive*; *you're so naive, Ruth, honestly*—but for two days running she had left Anna with her mother and taken the bus into Belfast to go to the Central Library and study the books written by people who had tried to track down Eden. Some were archaeologists, some theologians; some, it seemed, just plain cranks. But all set out their theories with meticulous care, and evidence: maps, dates, forgotten scrolls, carved tablets. Some said Eden was in Iraq, others in Damascus, a few in Jerusalem. A book by a Latter-day Saint had even argued that Eden was located in modern-day Jackson, Missouri. But a substantial number maintained that Bahrain was the most likely setting for Eden. And the ancient acacia in the desert, the only tree for miles around, nourished by a secret underground spring too deep for the roots of other trees, was all that remained; a reminder of paradise.

She had imagined the journey to the Tree of Life as a sort of pilgrimage: a long, bumpy drive through the desert, a beautiful desert, with mile upon mile of sand dunes like ripples of silk and a spice-scented sky. She had imagined arriving at

has no advantage over the animal. All go to the same place; all come from dust, and to dust all return.

Her vision was blurring; dizzy, she bent forwards.

'Ruth?' Farid was behind her, beside her. She tried to speak; she could not speak. She felt tears prickle her eyes, and before she could do anything, stop them, blink them back, they were spilling out and down her cheeks, more and more of them, rivers of tears.

'Ruth . . .' Farid's voice was coming from very far away. His hand was on her back, stroking, moving in firm circles, as she might do to Anna. 'Ruth, *humdillah*, what is it, what is it?'

She straightened up, lacunae still pulsing at the edges of her vision. 'I thought I'd find something,' she found herself saying, 'I know it's ridiculous because the Bible isn't literally true, I mean not even Euan'—another sob—'and it's not that, it's just, it's just'—her voice began to break down on her again—'I thought if I could see where things started, if I could—' and she stopped, dissolved into tears.

Farid had hold of her shoulders, was using the sleeves of his robe to wipe her cheeks. Then all of a sudden she was embracing him, falling against him, into him, clinging, as if once she let go she would plummet.

And Noor was there, too, she could hear her, but she couldn't stop crying, she couldn't stop crying.

10

When Farid left her back home that afternoon, Noor rushed straight down to her cellar, not even bothering with her usual precautions. Sampaguita called out a welcome, but Noor did not bother to reply, or to go into the kitchen to see what was cooking. That morning, Sampaguita had arrived with a package of cold, glistening rockfish, fresh from the early market, with which to make *lapu-lapu*. *Lapu-lapu* was practically a Filipino national dish and there were as many varieties as there were Philippine islands. Sampaguita sometimes fried the fish whole and served them *escabeche* with a sticky pineapple sauce—that was Noor's favourite—but other times she would steam them with slivered carrots and noodles or wrap them in banana leaves and bake them. She had also promised to make *crema de fruta* for pudding and that was a favourite of Noor's, too: the sponge fingers soaked in tins of Del Monte fruit cocktail and layered with sweet, chilled eggy custard, dolloped on top with glossy, gelatinous beaten cream. Noor could eat bowl after bowl of that.

But even though it was long gone lunchtime, Noor was not hungry: she did not care if the *lapu-lapu* was cooked *escabeche* or if there was a whole basin of *crema de fruta* waiting for her. She galloped downstairs, almost yanking the light cord from the ceiling in her haste, and pulled her diary from its hiding place to start describing the day.

She wrote pages and pages. She wrote until her hand was seized with splintering cramps, and still she was impatient to write more. She wrote, again, of how kind Ruth Armstrong had been inviting her on the trip, and she wrote of how adorable little Anna was, burbling and chattering away for most of the journey, happy to play endless games of peekaboo and This Little Piggy, shouting with joyful laughter every time Noor popped out from between her hands or got to 'all the way . . . home!' and tickled her soft, squashy little tummy, as if it was the best game in the world. 'You're good with her,' Ruth had turned and said at one point, and Noor copied this down, reverently. *I'm good with her.* She wrote of how disappointed Ruth had been when they reached the Tree of Life—and how she, Noor, could have saved her disappointment. The Tree of Life, although Noor had never actually been there herself, was where all the young Bahrainis went to drink and smoke spliffs and make out. The running joke was that it was called 'the tree of life' because so much sperm was spilt at its roots. She wrote of how Ruth had started crying—*crying*—at the Tree. She, Noor, had wandered off with Anna, and had been completely shocked to turn back and see Ruth doubled over against Farid. She had run back then, for a brief, horrible moment thinking they were kissing or embracing, but when she got close, she could see that Ruth was sobbing and Farid was trying to calm her down. She, too, had tried to help, touching an awkward hand to Ruth's back. And then they got back in the car, and came home. She had been disappointed at that: had imagined that they might go for lunch somewhere—Hardee's or Applebee's or one of the food courts at the malls—but Ruth had just said to Farid, Please take me home.

Noor stopped then, and frowned, rereading her narrative, wondering what was missing. She had put in everything that had happened, as detailed and accurately as she could, but still it did not feel right—did not feel complete.

*   *   *

She sighed. Then she took up her pen again and scribbled one last postscript to the day's entry.

The Diary of Noor Hussain

If it was me she'd come to convert I'd convert immediately. Or maybe I'd wait a while and act puzzled like my soul was in tumult and turmoil so that she'd kneel down and pray with me and maybe if I had a fever she'd (like they do in books) touch her cool fingers to my forehead.

Noor stopped, suddenly hot. She quickly closed and hid her diary and went upstairs.

III

1

These are the dust days. It is the time of change and instability known as the *sarrayat*, when the cooler days turn hot again. A simmering wind—a *suahili*, perhaps, coming from the deserts of Arabia, or perhaps the tail of an early *simoom*, that hot, dry, suffocating wind that scoops whole sand dunes from the desert floor and whirls them along for miles, reshaping the entire landscape through which it passes—whips the sand into four-foot demons that swirl along the streets like miniature, malevolent dervishes. This year the *sarrayat* has come earlier than usual. People say it is caused by the world's climate changing. People say it is a symptom of the political restlessness in the air, of nations blustering and waging war. People stay indoors, wear stones to ward off the Evil Eye. When they have to go out, they cover their eyes and mouths and noses, in case the demons get in.

The villa is constantly dusty, never mind that the maids sweep and mop it every day they are there, and Ruth the days between. It blows in even though the doors are kept closed, and their gaps stopped with damp, rolled-up sheets. It blows in even though there are no windows. Through the vents of the air-conditioning unit, through the cracks in the walls, she does not know how it gets in, but it gets in, and will not be cleaned away.

The days are long and the nights are longer; warped, elastic hours thick with the crackling pressure in the air. Ruth has strange, fitful dreams; dreams which, upon waking, she cannot put into sentences. The dreams do not have narratives; they are wordless dreams of pure distress and fear. She wakes shaking, sweating, gripped by nameless, nebulous dreads. Euan reassures her, time and again, it is simply the change of year. They must get the air-conditioning unit seen to, so it does not rattle so much. Its wheeze and clatter is probably what is waking her up, is seeping into her dreams. He spoons his body against hers and says the weather will settle and sleep will come again. She shakes him off: her legs are twitchy and her skin is tight and she cannot bear to be touched. Daybreak, when it comes, is a watery grey light that hurts her eyes.

She has not told him the real reasons for her restiveness. She has heard him talk before to people whose faith is shaken, many times; she knows what he will say. He will start by reassuring: even the apostles doubted, and begged Jesus to increase their faith, time and time again: they who had seen the miracles, who had seen the healing of the sick and raising of the dead, the walking on water and the armful of loaves that fed the five thousand. Even they doubted. Even Peter, walking on the water, lost heart and began to sink, afraid of the winds, afraid of the impossibility of what he was doing. And Thomas, at the Resurrection: *Unless I see the nail marks in his hands and put my finger where the nails were, and put my hand into his side,* he says to the others, *I will not believe.* And Jesus says to him, *Because you have seen me, you have believed; blessed are those who have not seen and yet have believed.* Faith, like the parable of the talents, can be increased; like the parable of the seeds sown on rocky ground, it needs care and cultivation, nurturing and protection. And faith without deeds is dead. She must pray, he will say; she must spend extra time reading the Bible. She must take a Sunday school, or lead a Bible study group; apply her faith, enact it, live it. He will end with Paul's words to Timothy: *Fight the good fight of the faith. Take hold of the eternal life to which you were called when you made your good confession in the presence of many witnesses.* And he will pray with her, using the words of the young boy's father in Mark: *I do believe: help me overcome my disbelief!* She knows this. She has seen him do it before. She has seen those who have wavered, strengthened. But she fears, deep down, that it is no use. And yet she lacks the words, or the ways, to explain this to Euan.

*   *   *

She has failed him. She knows this. And he is disappointed in her. He is disappointed with her reaction, which he considers an overreaction. He is disappointed that she is not the strength and support, the help-meet, that he had thought she'd be.

She met him when she was fourteen; he, at twenty-one, was seven years her senior. He was newly graduated in law, and had turned down numerous career opportunities, including one offer of a pupillage, in order to come back to Kircubbin to volunteer for the Citizens' Advice Bureau, work on an anti-drugs programme for teenagers and take an outreach group at church. Ruth's mother reported over dinner one night that the Armstrongs were bitterly disappointed. She did not know the family; the Armstrongs were not churchgoers. But

Armstrong Senior was head of the Rotary Club and drove a BMW with tinted windows; everyone knew who he was. He had high hopes for his son, she said; when the son came back to Kircubbin there had been a big confrontation; the father had demanded back the money spent on the university education and the son had walked out of the house and not come home for two days and nights. There was a picture in the local paper, a grainy, grinning curly-haired young man leaning awkwardly over a stile with the waters of the lough behind him, the headline 'No Place Like Home'. Ruth had kept an eye out for him after that, every Sunday scanning the heads in the rows in front and glancing round when they were required to stand until she found him: a glimpse of red hair, a flash of bright blue shirt. But it was idle curiosity, no more. She was a fourteen-year-old who had not even taken her GCSEs; law graduates who had been featured in the *Herald* belonged to another orbit.

That summer she joined the youth group, which met every Sunday evening for Bible study and quite often on Saturday nights, too, for barbecues or trips to the Ice Bowl or the bowling alley. Once they went to a rally to hear a famous American evangelist speak; another time to an open-air Christian rock concert where it bucketed down with rain and there was a very unchristian scrambling for the last remaining cagoules. Euan Armstrong was friends with Andy and Sarah, the group leaders, and he often joined them on Saturday night excursions. He had a girlfriend from Dublin that summer, who had an unpronounceable name and glossy, expensive-looking dark hair. The four of them were the celebrities of the youth group,

106

the idols, and they knew it. The younger teenagers would cluster round, competing to be the one to make a funny remark or to be chosen to lead prayers, to give the best interpretation of a Bible passage or to have adjacent seats in the minibus. Like any of the rest of them, Ruth mumbled and turned scarlet when Euan called on her to give her opinion; could not believe he knew her name, let alone was soliciting her ideas.

At the end of the summer, Andy left for England, and Euan took over as group leader. Now that the holidays were over, there were fewer excursions and parties: Saturday nights became trips to the cinema or table-tennis tournaments in the church hall, and fewer people attended. The Dublin girlfriend came less frequently; finally, she was not seen for four Sundays in a row and the rumour went around that they had broken up because she would not have sex with him—or was it the other way round? There were red faces and poorly suppressed giggles during the subsequent session's discussion of 1 Corinthians 7 and Paul's teachings on chastity. Ruth turned fifteen, joined the Young Farmers' Association, which met on a Saturday afternoon, and twice in a row she went away on outdoor pursuits weekends. A third weekend she had a bad cold, and a fourth one of the cows broke a leg and she waited with her father while the vet was called. The following Saturday afternoon she was helping her father fix a broken fence on the far boundary of the farm when her mother came through on the CB radio saying she had a visitor at the house. She ran back through the frosted fields, the crusted earth black and bare underfoot, the sun a low red lozenge in the sky, and arrived at the farmhouse flushed and breathless, Rosie barking beside her, delighted at the sudden chase. Euan Armstrong was sitting at the big wooden table with her mother, laughing, drinking a chipped mug of tea. He stood up when she came in, and waited while she prised off each of her wellies with the heel of the other, tossing them into the hallway. Then he took her hand and greeted her formally— because apart from the odd group discussion, they had never had a proper conversation before, just the two of them. Ruth's mother freshened the tea and brought out the leftovers of a Victoria sponge and said she'd leave them to it, bustled off to another part of the house on some pretext or other. Ruth felt acutely self-conscious. Her fork scraped against the plate and the wet noise of her swallow was claggy, too loud. But Euan Armstrong chatted away, seemingly oblivious, about how beautiful the farm looked, about how he liked the November weather, bleak as it could be, about what a lovely dog Rosie was. Rosie, lolling at Ruth's feet, twitched her ears and barked at the mention of her name: they both laughed, Ruth relaxed a bit. The conversation turned to youth group and Sunday Bible study, about what Ruth had missed over the past month. And then Euan asked, gently, if there was a particular reason Ruth had stopped coming. I haven't stopped coming, she tried to say, it's not like that, but the words were thick and dry as cake crumbs in her mouth. It was hard, Euan said, to stay true to a Christian lifestyle and the demands it made of you, especially at the age Ruth now was, when other things—parties, alcohol, even drugs— suddenly became temptations. He reminded her about the Sermon on the Mount, and especially

Matthew 13–14, the small road and narrow gate that leads to heaven and the broad road and wide gate that leads to hell. His eyes were wide and blue and utterly sincere, urgently fixed on hers. She felt a shiver of dizziness, a flutter in her stomach; she felt her mouth grow dry. When he had finished talking, Euan sat back and looked at her, his eyes grave, and she knew she would not miss another youth group session, no matter what else she had to sacrifice for it. He had brought her a small, leatherette-bound Gospel of Matthew. She took it and stroked the cover, her fingers clammy, and that night she slept with it under her pillow.

She was disappointed, the following week, to discover that she was not the only one Euan Armstrong had visited. He had been to the houses of five youth group members whose attendance had been shaky lately: and all but one of them returned the following Saturday and Sunday, and Saturdays and Sundays after that. Sometimes, Euan would give Ruth and a couple of others a lift to and from town. Her father's farm was furthest out, so he would drop her off last, and come in for tea and toast. He loved the farm kitchen, the old-fashioned larder, the rows of boots and Barbours, the cats curled up beside the Aga, the massive oak dresser and the milk jugs of bluebells, or tulips, or sweet peas, or whatever wild flowers Ruth had gathered from the fallow fields. To Ruth, the farmhouse was chaotic and shabby. But Euan loved to sit with her mother, and sometimes her father, eating slices of toasted barmbrack and last year's gooseberry jam, talking about the farm, the town, the world. That was always one of his strengths: he could talk to anyone about anything, and it was never forced or

109

sycophantic because he genuinely liked people and was interested in what they had to say.

Ruth turned sixteen, seventeen. She started to help out with Sunday school, and sometimes they went for hot chocolate afterwards, or a walk down the high street and along the harbour. But it was nothing more than friendship. He had girlfriends from time to time, she knew that, though he rarely talked about them. Ruth dated a couple of boys from school, nothing serious, trips to the cinema or to pubs that turned a blind eye to under-age drinkers, drives up to Scrabo Tower or down the coast to Portaferry, or maybe to Belfast and back. None of the boys lasted more than a few dates. She turned eighteen, and Euan gave her a pretty necklace—an enamel flower on a silver chain. She had a birthday party in one of the old barns, hired a DJ and set up trestle tables with barrels of beer and soft drinks. She invited people from church, Young Farmers, friends from school. Euan came, brought a bottle of champagne. She wondered if he might kiss her. But he did not.

She scraped through her A levels, getting grades just good enough to secure her place at Greenmount Agricultural College. That summer, she was the female leader at the church's summer camp: she and Euan took the teenagers abseiling and bouldering, rock-climbing and orienteering, sang songs and led praise groups in the evenings. Euan told her, one evening, that he thought he might have a calling. They talked about it, long into the night. People think God comes in a flash of light or a bush bursting into flames, Euan said, but it is not like that at all. He is the quiet, almost inaudible voice that you cannot quite ignore, the growing conviction that this, and only this, is the right and only way. She could not breathe when he said that; felt her skin tingling. She was the first, the only, person he had told.

On the drive back home, they detoured, down the length of the peninsula and across on the Strangford ferry to Castleward, all the way up the coast on the other side, past Killyleagh and Ringdufferin, the Sketrick Isles and the old monastery at Greyabbey. They drove mostly in silence. And then they pulled in to a little secluded bay and kissed for the first time, and Euan said he loved her, and she said she would always support him, help him; trust with him, hope with him, persevere.

        *   *   *

Anjali and Trudy drop by, sometimes two or three times a day, but Ruth is cagey with them; they ask too many questions about her husband and their church, her faith. Anjali perches on the ugly divan, smooths invisible (or imaginary) creases from her immaculate sari and tells Ruth about the Evil Eye, about portents and omens. She explains that in India, the Evil Eye is called *drishti* or *nazar*. In order to reverse it, you must burn a holy flame on a plate in front of the afflicted person's face; that flame will absorb the effects of *drishti* and when it is extinguished, so too will the power of evil be extinguished. In Arabic, you say *mash'Allah* to ward off evil. She makes Ruth practise it: *Mash'Allah*. She catches a wriggling Anna in her plump arms and tells Ruth to draw a spot of kohl pencil on Anna's cheeks or forehead, an imperfection that will keep

111

her safe, as the Evil Eye is attracted to whatever is good or new or perfect. Because the winds of the *sarrayat*, Anjali stresses, are inauspicious. Also inauspicious are a sparkle without smoke, bones, a snake, broken utensils, buttermilk, raw sugar. When Ruth asks her how she cooks, if raw sugar is unlucky, she laughs and says that until the *sarrayat* is passed, she uses honey and molasses.

Trudy makes fun of Anjali, and her superstitions. Trudy and her husband attend the NEC, the American evangelical church in Bahrain—and they believe, she brags to Ruth, in Intelligent Design; that the world was created six thousand years ago and the Devil plants fossils to throw us off course and test our faith.

Our faith: she speaks as if they share a kindred spirit.

Trudy talks a lot about the NEC, presuming it is what Ruth wants to talk about, too. It is the source of the most recent scandal in the expat world. The pastor—a hale, vigorous man in his late sixties, tough leathery skin and piercing blue eyes, a shock of white hair like an Old Testament prophet, a staunch Baptist and Vietnam veteran—is preaching the righteousness of holy crusades. He talks in parables, of course. He tells the Old Testament stories of Moses and the Egyptians, of how Moses's triumph gave the Israelites faith in God for evermore. *When I defeat them, the Egyptians will know that I am the Lord.* But everyone knows what he really means. Saddam Hussein has been given a deadline by which to comply with the UN weapons inspectors, just a few days away, now, and if he fails, war will be declared. What the pastor is doing is tantamount to warmongering: it is enough

112

to have him thrown into prison, or expelled from the Kingdom, if the Bahraini authorities get wind of it. A few kilometres across the water, in Saudi Arabia or in Qatar, it would be enough to have him executed. Trudy clutches her knees to her chest as she tells Ruth this, her eyes wide and delighted with the danger of it all. Ruth feels sick. She is uncomfortable with Trudy, as uncomfortable as she is with Anjali. She takes to pretending that she is not in when either of them calls round: she sits in the central room and does not answer the knocks at the door.

The edges of her world contract. Where once she felt wonder at the thought of existence—of the fact that we, that anything, exists—now she feels a sort of vertigo.

Noor comes over, and Ruth is relieved to have her: she seems happy to sit in the living room all afternoon and sing nursery rhymes or read story books to Anna, things that Ruth has lost the energy for. One day she comes over flapping a piece of paper and gabbling breathlessly: she has remembered that when she was little, an au pair once baked her play-dough; she has found a recipe online, all it needs is flour, salt, boiling water or vegetable oil, and colouring. They mix up play-dough for Anna, colouring it with the dyes Noor has brought from home: red, yellow, blue, green. Anna is delighted with the new game. They mould it into building bricks and stack towers for her to knock down, they make a green snake with red eyes, they make bananas and tomatoes and apples and pretend to have a fruit stall. Ruth feels sorry for Noor, so plump and awkward, so easy to please.

*   *   *

She sees nothing of Farid. She waits for Noor to mention him, to mention the life tree, but Noor does not. Ruth does not bring it, or him, up herself. She is embarrassed of how she broke down crying— and in his arms, a teenager, a stranger. She half hopes never to see him again, but yet the moment plays and replays in her head; the way he held her; what it felt to let herself go, completely.

One afternoon, after she has ignored another knock on the door, she finds a soft, square tissue-wrapped package on the veranda. She unfolds the paper and shakes it out: it is a deep blue cloth, the size of a bath-towel, a very fine, slippery material embroidered with a picture of the Tree of Life, blazing beautiful against a setting sun.

She rolls it back up and stuffs it into a corner of one of the suitcases, stacked in a corner of the spare room. She does not know why she does this. It is easier, she tells herself, than trying to explain it to Euan, explain its significance, its provenance. But that is not quite true.

2

The week was long for Ruth but for Noor it flashed by. *This week*, she wrote in her diary on Wednesday evening, *has been the best week of my life.* It felt highly significant that she finished one exercise book, and had to begin another. Before she Sellotaped up the old one and hid it away she

114

read through its entries, which began around the middle of February, when she came out to Bahrain. They seemed, she thought, to be written by another person. *Because when I was truly considering killing myself,* she wrote on the inside of the back cover, *and I mean I really, truly was, I didn't know that life was just about to change. As I was writing that entry on Thursday 6th March the world had shifted on its axis and everything was starting to fall into place only I didn't know it yet. And what it makes you think,* she went on, *is that in the broader scheme of things maybe things will be ok after all.* How unbelievable that she could write that sentence! She wrote it again, underlined it. *Maybe things will be ok after all.*

Her first entry in the new jotter was about how kind Ruth Armstrong was. She genuinely seemed to like Noor—to want her around. Anna was 'full of beans', she had said, the day of the Tree of Life—Noor loved that expression, copied it carefully down—and she could really do with an extra pair of hands to mind her. So Noor started getting up early each morning, showering and washing her hair, putting on Body Shop body lotion and her best jeans and top and going over to the Armstrongs' villa. She played dolls with Anna, read her stories, watched television. Sometimes Ruth joined them; other times she stayed in her bedroom; sometimes one of the neighbours would come over and Noor would keep Anna out of their way while they had coffee and talked. Needed and trusted for the first time, she was blossoming. Even her father saw the difference: he would look at her suspiciously as she kissed him on the cheek when he got home from work, chattered about her day. Once, he asked her outright what she had done, as if she was trying to

115

cover up for something. But even this just made her laugh.

Sometimes at night, as she recorded the day's events in minute detail, she thought: she would do anything for Ruth Armstrong. She could not explain what it was. All she knew was that she liked—wanted—needed—to be near her.

*   *   *

But Thursday was Ashura: the Day of Atonement. Noor had forgotten this. She came into the kitchen early to ask Sampaguita to iron her best T-shirt, ready to go over to Ruth Armstrong's, and there her father was, dressed not in the suit he wore into work but a *thobe* and *gutra*. It was Ashura, he said, and they were going to the mosque. Noor panicked at that. The day before, she had come up with the idea of making play-dough for Anna, and it had been a huge success. Today, she was going to suggest to Ruth Armstrong that they took Anna to the kiddie play area at Seef Mall, and go for a frappuccino at Cinnabon's or Dairy Queen afterwards. Her cousin could drive them again, or they could get a taxi: she had it all planned. But now her father was telling her to hurry up and get dressed, and wear modest clothing, not jeans.

She begged him to let her stay home. But he was adamant: attendance at the mosque on Ashura was not optional.

'You're living in Bahrain now,' he said.

'But I'm not Muslim!' she said, panicking even more. What would Ruth Armstrong, the wife of a Christian missionary, think if she heard Noor had been to the mosque?

116

When her father refused to listen to her she went on, and went too far, asking him if Muslims were meant to drink whisky and go to cabarets at the big hotels, and if a person who did such things could really consider himself a Muslim.

He was furious at that. He was more furious than she could remember seeing him, ever, and she thought for a moment that he was going to hit her. Instead, he seized her by the back of the neck and marched her into her bedroom, ordered her to be ready in five minutes or else.

'Or else what?' she screamed at him, and he shouted back that he would send her back to England to live with her mother.

She wanted to die, then. She could never go back: she knew that. The news all week had been dominated by Iraq, and Saddam Hussein. Even if you tried to ignore it, you couldn't help hearing it on the half-hourly news bulletins of the pop music stations, or as you flicked through satellite TV channels. It was just her luck, she had written in her diary, to share a name with the evillest dictator in the world. And the irony of it, which nobody in England wanted to understand, was that with a Western mother and Shi'a father, and half of her relatives Iranian, he would have persecuted her as much as anyone else. *I hate Julia Hazlehurst*, she had written in her diary one evening, in a burst of rage. *I hate hate hate Annabel Varley and I hate Lily Carrington-Villiers and I hate Emily-May Brierly.* She wrote so hard that the tip of her biro ripped through the next few pages of her notebook. She could never, ever go back, she was certain of it. So she had no choice but to get ready (the sack-skirt again, and a long-sleeved blouse, and a scarf to cover her head) and go with her father to the mosque.

She had never been to the mosque before—not to worship, anyhow. Her aunts had taken her and her mother there, once, one Easter holiday, because the Al-Fatih admitted strangers, and Westerners, for English-language tours. She remembered being bored: her mother had cooed at the huge chandelier and at the arched windows, the henna area for ladies and the displays of calligraphy. But to Noor it was huge and cavernous, exposing, and it smelt of feet and floor polish, like the school gymnasium.

But today was different: today was one of the holiest days of Muharram, and the streets and the square in front of the mosque were thronging with people. There were ordinary worshippers, like her father and herself, most dressed traditionally, those who weren't in *thobes* or *hijab* wearing sober black: because for Shi'a Muslims, today was a day of mourning. There were lines of young men beating drums and chanting *Ya Hussain*, and others beating their chests in time to the drums. And there were processions, too, circling the mosque and the streets around; bare-chested men with flails to purge themselves and others with razor blades, cutting themselves. They were: they actually were, slicing their skin so it bled, and howling, as the blood ran down their arms and soaked into their trousers. Noor had never seen such things before. Any time their holidays in Bahrain had coincided with Muharram and Ashura, her mother had kept her and Jamal indoors while the processions went past. Noor's head was spinning: she thought she might be sick. She had never felt less Bahraini,

118

less Arab, than she did now, pressed reluctantly close to her father as they negotiated their way through the crowds, the howls and the wailing, the heat and sweat and blood, to get to the entrance of the mosque. There were even tourists among the crowd, gawping and snapping away. Noor tugged her scarf down over her eyes as one particularly zealous man pushed in to get a picture of the entrance to the mosque: what if he was a news reporter, or posted his pictures on a blog, and people she knew saw them, saw her? What if Ruth Armstrong saw her? How disappointed, disgusted, even, she might be. Noor felt utterly miserable.

They reached the entrance to the mosque. They had to separate at the doors of course, because women and men had separate prayer areas. But Noor's aunts were there, and cousins, waiting to go in together, and her father pushed her towards them. She stuck close to them, for fear of getting lost, but she felt shy of them. Even those who did not normally wear the *hijab* or *niqab* were covered up completely. One of her cousins rewrapped and pinned her scarf for her—it was a plain pashmina, thicker and clumsier than their light slips of material—and it made her claustrophobic, bound in; it itched the back of her neck, muffled her hearing and reduced her vision at the sides.

It was a relief to get inside, out of the clamour and chaos of the square. But as more and more people made their way in, the women's balcony became packed, people pressing against each other on all sides. There were feet treading on Noor's heels, and elbows in her side. The balcony overlooked the main hall, but Noor was jammed in against her aunt's back and could not see down.

119

The thing to do was to release herself—release her self—give herself over to it. Then she would become one with the mass of bodies, and would not, holding herself tight and aloof, feel shoulders and stomachs of others an intrusion. But she did not—could not—and she felt all the more awkward, all the more other, for it.

When the service began, she thought she might faint: from boredom if not from the heat. The imam talked on and on, and her Arabic was not good enough to follow what he was saying. She did not know the responses to the prayers, or the words to the songs, and she seethed with anger at her father for making her come here. Her mother, she knew, would be horrified to hear about it. Her mother and father's compact had been that Jamal and Noor were brought up with no religion; if anyone asked them what they were, they were taught to say that both the Prophet Muhammad and Jesus Christ were good men, who taught us all to live a better life. But she would not dare tell her mother that her father had made her attend the mosque. It might be enough for her mother to insist she come back to England.

The one thing the imam said that she managed to understand, because he repeated it so frequently, was that *one tear shed for Hussain washed away a hundred sins*. But she could not work out what he meant: what sins counted, for instance, and what were unforgivable? Could one big sin take up your whole allowance?

She wished she could ask Ruth Armstrong about this. She could not, of course, admit to going to the mosque—but perhaps there was some other way of bringing it up. So far, she had

120

not been able to pluck up the courage to ask Ruth about God, or Jesus, or anything like that. She had been on the verge, a hundred times. But each time she was about to speak, her heart leapt to her mouth and blocked the words. She would have to be braver, she decided. And she resolved, then and there, that the very next time she saw Ruth, she would do it.

*   *   *

When the service was over, they all drove back to the al-Husayn compound. The only good thing about the day, Noor thought, was that it was *Fakah*, a day of fasting, so nobody ate. She could feel her stomach gnarling with hunger. She hadn't even picked at dinner last night—chicken macaroni salad with caramel flan for afters—and this morning she hadn't had breakfast, either. It was a grim, satisfying feeling. Unbelievably, she had found, and unintentionally, she had lost three pounds this week. Being around Ruth Armstrong made her forget about food. And when she did try to eat, it was as if she had somehow forgotten how, the chewing and the swallowing of it. Every bite of food she ate tasted like chalk and dust and rubber in her mouth. And not eating, she found, made her body feel pleasantly jittery, like she had drunk too much Coke, like she had all the energy in the world. She had taken to not eating in the evenings, telling her father that she had eaten already. Already her jeans were looser. She could wiggle a finger in between the waistband and her stomach, when only a week ago she'd had to lie on the floor to do them up and even then the top button wouldn't go.

121

She lolled against a cushion, her mind drifting in and out, as her relatives sat around talking about the situation in Iraq, lamenting the fact that during the whole of Saddam's rule, nobody had been able to make a pilgrimage to Karbala. Some thought it would be a good thing if he were deposed; others were against the intervention on principle. Noor listened for a while, but the discussions bored her, and eventually she managed to slip away, lock herself in the upstairs bathroom and write her journal. She filled pages and pages with the day, and with speculations about what Ruth Armstrong had been doing in her absence. It was the first day all week Noor had not seen her. She hoped Ruth was managing with Anna, without Noor's help. Only yesterday Ruth had said: I don't know what I'd do without you. Noor had written this down, incredulous, underlined it. *I don't know what I'd do without you.*

Now, she added, *I don't know what I'd do without you either, Ruth.* Then someone banged on the door and she almost jumped out of her skin, hot and flushed as if she'd been caught in some indecent act.

'I'm coming,' she yelled, too loud, and she bundled her diary back into her shoulder bag.

It was Farid outside, wanting to use the bathroom. She stopped, and they looked at each other. She had never had much time for Farid before: he was Jamal's age, and had been friends with Jamal during their childhood holidays. The boys had oscillated between ignoring the younger girls and running away from them, to teasing them, or inventing new ways to torture them. But now, suddenly, after the day of the *Shajarat*, they had something in common: almost a secret between them.

'Hello,' Noor said.

Farid nodded. He seemed to hesitate, and then he said, 'Have you seen the missionary's wife?'

'Oh yes,' Noor said, 'I see her a lot, actually. Ruth Armstrong'—she spoke the name carefully, savouring the chance to use it aloud—'has asked for my help with Anna, quite a few times. Yes,' she finished in a rush, 'I see her most days, come to think of it.' She felt the skin on her face burning. She stood her ground.

'So she's OK?' Farid said.

'Oh yes,' Noor said, 'I should think so. I think'— she lowered her voice, authoritatively—'I think she's finding it hard, away from home, and her husband working so hard. He's away most of the time, you see, most days.'

Farid looked at her. 'OK,' he said. Then he changed his tone. 'Well, if you'll excuse me . . .' and gestured towards the bathroom.

'Oh,' Noor said, 'sorry,' and she stepped aside to let him through. He closed and locked the door behind him. Noor stood for a moment. She felt, oddly, as if she had betrayed Ruth Armstrong by talking about her. It had felt so good to speak so confidently about her, to assert her, Noor's, closeness with Ruth. But now, afterwards, it felt somehow wrong.

Inside the bathroom, the loo flushed. Farid was coming back out.

She went quickly back downstairs, before she had to see him again.

3

He came for her on Friday morning.

When she saw him, she had a shock: she had been wanting, she realised, to see him. She was immediately self-conscious. It did not help that her trousers were creased and her shirt food-spattered, her hair unbrushed, and she knew there were shadows beneath her eyes. She smoothed down her shirt and tried to clear her throat. They looked at each other, and neither of them spoke. He was in a *thobe* again, but no headdress, and bright white trainers. His dark hair was gelled back, and a pair of mirrored sunglasses was pushed up on his forehead. The overall effect was somehow incongruous. He looked younger than she had remembered, fresher-faced, and she reminded herself that he was barely twenty.

'What are you doing here?' Noor's clear, crisp tones resounded down the hallway. Noor had come over shortly after Euan left, as the maids were arriving. She had been chattering, ever since, about Islam and the mosque, Atonement and Iraq—Ruth could not quite follow the thread of what she was saying, and she was starting to worry that the girl was making a habit of coming over, uninvited. It had barely been eight o'clock when she knocked on the door. But Ruth had not been able to bring herself to turn Noor away. Farid's eyes flickered to Noor, then back to Ruth. She felt a slow blush creeping up the back of her neck. They had been standing there, looking at each other, for several moments now, and neither of them had yet spoken.

the hard edge gone from it.

'Of course,' Ruth said. 'Sure you've been great with her, these past few days. She likes you. You'll be grand.'

'She likes me,' Noor repeated. 'You know, I think she does. I really think she does.'

'Of course she does. And you'll be grand. I'll give you my number, and you've got your cousin's. And the maids are here—'

'And Sampaguita's there, too,' Noor burst in. 'She used to look after Baba, when he was a boy. And I know first aid, we did it in school.'

'Well then,' Farid said in his velvet-accented English. 'It seems, *inshallah*, we are settled.'

'I'll pay you, of course,' Ruth said to Noor. 'I'll get some money out and—'

'Oh, no!' Noor interrupted. 'You don't need to pay me, Ruth! It would be a pleasure to look after Anna, honestly it would. You really don't need to pay me.'

And that was it: it was done. Ruth changed her shirt and trousers and buckled her stiff new sandals, washed her face and combed her hair, kissed Anna—who miraculously did not cry, or cling—and climbed into the car with Farid.

*   *   *

They turned out of the compound, and joined the slip road to the highway. She thanked him for the scarf—is it a scarf, or a wall hanging? she asked, and he just shrugged and said it was whatever she wanted it to be—and realised she had little else to say to him. He seemed equally nervous: his eyes were hidden behind his reflective sunglasses,

127

but his Adam's apple kept bobbing, as if he was swallowing, or silently clearing his throat. She was relieved when he turned on the radio. She was more self-conscious than she could remember being, ever: of her feet prim and flat on the floor, her hands sweating in her lap, the slight bulge of her stomach over the waistband of her jeans, how loud the noise was when she swallowed. The radio was playing the new Christina Aguilera hit, 'Dirrty'. It made her hot with embarrassment. She knew the song. Sometimes, when Euan was out, she turned on the radio for company; tuned it in to pop stations and danced along with Anna. He could not bear music of any kind as he worked, not even classical. If he turned the radio on in the evenings, it was to classical or current affairs stations. He had spent a whole sermon, once, talking about how debasing modern pop videos were, with their spray-on clothes and sexual moves and stripping. After that she was ashamed to tell him that she watched the music videos, sometimes, and could sing along to those songs. She felt a ripple of giggles rising in her throat and tried to keep it down, disguising it with a cough. She felt Farid looking at her and she tried to think of something to say, but her mind was a racing blank and her tongue had thickened to take up the whole of her mouth. Her legs were tight in her jeans. They were a stiff, new pair, bought specially—for camping in the desert, she'd thought, Jeep rides into the sunset. She could feel every seam, every stitch, against the inside of her thighs. The central seam pressed into her crotch; she was pulsing, almost itching. She shifted in her seat to try to release the pressure as the song came to its tacky, glistening, provocative end, and tried to banish such thoughts—such physical thoughts—from her mind.

*   *   *

The Bahrain National Museum was on the Al-Fatih highway west of Manama, overlooking the Gulf. It was an impressive complex: sprawling, monumental exhibition halls and wide, open plazas; glossy marble floors and inscribed marble walls, everything hewn from the same sumptuous pale stone. Farid bought their tickets from a desk in the cavernous foyer and they joined a group of jostling schoolchildren filing through to the main display: a history of Bahrain from 6,000 BC to the present. It was a relief to have something to do, something to concentrate on. They followed the school party up and down the aisles. They saw cases of skulls and reconstructions of ancient burial chambers, the skeletons buried on their right-hand sides, curled in the foetal position, with pots of water and jars of spices at their heads to help them on their journey through the afterlife. They saw large urns holding children's bones and archaeologists' representations of graves from later civilisations, built together like the cells of a beehive. They saw ancient clay tablets from Mesopotamia, inscribed with blessings and curses, verses from the Sumerian epics of Gilgamesh and Lugulbanda in a pre-cuneiform script. Ruth dutifully read the translations: *Tears, lament, anguish, and depression are within me. Heart-sickness overwhelms me. Evil fate overcomes me. Malignant sickness overburdens me.*

'Not exactly happy-chappies, are they, these Sumerians?' she tried. It was a poor attempt at a joke: the first time either of them had spoken. Her

129

voice echoed against the cold, blank walls.

'Pardon?' Farid looked startled.

'I just said—' She felt foolish now. 'It's all so—melancholy.'

'The Sumerians were not an optimistic people. They believed that once your life is over, you wander as a ghost, a *gidim*, in a damp, unlit underworld, for ever.'

Ruth looked at him, his face sharp and shadowed in the thin artificial light of the windowless hall, and swallowed the urge to laugh, or weep. What on earth—she said the words aloud in her brain, almost like a prayer—what on earth was she doing here? She imagined telling Anna, one day. You won't remember, pet, but one time when you were little, we spent a few months in Bahrain, in the Middle East, and I left you to go around a museum with an awkward Arab teenager, and it was the most daring thing I had ever done.

She stared at the bones in the pot in front of her, bubbled like honeycomb. Her head hummed with emptiness. She blinked, caught her own reflection in the glass. She shivered. The conditioned air was dry and chilly and gooseflesh was rising rough on her forearms. The schoolchildren had left the hall now: save for an attendant or two lurking in the shadows, she and Farid were the only people there. She suddenly remembered a story she had read, or been read, a long time ago: a young boy left behind in a museum after dark and the exhibits coming to life. The half-shattered Sumerian skulls in the backlit case gaped at her. She rubbed her arms briskly and followed Farid on to the final aisle.

'This one,' he was calling, 'this one is happier. This is what I wanted to show you.'

130

These plaques showed artists' impressions of a land called Dilmun, place of eternal youth and happiness. There were more clay tablets, elaborately inscribed: *Utnapishtim, whom they call the Faraway, has entered the assembly of the gods*, ran the translation, and *What is this sleep which holds you now? You are lost in the dark and cannot hear me.* Gilgamesh, Farid read aloud, mourning his comrade Enkidu, journeyed through the desert and the grasslands to beseech Utnapishtim-the-Faraway in the land of Dilmun, eastward of the mountains, garden of the sun, the place of everlasting life. But although he passed through the trials of fire and water and won the rose that restores eternal life, he was tricked by a serpent bathing deep in a pool, who sensed the sweetness of the flower and snatched it from his hands. *Was it for this that I toiled with my hands,* Farid recited, *Is it for this I have wrung out my heart?* And Gilgamesh went back to his people and the land of the dead and dying, grown frail with the knowledge of mortality.

'Look,' Farid said, pointing to the final tablet in the display. Ruth stooped and read, shielding her eyes against the glare of the spotlights.

Though he was strong of arm, he will not rise again;
He had wisdom and a comely face, he will not come again;
He is gone into the mountain, he will not come again.

The words sent a rush of something uncomfortable, a tremor, intimations of mortality, through the whole of her body.

'You said this one's happier?' she said—a stupid, clumsy, meaningless thing to say, for the sake of saying something.

Farid was staring at her eagerly, as if she should understand. 'It's Bahrain,' he said. 'Dilmun is Bahrain. Dilmun is our ancient name, you see. The land of paradise and eternal life. Look.' He turned to the display cabinet, and read aloud the translation of one of the stone tablets.

'The land of Dilmun is holy, the land of Dilmun is pure.

'In Dilmun the raven does not croak, the lion does not kill.

'No one says, "My eyes are sick, my head is sick".

'No one says, "I am an old man, I am an old woman".

'You see? Dilmun is paradise. Your Eden. It did exist, once. It existed here—this was it. You are in it right now. The most sacred place in all Arabia—in all the mythologies. That's why there are so many graves—I will show you, later, some of the graves. People rowed here from the bigger islands and from the mainland to bury their dead, to send them on their way to the afterlife. And the *Shajarat* is there to guide them, to mark the place of entry.'

He was close enough that she could smell his breath: warm, and slightly sharp, unfamiliar. She felt the breath stop in her lungs, and her heart was thumping.

'It existed once,' he said. 'You weren't wrong, you weren't mistaken. Once, it existed, and this is the proof.'

That day, when they returned to the compound from the Tree of Life, Noor had rushed inside;

132

but the two of them (and Anna sleeping in the back) had stayed in the car for half, three-quarters, almost an hour: until Anna woke up and began to cry and Ruth had to go in. She had been seized with a peculiar dread of the airless, sunless house, of being inside there, shut away, a body buried before it has grown old. It was irrational, she knew, hysterical, but she could not bear to go back in, not yet. And so Farid (how odd he must have thought her, she thought only later) had sat with her.

She stared at him. Neither of them moved.

A new party of schoolchildren came clattering into the hall and Farid smiled, not the curved, superior smile he had smiled the first time they met, but a soft, tentative smile with his eyes.

And then he turned away, the moment was over, and they walked quickly through the rest of the exhibits. The upper hall was devoted to modern Bahrain, waxworks of women in traditional dress grinding herbs, weighing spices, crouched cooking over pits of fire. Photographs of *thobe*d men and camels, of pearl-divers, a reconstruction of the inside of a basket-weaver's house. They flitted around, overtaking the first group of children, who were sketching baskets and copying down inscriptions. And Ruth felt giddy, unreal, her feet light and her head ringing.

*   *   *

Out of the museum and into the bright light: the marble of the plaza reflecting the sky, reflecting the sea, the world whited out. Sharp edges and sheering façades, knife-edged sculptures of sails and sharks' fins dazzling in the sunlight, the sea-light. They walk to the edge of the waters, right up to where the Gulf begins, a zinc sheet sliding against the marble slabs, and the slippery, dizzy feeling grows: shimmering possibility, insubstantiality. They are standing side by side, looking out across the waters, out into the sun. She feels laughter rising, and this time she lets it out. Farid looks at her for a moment, and then he starts laughing too, and she thinks that neither of them knows what they are laughing about and she doesn't care and it doesn't matter. She has not brought sunglasses, and she cannot see his eyes behind his, so she reaches out and tugs them down, off. She does it without thinking, and as she does so a jolt runs through her. It is the closest either of them has come to touching the other and it suddenly seems too much, too intimate, to have pulled his sunglasses from his face. She holds them out to him, sober now, and he takes them back, carefully, his fingers on the opposite arm, not meeting hers. He folds them and places them in a pocket, and they stand for a moment, facing each other.

'I'm sorry,' she says, 'I—'

'No,' he says, 'don't be sorry.' But she is awkward now, and it is almost lunchtime, and Anna—and so they go back to the car.

*   *   *

On the way back, he stops by a dusty roadside stall and buys a pomegranate. Its skin is glossy and unblemished, perfect, a Christmas bauble. He gives it to her to hold. It is surprisingly heavy, dense, its skin taut as a drum. When she taps it, she can feel it quiver. Back at the compound, the maids have gone and Anna is sleepy, lying placid in Noor's lap. It is

134

a relief to see them again, to see that nothing has happened to them. She has been gone only a couple of hours, she reminds herself, although it feels as if she is arriving back from years away. In the kitchen, over a bowl of cold water, Farid shows her how to score the skin of the pomegranate with a knife, then twist and split it into two halves. The scarlet juice, brighter than blood, beads across the worktop and flecks Ruth's face where she is leaning in to see. Farid laughs and wipes his own face, spattered too. She touches her tongue tip to the back of her hand; the sourness of it glisters. Farid submerges the fruit in water for a few minutes, then lifts it out and begins peeling back skins of white membrane, twisting and pushing out clusters of seeds—the *arils*, he calls them—onto a plate. The seeds are like jewels, heaped rubies on the plate. They eat them standing, with teaspoons. The taste of them is glassy, astringent. They are like nothing Ruth has ever tasted before. Pomegranates are used a lot in Persian food, Farid tells her. His mother was from Iran—*was*, he says; she died when he was young. She fled her homeland with the Revolution, and could never go back. She taught them Persian stories, and cooked them Persian food. Pomegranates featured heavily: stewed with dried plums and lamb, or boiled to a syrup and drizzled in sauces. And in the Qur'an, too, he says, the sixty-eighth verse of the fifty-fifth sura speaks of paradise: *In it are fruit, the date palm and pomegranates.*

Later that evening, when Euan sees the remaining seeds in the fridge, he tosses her a fact. Did you know, he says, that there's a mistranslation in the Bible: it was a pomegranate Eve gave Adam, not an apple? The word comes from the same

135

root, the Latin *pomum*, for apple, but they are completely different things.

She feels her blood slow when he says that. He picks at a seed with his finger and thumb; presses it until it bursts then licks the pulp up. He does not ask her where the fruit came from, and now that he has talked of Adam and Eve, of knowledge and betrayal, she does not tell him.

4

Noor woke late on Saturday. She had gone to bed jittery with hunger, unable to sleep, her stomach gnarled and her mind racing. When she did sleep, her dreams twisted and swirled, like winds whipping round the centre of a hurricane. When morning finally came—the sharp slice of light through the slitted window—she felt sluggish and heavy. Her mouth tasted foul and she had a pounding headache. She lay in the tangled, damp sheets until she summoned the energy to haul herself out of bed and into the bathroom, where she peeled off her nightdress and stared at herself in the mirror with loathing. It was time to confront herself full-on: it was time for a change. She pinched rolls from her stomach, slapped the wobble of her arms, clambered up on the toilet seat in order to scrutinise her thighs from behind. Close up, her skin looked ashy and her teeth and tongue were coated in some sort of dry fur. She stood in the shower tray and scourged her skin from toes to fingertips with a bristled kitchen scourer—she did not have a loofah or a body brush, as beauty magazines advised—and then had a cold shower to try to wake herself up. It worked, to an extent: the freezing water felt like needles driving into her skin and she whimpered aloud, but she left the bathroom feeling clearer-headed, with her skin tingling. One or two of the recent practice cuts on her inner arm had reopened with the brushing, and they smarted. She tried to ignore them. In the kitchen, she boiled the kettle and made herself a cup of strong black tea, mashing the colour and the caffeine out of the tea bag with the back of a spoon. No milk, because the only carton in the fridge was full-fat, so she hacked off a wedge of lemon to combat the tongue-curling tannins. Sampaguita was in the utility room, sorting out the washing. She heard Noor and came clucking into the kitchen, flapping her hands and muttering hissing bursts of Tagalog. She took Noor's chin in her hand, tilted it upwards, clicked and fluted some more. She filled a cereal bowl with honey-nut cornflakes, glugged milk over, stuck a spoon in and shoved it pointedly towards Noor, then stood there, beady-eyed, hands on her hips. Noor started to protest. But that only prompted another shrill string of invective, and she was too tired to resist. She took up the spoon and dipped it into the flakes, lifted it up and dribbled the milk back out. Another barrage.

'All right, all right,' she muttered. 'Keep your hair on.'

Sampaguita frowned, and took a step closer, not catching the words, but understanding.

'Noor!' she said. *Noh.* 'Noor-miss!'

Noor sat down, took a spoonful of cereal and raised it slowly to her mouth. The taste was almost too much, too rich—and then it was heavenly. So sweet, so creamy. She felt the liquid soaking

137

into her parched tongue, manna. The day before, she had eaten only an apple and Anna's leftover yogurt, the day before that (Ashura) nothing at all. She took another spoonful, greedy now, her body overriding the part of her mind that was screeching at her to stop. Sampaguita stepped back, satisfied. Noor coughed, her mouth too full of food. Damp lumps of cornflakes spattered the breakfast bar. She stopped, overcome with a lurch of disgust. She put the spoon down and gulped a mouthful of tea. The bitter taste cut through the creamy milk, washed the taste of it from her mouth. She took another swig. Her self-control returned. She stood up, tugging the flimsy T-shirt material of her nightdress over her bottom and thighs, where it clung and creviced.

'I'm going to finish this in my room.'

Sampaguita narrowed her eyes, but said nothing. Noor lifted the bowl, turned and left the room, making a show of closing the door. When she was satisfied that Sampaguita had gone back to work, she slipped back into the bathroom and scraped the softening remains of cereal into the toilet bowl, leaving a few clots and a pool of milk behind to make it look realistic. She wanted so badly to lick the spoon—to run her finger around the bowl—but her willpower held firm. She left the bowl on the draining board, unwashed, where Sampaguita would see it—and set about making her plan of action.

Because Ruth Armstrong had invited her to church tomorrow.

'Of course you can come,' she had said, 'if you're interested.' Then she had frowned and said, 'Except, well, would your father not mind?'

'Oh no,' Noor had said. 'Oh no, honestly he wouldn't,' and she had rushed to explain that her mother was English, that her old school was a Church of England school, with a chapel and Sunday services, everything: of course he wouldn't mind. This wasn't quite true. Chapel at boarding school, in England, was one thing: but here in Bahrain, it might be quite another. And this newly devout father of hers, who dressed in a *thobe* and tried to practise *wudu* and *salah*, would surely object, at the very least, to her going to a Christian church.

When Ruth Armstrong still looked dubious, she promised she would check with her father, to be absolutely sure. This was an outright lie. She had no intention whatsoever of telling her father. He worked on Sundays—it was a normal working day in the Gulf, a Tuesday back home—and so he would just not know of her going.

She hated lying to Ruth Armstrong—felt physically sick as she was doing it—but she could not bear for the invitation to be rescinded.

'Well,' Ruth had said, 'only if you have his explicit permission, all right?' They were absolutely, categorically forbidden from evangelising to Arabs, she said: if it was discovered they were, they could be thrown out of the country, and there could be consequences for St Thomas's. Christianity was tolerated in Bahrain because of the country's long-standing ties with England, but that tolerance was conditional, Noor must understand.

'Oh yes,' Noor said. 'I understand, absolutely I understand. I mean—of course. And I will of course get Baba's permission, I honestly will.' Again, the lie: she felt sure it was flashing and shrieking, like the siren on a police car, and she felt a flicker of fear, a sudden, tilting intimation of vertigo, as if she was teetering on the edge of something deeper and bigger than she had known. But she couldn't *not* go. She didn't know why: all she knew was that she needed to go, had to be there, near Ruth.

'Well—' Ruth said, and before she could waver, or suggest that *she* spoke to Noor's father, Noor said, as confidently as she could: 'I promise it's all right, Ruth. I promise.'

And she left glowing. Ruth Armstrong was so caring, so considerate—so compassionate. She was so trusting—the way she had trusted Noor to look after Anna, alone—nobody had ever trusted Noor like that, before. Ever.

The Diary of Noor Hussain

Saturday, 15th March 2003

PLANS FOR A NEW ME

Things I Hate About Myself
– A stone (at least) more to lose
– Hair greasy and split-endy
– Glasses
– I look like a Bearded Woman
– Eyebrows join together in the middle into one fat hairy caterpillar
– Nails raggy and bloody where I've bitten them
– The scars on my left arm and thigh
– Legs lumpy like cottage cheese
– No nice clothes
– ~~My stupid name~~   RA said it was a 'very pretty name'.

Things I Like About Myself
– ~~I'm clever~~   What use is that when you just get called a swot?
– RA says I'm kind
– I looked after little Anna all morning
– ??

To Do By Tomorrow
– Bleach moustache (again) and also hair on chin and cheeks
– Dab Dettol on spots
– Hair mask out of egg-yolk, avocado, olive oil
– Pluck eyebrows (tweezers in First Aid kit in utility room cupboard??)
– Fitness routine: 100 sit-ups and 3 sets of bicep curls using back of chair and as many star-jumps as possible in 3 minutes

ALSO: <u>find out about Inishargy.</u>

Things to talk about so far:
– the cut-away bog nearby is a prominent feature of the peninsula
– The issue of EU Milk Quotas and stifling over-regulation in dairy farming (N.B. find out more before you bring this up!!)
– Has she ever visited the nearby Temple of the Winds at Mount Stewart or the brooding Tower of Scrabo which at dusk is silhouetted against the sky like an ominous watch-tower from Lord of the Rings?
– Does the name Armstrong come from Viking times when raiders crossed the Irish Sea, hence the word 'Strangfjord' from Old Norse meaning 'Strong

Ford'? N.B. what was Ruth's name before she was married?

Noor closed her diary. This last section had taken her quite some time: hours of Googling Strangford Peninsula and Inishargy, where Ruth had said she was from; looking at photographs, following links. She had found Ruth's farm on a map, she thought. She had also found minutes from the parish meetings, and photographs of Euan on the church website. It was a strange, illicit feeling, amassing information, gathering and noting and possessing all you could of someone. She was doing nothing wrong, she told herself. She was only looking at what was there, and the information was there, for anyone to see. Nevertheless, she had been careful to delete the browsing history after each time she used her father's computer; she was not sure why, but she did so, all the same.

Time to get started. She went back to the kitchen to amass ingredients. Dettol she found under the sink, a big bottle of it. There was plenty of olive oil, and a whole box of eggs. But no avocados. The recipe she had found online stated that two avocados were needed: ripe, mashable ones. But Sampaguita was gone now—she worked only until lunchtime on Saturdays—and there was no point asking her father to buy avocados on his way home from work, because he might not be home for hours, or he might be in a bad mood and point-blank refuse. It was bucketing down outside. The storm that had been brewing for the past few weeks had finally broken, and the sky was cracking with lightning. But there was nothing for it: she would have to brave it. She put on her hated old gym shorts—there was no point getting her jeans soaked—and a hooded top and gathered together as many loose coins as she could from her father's dresser. She paused on the veranda, and almost turned back: the rain was coming down in solid sheets. But her determination got the better of her and she jumped down into the deluge. She could not resist knocking on the Armstrongs' door. But it was Mr Armstrong who answered it—Reverend—and she was suddenly tongue-tied. She mumbled something about coming to church tomorrow, and what time they would be leaving—it was half past eight, she knew this, she had checked twice with Ruth, in case she missed it—and ducked back into the rain, feeling a strange swell and surge of disappointment that it had not been Ruth who answered the door.

The cold store was only ten minutes away, but by the time she got there and back, she was soaked to the bone, her hair so plastered to her head that she would not even need a shower to wet it before applying the conditioning mask. She peeled off her sodden clothes and towelled herself dry—remembering with a sudden pang the bathtimes when she was little, when she and Jamal would be bathed together, and their mother and father would catch up each of them in a fluffy towelling robe and rub and tickle them dry.

She pushed the thought from her mind.

In the kitchen, she cracked two eggs and separated their yolks, beat them up with the avocados and enough oil to form a thick, slow sludge. She spooned it onto her hair, trying not to gag at the smell, and wrapped her head in cling film, as the recipe instructed. Once that was

143

done, she mixed up the hair-lightening paste and spatulaed it liberally over her upper lip, cheeks and chin, then dabbed the stinging Dettol on the worst of the spots on her forehead. She lay carefully down on her bed to wait the necessary twenty minutes. It was impossible to read—even the slightest movement displaced the fuzzy bleaching cream— so she closed her eyes and let her mind slip into the grooves of her new fantasy. It was elaborate, now, each detail considered, turned over and over and added in only when Noor was satisfied with it. She was in bed, with a fever—not an ugly, sweaty fever, but the sort of fever they had in novels, where the heroine's cheeks were delicately flushed and her eyes were dark pools. She lies there, drifting—and Ruth Armstrong comes in, pausing at the door and then rushing to the bed, dropping her bag. (She is carrying a bag, filled with grapes and flowers, because she has heard that Noor is ill. How exactly she heard had caused Noor quite some thought—but she had settled on the maids, Sampaguita mentioning to one of Ruth's maids, and knowing the name of the hospital.) Noor's father is not there, nor is her mother—her father has been called away to some medical emergency elsewhere and her mother does not know she is ill, and Ruth is the first, the only, person there. She is kneeling at Noor's side. Noor's eyes are closed, and Ruth thinks she is sleeping, and so she just strokes, gently, the hair from Noor's forehead with her slim, cool fingers—and she murmurs a prayer, so softly, like a lullaby. And then Noor opens her eyes, and Ruth's face is inches from hers, eyes wide, lips parted in concern. And Ruth says, *Shh, now, shh, it's all right, everything's all right* in her low, lilting

144

Irish accent, and Noor closes her eyes again and Ruth kisses her forehead, so gently, so gently she can hardly feel it . . .

*   *   *

Noor is hot, suddenly, and it is difficult to breathe. She feels hollow inside, as if the floor of her stomach has fallen away. She is tingling, all over. She touches her fingertips to her stomach, lightly, so lightly she can barely feel their touch, and it is as if her fingers are someone else's fingers. She has never known before this yearning, such emptiness.

*   *   *

When she scraped the cream from her face, the skin below was pink, but the dark hairs were definitely thinner and lightened. The Dettoled spots looked red and shiny as always—but perhaps, she reluctantly decided, one application was not enough; she should do it again before bed and then perhaps she'd see results tomorrow. Lashings of Rimmel concealer would have to do, otherwise. Her hair was another matter. As she washed the mixture out, it congealed into smelly, drain-clogging lumps and she was forced to kneel with an unbent metal hanger and poke the plughole clear. And there was an odd, sulphurous smell that seemed to trail with her wherever she went. It was only as she was drying her hair that she realised: the yolks had scrambled in the hot water as she rinsed them, and her hair was caked with clumps of rank-smelling egg.

It took five shampooings before her hair had ceased to smell. Any benefit from the hair mask was undone by the number of times she had to wash and dry her hair, and by the time it was finally clean again, she was behind her schedule. She found the tweezers and got to work on her eyebrows, but she was het up and rushing; she could not seem to get them even, plucking first too much from one side, then the other. Eventually she threw the tweezers down in a panic and decided she would have to draw the missing parts of her eyebrows back in.

It was six o'clock now. She had not even managed one set of her fitness routines, and her father was home. He was annoyed at the mess of mixing bowls and whisks in the kitchen, furious that there was no hot water. He cursed Noor in Arabic as he stomped about, boiling a kettle for hot water to shave, trying to wash over the sink with a wet flannel and bar of soap. He was going out tonight, he said, how was he supposed to go out tonight? *Sakheefa*, he shouted, *hablah!*

It took all of Noor's wit to apologise and pacify him. A few weeks ago, she would have screamed and sworn right back at him: but this was no longer the way. She needed him to be as calm as possible. She grovelled.

By the time he left, she was exhausted. Her body, though purged, felt raw and sore, and her limbs were heavy. She weighed herself—that was the bright spot of the day, she had lost another two pounds, which meant almost half a stone in total—then curled up in bed, ready for tomorrow.

5

Saturday was her first full day with Euan since they had arrived in Bahrain. It was miserable. They had planned to go sightseeing, or to the souk, but a thunderstorm broke: the *mawsim*, heralding the start of the hot season. From now, the temperature would rise almost daily; in a few weeks it would be reaching 40° with the ease of a stretching cat, a panther, effortless and languid and terrifying. *Almighty* was how Euan described the storm, as they stood by the front door watching the rain lash down. It bounced up metres where it hit the ground, churning the dusty road of the compound into a seething, semi-viscous mass.

'If we lived in another age,' he said, 'we'd think that the storm was the wrath of God.' He was making a joke. But privately, Ruth agreed with him. Storms like this were the reason people did believe in God, she thought to herself. It was too easy to believe, if you knew no better, that a vengeful, furious god was hurling the lightning bolts, spitting the winds. *I, the Lord your God, am a jealous God, punishing the children for the sins of the fathers to the third and fourth generation of those that hate me.*

Inside, there was little to do. Anna was restless and badly behaved; she had not seen enough of Euan recently and she was punishing him for it. He tried to read her story books, but she wriggled and bit him—she had never bitten, never—and she howled when he tried to punish her for it by taking her toys away.

'How do you do this all day?' Euan said to her,

147

and there wasn't admiration, but incomprehension, and even condescension in his voice. When Anna was born, he had been a dutiful father, taking his turn to get up in the night and change nappies, mix up formula and sterilise bottles. But she had never shaken the fear that he resented the baby—even if only at some deep, barely conscious level—for forcing them too early into marriage and curtailing his options, making his final months at Braemore so difficult. Now, he prayed over her at night and tried to teach her grace and other simple prayers, patiently, over and over again; he read her story books and engaged her in conversation. But Anna was at a difficult stage, contrary and stubborn, and Ruth was beginning to sense anew his exasperation with the child, how eager he was to throw up his hands and leave her to deal with tantrums.

Was she sensing it, or was she just imagining it? Suddenly, she could not be sure. He was busy, she told herself, that was all. But since their arrival in Bahrain, and the realisation of what—or how little—they both meant to him, she was starting to see all of his behaviour in a new light, registering every flicker of annoyance towards them.

Eventually, as she expected, Euan shut himself in the bedroom with his notebooks and his Bible and she was left with Anna. She turned on the TV to distract and soothe her. They found a children's channel and curled up together to watch it. It was a cartoon adventure about children discovering a new world. She thought it might be too old for Anna, but Anna seemed to follow the story, and the bright colours and music were hypnotic. Anna's shuddering breaths lengthened. After a while, Ruth stopped watching the television; watched her daughter, instead. How avidly she watched it, how trustingly. For the first time, Ruth felt a twinge of real, ineffable sadness. It was something she could not have put into words, even if she had tried. It was a feeling of pure loneliness, an understanding of the stories we tell ourselves to combat that loneliness, and the loss that knowledge brought.

She sat there, tears rolling silently down her cheeks, and she wondered what Euan would do, if he came back in to find her weeping at a cartoon. Would he laugh at her, or would he be concerned, take her in his arms and hold her close?

*   *   *

They made love that evening. It was the first time they had done so since arriving in Bahrain. Ruth clung to her husband, pressing him deeper in her, as if by doing so she could press herself into him. But it was no use. Afterwards, she curled up against him, fitting her body to his, shaping herself along the curve of his back, her knees spooned in behind his, her arms around him. She matched her breathing to his, but it didn't work. She could not stem the creeping rise of a slow, wordless terror.

*   *   *

She has been trying not to think of Farid, but it is no use. He has been in her thoughts; he has been her thoughts. He had given her a piece of paper when he left the house yesterday. It was lined paper, torn from a file pad, written with neatened spidery letters in black ink. *THREE STORIES ABOUT GOD* was written at the top, in capital

149

letters. The stories were short, little more than a line or two each. *One. A prostitute sees a thirsty dog scratching at the ground. She goes to a well, and fetches water for it in her shoe. Two. A man who has killed ninety-nine men goes to an imam to ask if Allah will forgive him. The imam says yes, and the man kills the imam to make it a round hundred. Three. An unbeliever watches a flower unfolding in a garden.* The imam had told him these stories, Farid said, when he was twelve, and his mother died. She had ovarian cancer, which ravaged her so quickly, so comprehensively, that she was dead within three months of the first diagnosis. He had been angry; bewildered; raged at Allah. The imam, a kindly old man who meant well, had recited these stories to him, and although he did not know what they meant, and although he had scoffed at the imam and at Islam, he had not been able to forget them. The following year, he had stopped attending the mosque, and his father had not forced him. But he had always remembered the stories, and perhaps they would mean something to her.

He had been embarrassed as he handed the folded sheet of paper to her, and she had not known what to say, either. She had read the parables—for that is what they surely were—twice, three times, then folded the page up and hidden it in her phrase book. When she thinks through the parables now, what she decides they are saying is: there are no gods but the gods we create, the gods formed out of the stuff of need, or fear, or wonder. Or: there is nothing more than what we do, here, in this life, on this earth. There is no heaven, no paradise, only this, here, now.

She cannot decide if this is a liberating or a

150

terrifying thought. All she feels is an engulfing sense of loss, the meaninglessness of all things, now that the meaning has been stripped from them.

*   *   *

He called for her again on Sunday afternoon. She was ready this time. She had changed out of her church clothes, plaited her hair back, rubbed some cream blusher into her cheeks. Noor was there, too—she had come back with Ruth after church, wanting to talk about the sermon, and what it meant. Euan had given the sermon this week, and Ruth had found it contradictory and overzealous. It was one of his set pieces about the life of Jesus, the baby born to a peasant girl; she had heard it tens of times before and found it disingenuous. It was not even Euan's sermon, really: he had taken and elaborated it from someone else; she remembered hearing it with him at a Mannafest when she was a teenager. But beside her, Noor had listened avidly, hanging on Euan's every word. She had watched Noor for a while. The girl's lips were parted and her tongue was slightly out of her mouth, as if it was not enough to hear, she had to inhale, to suck in Euan's words. Noor's skin was scattered with a fresh burst of pimples and she had dark, sunken circles under her eyes, badly disguised with concealer. Ruth felt a fresh wave of pity for her, so obviously lonely, and she had taken care to be patient with her, to invite her back to the house to continue their conversation.

It was the charitable thing to do, she told herself.

But perhaps this was not quite, or not entirely true. She was nervous of seeing Farid, equally

151

nervous as she longed to see him. With Noor there—for she would invite Noor along too, on the pretext of needing help with Anna—she would be safe. She could indulge, whilst being protected from, her strange sudden feelings and longings. She was safe, she told herself. With Noor and Anna there, she would be safe.

They drove south, away from Manama, along the eastern coastal road towards Dar Island and the resort of Al Bander. They stopped to look at a flock of upraised dhows, the salted, stippled bows being planed and sanded by dark-faced boys in white headdresses and loose brown kaftans, oiled and repainted by other, older men, who took turns to squat in the shade of the curved prows, or under makeshift canopies of canvas and sackcloth draped from ladders and scaffolding. They stopped a second time when they crossed the causeway bridge from the mainland to Dar Island. Now the view to the east was clear and unimpeded: miles of glittering white sea and whitened sky, past the tip of Qatar and right across the Gulf, hundreds of miles, past uninhabited scattered islets to where the tip of the emirate states reached towards the curve of Iran. As Farid pointed it all out, Ruth laughed and compared it to the Irish Sea—seen from Portavogie, say, or Ballywalter, equivalent little towns and fishing ports—the oily black waters and slapping waves, the roiling, scudding clouds that could in a matter of minutes obscure the view, so you could see no more than a hundred metres out to sea and could only guess where the westerly parts of Scotland were, or the Isle of Man.

'I would like to see Ireland, one day,' Farid said. 'I would like to see your world. It is so much part of

152

you.'

She thought, involuntarily, how dark his eyes were, how steady, how his gaze held hers—

And then Noor jumped in: 'Me too!' she said, 'I'd love to see Ireland, too,' and she started babbling about Vikings and monks and cats, and the moment was gone—just as Ruth had intended, just as she had hoped.

And yet.

They got back in the car, and drove on.

*   *   *

Al Bander, when they reached it, was cool and airy, the illusion of a breeze conjured by tiers of fans. The main restaurant opened into a terrace, scattered with round glass tables under striped awnings, and beyond were deckchairs and sunloungers arranged in rows by a split-level pool. Only a handful of the tables and loungers were occupied. They chose a table at the very edge of the terrace, facing the sea, and ordered drinks from the waiter: a tiny Indian man in an immaculate white suit. Farid ordered a bottle of beer and Ruth, in a burst of extravagance, asked for an 'Egyptian Champagne': white wine and soda water. When it came, it was a crystal chalice the size of her cupped hands, adorned with papery pink blossoms—*muhammadi*, Farid said they were called.

'*Muhammadi*,' she repeated, and he smiled at her accent, and she blushed, and knew he saw her blushing.

Noor had taken seriously her charge of looking after Anna. The two of them had run down to the edge of the shallow pool, and taken their shoes

153

off to splash their feet in the water. Their laughter rippled through the air on the currents of the fans. She and Farid sat in silence, watching them, watching the waterfalls—designed to look like large terracotta pitchers—spilling their contents from the upper to the lower-level pools. She felt a slow warmth in her stomach from the wine, and her head felt light in the heat.

They talked of this and that; of Ireland, of Bahrain. He did not mention her husband, and neither did she. They talked of the parables he had given her, and what she thought they meant. He talked a little of his mother, of when he lost his faith in Allah.

*   *   *

She says, for the first time aloud, *When I lost my faith in God.* She says it, and nothing happens: nothing. The air shimmers, the fountains plash, the children laugh. The waiter comes by to offer more drinks. She says the words again: nothing. No shaking of the earth, no sudden cloud of darkness, no splitting of the rocks. Yet it is done. How can it be done? But it is done: she has lost her faith.

*   *   *

He leans forward, asks her if she is going to cry. His eyes are dark and liquid; you could lose yourself in those eyes, she thinks, forget yourself. She should have looked away from him by now, broken the gaze: but she has not. Again, softer, Is she going to cry? No, she is not—she knows she is not, it is all right. She is past that, now.

154

The sun begins to set. Beyond the palm fronds, the sea is green, shot through with rippling veins of orange light. The sun sets so rapidly here; you can watch it falling through the sky like a dropped coin.

It is too romantic, she knows. Being here, with him, in the sunset, drinking wine. It is wrong, she knows this, too. She knew it before she came; she should not have come. She pretended to herself that having Noor there, having Anna, would make a difference, or at least be camouflage, or ballast. But she was deceiving herself, or letting herself be deceived. And at the same time, even as she knows she should not be there—here—she is strangely, helplessly excited, as if not being here, not coming here, was not a choice, was never an option.

Time slows. She is acutely conscious of the fuzz of sweat on her empty glass quietly beading into droplets; the quivering cyan blue of the pool; far off, seagulls skimming over the glistering sea. Against the last blaze of light, they are become silhouettes. Noor and Anna are laughing again, she hears them run past, playing chase, the slap of their bare feet on limestone paving. She does not move. Her hands are palm-down on the table, stilled, where they had been picking at the edges of a place mat, worrying the beginnings of a fray. Farid reaches forward, turns her right hand over, then her left, holds them cupped open, wrists up. It is the first time they have touched. She has never felt so exposed. With his thumb, he traces a vein down her wrist and into her palm. She can feel his breath, warm and more ragged than hers.

She does not look at him.

Time is away and somewhere else. Each moment is an entirety; pearls on a string. There is nothing else beyond them, here and now.

Stretched out into streaks of red on the horizon, the day shimmers, settles; night-time stirs and rises. The first flickerings and flitterings of an evening breeze, the click and whisper of the sprinkler on the lawns behind, the husky scent of jasmine as pale, open petals bruise with water. Her hands are shadows, he is a shape of shifting shadows, somewhere a bird—is it a bulbul?—burbles its liquid, plaintive call.

What is she doing?

What has she done?

Noor and Anna run over. It is night-time, they are hungry, wasn't the sunset pretty? Ruth stands: the scrape of the heavy chair against the tiled ground is discordant and ugly. Euan will be back soon. She is a wife, and a mother. He is a boy, not yet twenty, and a Muslim. Adultery is illegal, not just by the law of God, but the law of the land. What if the waiters have seen, what if Noor has seen?

Her whole body is tingling.

'We have to go.'

'Ruth,' he says. It is the first time he has called her *Ruth*, has not called her *Mrs Armstrong*. Her name in his mouth is a ruby.

'We have to go.' She turns and picks up Anna, feels her voice and body slip into the familiar rhythms of motherhood. Did you have fun, are you thirsty, let me wipe that smudge from your face, oh my goodness your nappy needs changing. Noor is trotting beside her, relating in minute detail the tale

156

of some game played, some elaborate imaginary escapade. Ruth strides ahead, back through the clubhouse, down the gravel pathway to the bougainvillea-laden canopy, leaving Farid to pay the bill and follow. The night is thrumming with the creak-chirp of crickets, already a moon is rising.

How has this happened? she thinks, and the night come so fast?

'Lady moon, lady moon, sailing up so high, drop down to Baby from out yonder sky,' she murmurs into Anna's ear, Anna already beginning to grizzle, overtired, overexcited, not wanting to leave, to be strapped into the car seat. Anna wriggles, and kicks out at her. 'Babykin, Babykin, far down below, I hear you calling, I hear you calling, but I cannot go,' she croons, only half-conscious of what she is saying, feeling a bubble of laughter or tears rising in her throat and trying to swallow it down.

'What's that?' says Noor. 'Ruth, what is that?'

'Oh, it's silly, it's nothing, it's just a silly song, isn't it, Annie?' she says, jogging Anna in her arms.

'My mother never sang songs to us,' Noor says wistfully, her eyes round and glinting behind her glasses. 'Never.'

'Well, it's meaningless, really, I don't even remember how it goes. Here's your cousin.' She turns away, so that she does not have to see his expression as he walks towards them. She is going to tell him, she decides, when he leaves her back at the compound, that she cannot see him again.

'It's been a wonderful day,' Noor bursts out, 'oh, such a wonderful day.'

157

That was the first thing Noor wrote in her diary: Today has been a wonderful, <u>wonderful</u> day. She had been rapt by Euan Armstrong's sermon: thrilled and terrified, in equal, exhilarating measure, by the urgency with which he talked of the wages of sin and the cost of forgiveness. He talked about the word *wage*, and where it came from. To wage war, to wager, to receive your wages. The wages of sin was death, but the gift of God was eternal life. '"I tell you the truth,"' Euan quoted, his voice rising to rebound off the blond wood and whitewashed walls of the little church, '"whoever hears my word and believes him who sent me has eternal life and will not be condemned; he has crossed over from death to life."'

There is a way, Euan went on, punning on the almost-homonyms of *wage* and *way*. There is a way out of darkness and despair, of war and death and suffering, and that Way is Jesus.

His face shone, now, when he talked of Jesus: Jesus as our saviour, Jesus as the example by which we must live our lives. This was a man, Euan said, who was born in ignominious circumstances to a peasant girl, and spent the early years of his life as a refugee—an asylum seeker—in foreign lands, after his parents were forced to flee their homeland with little more than the clothes on their backs. He worked as a carpenter alongside his father until he was thirty, and then he became a wandering preacher, roaming the desert lands and small settlements. He never owned land, he never held political office. He was never rich, he was never powerful—as we on earth define wealth and power. He travelled, all in all, no more than a few hundred miles from where he was born. He was mocked, derided, deserted and denied by those he thought his closest friends—a motley collection of itinerants, lepers, prostitutes and tax collectors. He was executed alongside petty thieves at the age of just thirty-three—*thirty-three,* Euan said, beating his own breast, *the age I am now*—and when he died, he would have been thrown in disgrace into a pauper's grave, but for the pity of an onlooker. And yet, Euan said, dramatically dropping his voice and swivelling to meet the gaze of every single person in the church, and yet: two thousand years later, he is the most important person who has ever lived: he is the centrepiece, the climax, the apotheosis, of the entire human race. All the kings who have ever reigned are nothing beside him. All the armies that ever marched, all the warships ever built, all the bitterest battles ever fought, they are nothing beside him. Earthly baubles turn to dust: heavenly treasures are incorruptible. The life Jesus lived shows us we are not insignificant, however small or ignorant or unimportant we are or believe ourselves to be. The first shall be last and the last shall be first: the meek shall inherit the earth.

Jesus, Euan finished triumphantly, came for the least, the last and the lost.

The least, the last and the lost. When he said those words, Noor felt that he was talking directly to her. She felt her whole body start to shiver, and her skin was tingling. She turned to look at Ruth Armstrong, but Ruth did not notice her: she was gazing at her husband as if she was in a dream. When they

159

stood to sing, Noor sprung to her feet, light as air, feeling that she might float to the ceiling, feeling that part of her *was* on the ceiling, looking down on herself, borne upwards by the streams of laughter rushing up inside her. Her fingers were trembling. She tore a page of the hymn book in her haste to get to the psalm. She was not a good singer; her voice was croaky and tuneless, but she did her best to sing along as lustily as she could, matching the rhythms of her voice to Ruth's, thin and sweet beside her. The words of the psalm were rousing, admonishing—fires blazing through the Israelites and consuming the wicked, who had strayed from God—and then abject, humbling. Noor felt every surge and scourge as if it was amplified a thousand times. They ended by repeating the first verse, *Blessed are they who maintain justice*, and when Euan led them in prayers of peace and reconciliation for themselves and their families, for the leaders of the world and the warmongering factions in the world, Noor squeezed her eyes and clenched her hands and tried to mean every word, to truly mean it. For the first time in her life, she had a glimpse of what it meant to matter.

*   *   *

After the service, she hovered by Euan and Ruth's side as people flocked around to thank the Reverend for his service and pay their respects to his wife. They were the centre of attention. And she, too, basked in the reflection of their light. She had never received so many smiles and greetings, gentle enquiries: who was she, was she a family friend, was she from Ireland? (Oh to be a family friend! she thought, thinking her heart might burst with happiness. Oh to be from Ireland, with Ruth and Euan Armstrong!) In the whirl of it all, she quite forgot her worries that her father might find out she had come to Christian church. And when the thought did occur to her: so what? she thought, emboldened and buoyed by the service, by the solidarity of being among these people, being one of them, welcomed and accepted by them.

*   *   *

Euan Armstrong turned to her at one point—turned to her, out of all the people there clamouring for his attention—and said, 'One of these days we must have a chat,' and when she cried, 'Oh really?' (everything seemed to be a cry or an exclamation suddenly, as if life had been turned up to a higher volume) he said, 'Yes, of course we must.'

'I have such a lot of questions,' Noor said. 'Such a lot.'

'Write them down. Write them all down, and we'll go through them.'

'Euan,' Ruth said then, and for the first time ever Noor heard an edge to her voice, a hardness. 'Perhaps it isn't entirely appropriate. Noor's father is a Muslim. It's one thing to let her come along with us, but quite another—'

'It's only a chat,' Euan interrupted smoothly, turning to smile at Noor. 'It's only a friendly chat, to help her answer the questions she has in her heart.'

There was a slight, taut silence then, even in the midst of the bustle. But Euan's calm smile did not falter, and after a moment Ruth shrugged and turned slightly away.

'It would be all right, wouldn't it?' Noor said to Ruth, anxious not to upset her. 'After all I am part English, too'—remembering the proselytising conversation—'and so it wouldn't get you into any trouble, it really wouldn't. And, Ruth, I do have questions, so many of them,' she went on in a rush. 'I've done some such bad things, Ruth, I really have, and—'

'You, do bad things?' Ruth said. 'You're practically a child, Noor. Heavens above, you haven't done bad things.'

'Oh, but I have,' Noor said. But Ruth just shook her head and smiled at Noor so sadly, full of so much love and compassion—Noor could feel it, coming in waves, like warmth—that Noor did not say any more.

*   *   *

It was further evidence of Ruth's compassion when she invited Noor to stay for lunch—and when Farid came by and offered to take Ruth and Anna on a drive, to show them some of Bahrain, she insisted that Noor came, too.

Noor wondered, briefly, at Farid coming by. He was the black sheep of her cousins, the outsider; a bit of a loner. He and Jamal had been good friends when they were younger—there was less than a year between them—but in his adolescence, after her aunt Azar died, Farid had become odd and introverted, moody, liable to lash out and unwilling to take part in games or excursions with the rest of them. But it was testament to Ruth's kindness, she decided, that he was somehow changed: warmer,

162

more open, than she had ever seen him before.

They drove to Al Bander, and spent the afternoon there, until it grew dark. And as she played with Anna—splashing their feet in the kiddie pool, playing hide-and-seek behind the potted ferns and miniature palm trees, ordering lavish fruit cocktails with cocktail cherries on sticks (as many as they wanted, Farid said, it was all on him)—the first germ of an idea occurred to her.

The Diary of Noor Hussain

Sunday, 16th March 2003

QUESTIONS FOR EUAN ARMSTRONG
(rough draft)

1. What about evolution because everyone knows that God didn't create the world in six days with light on one day and water on the next and trees and animals on the next etc.

2. If there is a God why does he let wars happen and why does he let people die of horrible diseases especially babies

3. What about all the bad things that are done e.g. the Crusades which you learn about in school as this amazing thing but in actual fact when you hear the story from the other side i.e. your Muslim father and uncles then the Crusaders were a bunch of raping pillaging madmen

4. How do you <u>know</u>???

5. What happens if you've done something really, really bad, something that even a non-Christian knows you're going to burn in hell for?

6.

7.

8.

9.

10.

Come on, Noor! WHAT ELSE? You mustn't waste his time! You're not allowed to go over until you have ten good questions to show you've taken things seriously and thought about them properly ok!!!

7

She told Farid she could not see him again and he nodded, grave, and did not protest. She does not see him again. The days pass, long and hot and suffocating, and she is wretched.

*   *   *

Euan brings home a sheaf of papers, hole-punched and bound with a treasury tag.

'What?' she says.

The print is so small, and so smudged, it is almost impossible to read. He takes her by the wrist, impatient, and pulls her to a lamp. It is a photocopy of the King James Bible—a photocopy, he says, imagine. The internet connections in the country cannot always be trusted: you cannot read the Bible online, or download it to your computer, and many of the converts are Filipino or Pakistani, servants and indentured labourers, who do not have their own computers. And so someone in Riyadh, or Jeddah, has worked through the night, photocopying their Bible a page at a time.

'Isn't that love,' he says, 'isn't that devotion?'

'A man killed ninety-nine men,' she says, 'and went to a priest to ask if God would forgive him.' She stops.

'What do you mean? Is this some kind of riddle?'

'It doesn't matter,' she says.

He flips once more through the photocopied Bible. 'I just had to show you this. It just puts everything in perspective, you know?' He holds it gently, gingerly; as if, she thinks, it was the Book of Kells.

*   *   *

Noor comes to their door with a list of questions. Her questions are neatly written out, numbered, headings and subheadings underlined. She sits, stiff and formal, flushed with embarrassment and importance, on the edge of the divan. Euan sits opposite, heaving an unwitting groan of air as he settles back. He is exhausted. Whatever the preparations are for his impending trip to Saudi— he will not speak of the details to Ruth, for her sake as much as his, he tells her—they are wearing him out. But weary as he is, he would never turn someone in need away.

'Well now,' he says, smiling a particular smile, a smile Ruth recognises, where he tilts his head to one side and presses the tips of his fingers together just below his chin. It is his encouraging smile, his disarming smile. He smiles as if he is all yours, and only yours, with all the time in the world.

Ruth goes to make tea. She makes an infusion from a paper twist of *babunag* or camomile, stirring and mashing the dusty, apple-skin-scented flowers with the back of the teaspoon. Camomile grows wild in the meadows at home, creeping along the lee side of the hedgerows and ditches, sending its feathery leaves flittering into the air. Her father always warned her against picking it, in case she picked its impostor, stinking mayweed, instead: blistered hands and severe vomiting, if you brewed and drank it by mistake. It is impossible to tell, from the appearance alone, which is the real and which the poison. By their fruits you shall know them. She strains the straw-coloured liquid into three mugs and adds a spoon of honey to each. The smell, of farmyards and hay and the inside of barns in summer, makes her ache for home. But it isn't a home she can go back to, any more: it is a time, not a place, and she left it long ago.

When she goes back into the living room, carrying the mugs on a tray, Noor is folding and unfolding her piece of paper and frowning. She glances at Ruth, quick, beseeching, and Ruth feels suddenly sorry for her, and sad. A far-off, distant sort of sadness: for the time when she was Noor.

'Evolution,' Euan says. 'Noor was asking about evolution, saying she's pretty sure she believes human beings grew from monkeys.' He smiles,

166

sips his tea. He is on firm ground. 'I was just explaining to her that the Anglican Church is not against theories of evolution, not at all. The Church recognises that scientific findings in fact make a significant argument for the likelihood of evolution. And what's more, Noor –' he says, turning back to the girl, leaning forward, about to deliver the *coup de théâtre*, 'considered in the correct light, there is no conflict between evolution and faith. None at all! Because, you see, they are two different things entirely. Theories of evolution seek to explain how things came to be, whilst doctrines of faith deal with the meaning of things. You with me?'

Noor darts another glance at Ruth and nods dubiously.

'The thing is,' Euan carries on, eyes glistening, in his element, 'the two deal with different realities. The story of Adam and Eve—the dust of the earth and the breath of God, the rib fashioned into a female form—it does not explain how things came to be, but *what they are*. Do you follow? Evolution is one way of trying to understand how humans came to be, how we developed and grew, but it can't— and, actually, doesn't even try to—explain what we are here for, what our *purpose* is. The two realities are complementary, not mutually exclusive.'

Noor is frowning. She folds and unfolds her page again. 'But—' she begins, then stops. 'But—' she tries again.

'Yes?' Euan says. 'Yes, go on.'

'Evolution—I mean I don't know, but what I mean is—evolution just says we're here, and that's it. It's not about why, or any of that. We just are because that's the way things work.'

'Exactly!' Euan says. 'But that's not enough, is

167

it? You know there's more. I know you do, because you wouldn't be here, asking these questions, if you didn't. You know there's more to life than that, than a simple, arbitrary accident of, of bacteria in the Petri dish of a universe, if you will. And the mystery, the why, can only be explored within the realm of faith.'

'OK,' Noor says, slowly.

'You follow me?'

'I—'

'I can see you're a bright girl, I can see that straight away.'

Noor reddens, unaccustomed to the praise. She bends down and lets her black curtain of hair fall to hide her face. 'Can I ask another one?' she mumbles.

'Of course,' Euan says, 'ask away, ask away. The only way to learn.'

'OK. Um—this is probably an obvious one, but—suffering in the world, right?'

Euan puffs out his cheeks, exhales, and leans back. Ruth gets to her feet. They are always the same questions, always: already she has heard them all before. But it is Euan's job to treat each question, each statement of doubt or accusation, as if it is the only question, asked for the first and only time.

'Well,' she hears him saying as she closes the door to, 'that's the biggie, isn't it?'

She knows what he'll say. He'll start by saying the Bible itself tackles the very same issue, head-on. He'll quote from the third book of Job (she always imagines Job as high-voiced and querulous, though goodness knows he has enough reason to be), *Why is light given to those in misery, and life to the bitter of*

168

soul, to those who long for death that does not come,
who search for it more than for hidden treasure . . .
For sighing comes to me instead of food; my groans
pour out like water. What I feared has come upon
me; what I dreaded has happened to me. I have no
peace, no quietness; I have no rest, only turmoil . . .
He'll talk about free will, about how we have to be
responsible for our actions. He'll say that however
much we suffer, it is only a fraction of how God
suffers, to see us, his beloved, his creation, abusing
and hurting and killing each other. He'll go on to
explain how the emphasis of the Old Testament—
Job's plaintive outcry of Does God care? Has He
forgotten to be merciful?—is replaced in the New
by God-made-man, made manifest in the person of
Jesus, who came to show us the way, and to remind
us that in Him is to be found a joy, a security and
hope that even the greatest suffering cannot
overwhelm. He'll talk about living a Christian life,
to make sure you minimise your capacity to injure
others; he'll quote passages from the Sermon on
the Mount as the only viable code by which to live.
He'll talk about giving unconditionally, so that the
left hand does not know what the right is doing, and
he'll probably quote from 2 Corinthians, Whoever
sows sparingly will also reap sparingly. He'll talk
about how we do not and cannot ever understand
or hope to understand God's plan, and that how
we find ourselves on earth—alone and miserable
and sinning—is in one sense all we can ever know
of humanity. When Noor persists—as she will, as
people always do—and asks why God lets babies
die and innocent people suffer horrible illnesses,
sufferings that do not occur at the hand of others,
he'll sigh and look grave and say: he does not know:

169

he admits that there are no answers. He will not talk about the pain of childbirth as a punishment for womankind, or the sins of the fathers being visited on the children. He will say instead that not a single sparrow falls to the ground apart from the will of our heavenly Father, and that in His eyes even the very hairs on our head are numbered. This we know, he will say, and we must take on trust that there is a plan for the rest of it, for us, for the world. That is what hope is, that is what faith is. He will speak sadly, and solemnly, and persuasively. It is hard not to believe him, when he talks like that. Noor will believe. She believed.

She wanders through the kitchen and out of the back door, into the narrow strip of wasteland running between the back of the house and the rough-bricked compound wall. It is dim here, and dank; it smells of gutters. The air-conditioning unit is dripping steadily down the wall; the flaking white paint of the house is stained a dull rusty colour, like dried blood. She has not come out here before. The pathway is scarcely wider than the width of her body. She walks a few steps along it. A low wall marks where their villa ends and next door's begins, but it is little more than waist-high; you could easily clamber over it. She shivers, in the heat: thinking suddenly of escape routes and smugglers, burglars, illicit activity. You could sneak around the compound, if you were so inclined.

Not that it would get you anywhere. The flat, blind backs of the villas were still bookended by the dilapidated tennis court on one end and the barbed-wire fence and sentry box on the other. There was no real escape, not really.

She goes back inside. Euan is on the sparrows

bit. She listens for a moment, hovering behind the door. Love cannot exist, he is saying, where there is not the freedom to choose. His voice, melodious and gently insistent; Noor's stilted, marble-mouthed interjections or capitulations. It is not an even contest. It will not be long.

She checks on Anna—fast asleep—and goes into their own bedroom.

*　　　*　　　*

Rosa had come, one afternoon, to take her to the souk, as promised. Ruth left Anna with Noor, and they wrapped silk scarves around their mouths and hair against the dust and the taxi driver dropped them at the Bab al-Bahrain, the entrance to the markets. The souk was not what Ruth had imagined. It was a grid of concrete streets lined by metal-box shops with corrugated-iron canopies. The shops were cluttered with tat: viscose dresses and fake designer sunglasses, handbags that looked more plastic than leather. Misshapen pouffes and overpriced *sheesha* pipes, carpets in lurid colours and strings of stuffed toy camels. Rosa led her along, chattering happily, pointing out shops that sold mops and mop buckets, cut-price cleaning fluids, tinned food and crates of soft drinks. They turned down one street made entirely of gold merchants' stores, the windows crammed with flashing, vulgar yellow-gold bracelets and necklaces that looked like chains. The souk was hot, airless and claustrophobic; everywhere you went men called or leered after you, followed you the whole length of a street entreating you to come into their shop, promising you the best prices for saucepans, kaftans, dinner sets and wall hangings. Ruth bought a sticky cardboard box of baklava, a bottle of rose water, one of the tacky toy camels, just to have bought something, just to appease Rosa. Rosa treated her as if she was a young girl, naive, able to be excited by baubles and glitter. Rosa slipped her arm through Ruth's, and asked innocuous questions about Anna, about Easter, as if Ruth is stupid. Ruth thinks that she might despise Rosa.

*   *   *

The magic is gone from Bahrain and she misses Farid. She cannot stop thinking about him, even as she tries so hard not to think about him. Her thoughts—though they are not quite thoughts, more images half-glimpsed, conjured without her mind's permission—are of his curved lips and sinewy arms, the tautness of his body underneath its clothes. At night, strange, unlikely pictures come to her: him pinning her by the wrists, crushing his mouth against hers, licking her, biting her. She is scared, and troubled by these pictures. This, she knows, is desire. She feels it low in her sacrum, her pelvis, dark, hidden places: a dull, pulsing ache. She has never felt desire like this before. She has never been so miserable in her life.

8

The Diary of Noor Hussain

Thursday, 20th March 2003

Well, life as we know it may very well be coming to an end because WAR HAS BEEN DECLARED. Baba woke me up at half past six this morning to tell me and we sat in his bedroom for more than two hours watching it on TV, flipping back and forth between Al Jazeera and BBC News 24 and a couple of the American stations to see what they were saying. Neither of us said much, we just sat there watching. A lot of it was shaky, filmed from the distance, so it just looked like dodgy camcorder footage of someone's firework display. It was so hard to believe in it. Al Jazeera had footage from inside Baghdad, but it was mostly just anti-aircraft guns rattling and deserted streets. And then of course all the pundits and politicos, the American ones saying it was to free the People from the tyranny of Saddam Hussein, and the English ones saying it was WMD—which Baba says is a total lie. Any weapons in Iraq, he says, are left over from the last Gulf War and everyone knows it. It's the West, asserting their dominance over the East, that's what Baba says.
Al Jazeera says there's going to be big trouble in the Middle East.

Then of course Mummy rang, quite hysterical.

173

She had woken up to it on the radio and she was watching it on the TV and crying. She said she'd logged onto the Foreign Office website and there was 'a high risk of terrorist attacks against Westerners in the Middle East' and they were 'advising against all non-essential travel' and she wanted me to come home immediately.

No way—NO WAY—am I going back there. I actually will kill myself if they make me go back there.

I put the phone onto speakerphone during Mummy's rant so Baba could hear it, and he took the phone from me and started trying to calm her down. Bahrain is millions of miles away, Bahrain is the safest place in the Middle East, Bahrain can't and won't do anything to alienate the Western expats it relies upon. But what about fucking Saudi? Mummy said. That's only a handful of miles away and it's the most fucked-up crazy country there is. What if something happens from that direction? And every time Baba tried to calm her down on one count she went off on another one. He said: think of Kuwait. It was over in days. He said let's see how the next few days pan out. Then he got cross and said For God's sake Veronica it's not as if you didn't know this was coming and Mummy started yelling back at him. She wasn't on speakerphone any longer but I could hear her as clearly as if she was.
When Baba was finally off the phone I said, I'm not going back there, I swear I'm not, and he said, We'll see, and I said, You have no idea what it was like there, you and Mummy have no idea, which is

174

the closest I've come to telling either of them what really happened.

But he just looked away. I'm going to have to move fast, this means. I'm going to have to think and plan and move fast.

After the phone call I made Baba a cup of tea with brandy in it and we sat watching the TV some more. They'd started to show footage from inside the actual war itself, from the Coalition perspective. Because the thing is: they've got camera men in with the troops, actually alongside them. It is <u>fucked up</u>. It looks like the Blair Witch Project, all shaky and green, because they did it at night to take Iraq by surprise and so the cameras have night-vision filters on.
On Al Jazeera they had amateur footage of a market place and a children's health clinic that had both been bombed. While we were watching, the American woman from No. 4 came banging at the door really distressed saying what did Baba think would happen, and that her husband had insisted on going into work that day because they were closing a big contract and was he going to be ok, etc. etc. And it was only THEN that I realised I hadn't thought of Ruth and Euan and Anna, not once! I was sick to the stomach when I realised that: it was like I'd betrayed them. I went straight over to their house but they didn't answer the door. So I went down the back passage, behind the sentry box and over the walls, to see if maybe they were inside watching TV and hadn't heard the door. But their utility door was locked, too. And then when I got back Baba said we were going to drive across

town to Amm al-Harun's and we spent the rest of the day here and we're probably going to spend the night here, too.

I hope they're ok. I really, really hope they're ok. I would die if anything happened to them. I texted Ruth, but I haven't had a reply. About five minutes ago I texted her again, just in case the first one hadn't got through, but there's been no response to that, either.

Text messages have been going round all day, from distant cousins and random numbers I don't even know, saying things like, 'God once drowned Pharoah and his court may he now sink an American aircraft carrier', and 'God protect Iraqis from the boots of American soldiers'.

It's a weird thing—and there have been shouting matches all day about it—because most of the family are in favour of the invasion, but only because of Saddam. And others are saying that America has gone too far and we shouldn't be in favour of them because think of the last Gulf War, when they'd liberated Kuwait but just watched— and I mean literally watched, they were flying their aircraft overhead the whole time—while Saddam bombed to smithereens the Shia rebels in the south. Some of the aunties are just shaking their heads and crying and saying, Remember how the Americans used to lick Saddam's backside and it's all politics and it's the innocent people who always get shat on in the end. And about five minutes ago it erupted all over again when someone pointed out that today is the Changing of the Qiblah, when

176

Muhammad told Muslims to pray towards Mecca instead of in the same direction as the Jews, and that America chose today because it's just giving the finger to the Muslim world.

I was getting a bit tired by all of it then, the shouting and the tears, so I came up here to the roof to write this. But Farid followed me. He and I were practically the only ones who hadn't been waving our arms and shouting and wailing. We shared a cigarette and he told me I looked thin. (!!) I told him he looked thin, too. He does. His face is sunken, and his eyes look like bruises. But when I asked him what was the matter he just said, Nothing, *lashay jaded*, and then he repeated it in Farsi, *khabari nist*.
So it obviously was something, but I didn't say any more. We just shared the cigarette and then he left. Poor Farid. I wonder if he's going into one of his depressions again?

It's dark now, and I'm going to have to stop writing because I can hardly see any longer.

Still no word from Ruth. I hope she's ok.

9

Christopher phoned to tell them of the invasion and within minutes Euan was up and dressed and ready to go.
  'Go?' Ruth said, jolted fully awake. 'Go where?'
  To Christopher's, Euan said: they had been

expecting this would happen and they've made contingency plans for it that now need to be activated.

'"Activate"?' she said. '"Contingency plans"? You sound like you're the ones making military manoeuvres.'

'But we are,' he said. 'That's exactly what we're doing. We're fighting a battle, Ruth.' It was even more important now than ever, he went on, that they were braced for a backlash against Christianity and all things Western. And there was even more danger, now that war had been declared. They had to go through their plans, check and double-check details, prepare for the trip into Saudi. He was excited, she saw. Despite his pacifist sermon, despite the lip-service to peace, he was wildly excited now that the war was real.

She thought of the Stop the War march, the day after Valentine's Day, in Belfast city centre. She had left Anna with her mother and gone with a group from church, in a minibus; fifteen or sixteen of them piled in with their placards and banners, cracking jokes and singing songs. Euan had been unable to come: he was meeting Richard Caffrey that day, she suddenly remembered. He had been vague about the reason and the arrangements, but she had not thought to question him further at the time: why should she? Now she thought: that was the day he collected the contraband Bibles; they must have planned to use the distraction of the day as a smokescreen.

He was still talking, but she had stopped listening: just saw his mouth moving, a fleck of spittle on the corner of his lips.

They had walked up Royal Avenue, from the

178

Arts College to the City Hall. There had been a sense of carnival: people in fancy dress, like Victorian undertakers, tribal drummers and chanting. Politicians had been there, too, from all of the parties. They had laughed at the cries of *Ulster Says No!* and even at the speaker who said, *The last time we listened to a Bush we spent forty years wandering in the desert.* She had been back much later than planned—by the time the march was over and their party reassembled, the roads were chock-a-block, with traffic ground to a halt for miles out of the city centre. Her mother had been cross when she got back, and they argued, once more, over the forthcoming trip to Bahrain. And Euan, later on, watching the footage on the news, had said the marchers were naive.

'You wanted this to happen,' she said, interrupting him. 'All along, you wanted this war to happen.'

'Ruth—' he said, and heaved a sigh, and looked at her as if she was unspeakably simple-minded. 'The first Gulf War,' he said, 'brought about tremendous persecution of Christians in Saudi by the *Mutaween*, the religious police, who are a very powerful authority there. People were thrown in prison, their families threatened, their homes trashed. Many were horribly tortured. Believers need to know, now, that they are not alone. That we walk with them. That we will enter the lions' den alongside them.' He slapped his hand on the wall for emphasis. Then he said, 'Look, this is ridiculous. I haven't got time for this. I have to go.'

'You're not leaving me,' Ruth said, the initial stab of fear twisting into a mounting fury. 'You're not leaving me and Anna alone here when war has

179

just broken out. You're not doing it.'

She could see Euan trying to calm his mounting exasperation and this made her even angrier.

'You think it's appropriate to leave your wife and baby daughter in a strange house in a strange country when war has been declared?'

Again, he was betraying her: again.

Euan said, keeping his voice steady, that he thought she was exaggerating, that of course it was unsettling, the news of war, but it was hundreds of miles away, she was safe here, she had a TV and radio to keep up with what was going on and she had friends nearby—your Indian friend, he said, the American, and she caught his flicker of annoyance at himself that he could not remember their names, because he prided himself on such things.

She did not back down.

Christopher arrived at the door: he had already been on his way to collect Euan when he phoned. Ruth felt stiff and cold with anger. It was all planned, she realised. They had planned for Euan to go off with Christopher without a second thought for her or Anna, left behind to fend for themselves.

She told Christopher that he must wait for them: that she and Anna were coming, too. Euan's jaw tightened and his eyes hardened but he would not argue with her in front of someone else, especially not someone from the Church. So the men waited while she got dressed and woke Anna, packed a bag with things they might need—nappies, baby wipes, beaker; some bananas and biscuits and a couple of soft toys.

She took her time getting ready, daring Euan— just daring him—to tell her to hurry up.

The sun had not yet risen as they drove through the city. She had never seen the streets so empty: they were strange, flat, ugly places, devoid of movement or life beyond a few stray cats and dogs and the occasional labourer trudging to work, bent double under his dirty bundle. How bleak this city was, she thought. How man-made and makeshift and lonely. It was nothing like the city she had seen from the plane, nothing like the land she had glimpsed with Farid.

None of them spoke. Christopher had the radio tuned in to the BBC World Service. The reception was patchy, but they could make out the calm, mournful voices of the announcers describing that at half past five local time, ninety minutes after the forty-eight-hour deadline had expired, the so-called Operation Iraqi Freedom had begun. She clutched Anna close to her. There was no child seat, so Anna was strapped in on her lap, sharing her seat belt. It was dangerous, she knew. She imagined something happening—some accident—and Euan blaming her. Well, she would blame him right back, she thought. She thought, with a rush of nausea, that she almost hated him.

*   *   *

There were several men at Christopher's and Rosa's apartment already, mainly Indians, drinking chai tea or coffee brewed in a pot, clustering round the television in the living room, talking rapidly and waving their arms.

So this is you, Ruth thought, taking them all in.

You're the cell. There was something alarming about their animation, their intensity. It was nothing she could put into words, but it was there, palpable, as present in the room as any of their physical bodies.

She watched Euan greeting them. He talked to them not with the easy smile and self-deprecating humour he used with acquaintances, nor with the authority and vigour he used as a preacher, but with something else entirely, something Ruth had never seen before. It was a peculiar sort of animation: a quickness, a concentration, almost a furtiveness. It was something she had not known he possessed.

'Come,' Rosa said, smiling her white smile and slipping her arm through Ruth's. 'We will leave the men to it.' If she was surprised to see Ruth and Anna, she did not let it show. She led them into the kitchen, keeping up a steady stream of conversation, not seeming to mind that Ruth was not engaging. If Ruth had not known better, she might have thought Rosa slightly simple: charmingly, childishly talkative. But the wall of words was a deflection, a distraction, thrown up to disarm you. It was a weapon, used against her: because she, though not the enemy, was not one of them, either.

Euan, she knew, had not told them he had confessed to her: it might throw all of their plans in jeopardy, because while he knew he could trust her, they did not. She imagined what a silly, trembling, coltish thing they must think her, how simple, how easily deceived.

It was an effort to control her breath and the sudden shaking of her hands. She bent down and fussed over Anna, who was squatting in a corner watching a curled-up cat.

'Careful, Annie, don't touch her, she might get angry.' She propped Anna up on a cushion and gave her a beaker of milk, scattered her toys around her, then took up a knife to help Rosa, who had started chopping vegetables and grinding spices to make dhal and other curries. It was not yet eight in the morning and the smell of onion and garlic made her feel queasy but she took a gulp of her milky tea and got to work, trying to keep her face as blank and her voice as light as possible, all the while feeling hatred, anger, treacly black rage, bubbling inside.

She had had enough.

*   *   *

The following day, she phoned Farid. She got his number from Noor. Noor had texted, three times, to check that Ruth was OK. *Thanks for your concern*, Ruth texted back. *We're fine. I hope you and your family are OK too. And your cousin. Could I have his number, to send him our regards?* She hesitated for a long time over that last phrase, and over the phrasing of the whole thing. But in the end, she just pressed SEND—and there, the message was sending, sending, sent. Her phone bleeped with a reply only minutes later. *SO GLAD 2 HEAR UR OK. F WITH US SO NO NEED 2 WORRY. ILL SEND HIS NO NE WAY.* And there it was. She took a breath, and dialled it, before she had time for second thoughts, before she had time for any thoughts.

*   *   *

183

He took her to a restaurant downtown, a Persian restaurant. It was secluded, he said, and discreet; they could have some privacy there. Anna came too, of course: Ruth knocked on Noor's door but she was not there, so there was nobody to babysit. Farid was distant in the car, polite; they talked of the war, but little else, and neither of them mentioned Al Bander. But Ruth thought the air between them hummed, and wondered if he could feel it, too. She had never felt so nervous or so sick in her life as when she was waiting for him. He had answered the phone immediately she rang, and said he'd come over that morning. But even so, she had paced the house, restless, unable to sit for a minute, waiting for her phone to ring and him to cancel. When she saw him, when he was finally there, she had hardly been able to look at him.

The entrance to the restaurant was nondescript, on a nondescript street of apartment buildings and office blocks, shabby steps leading up to an unmarked door with a bell, and no sign or menu displayed outside. But inside was luxurious: wood-panelled walls hung with swirling Persian tapestries, antique brass lamps swinging low from velvet-draped ceilings, thick-pile rugs lining the floor. Farid slipped off his shoes; Ruth did the same, and unbuckled Anna's, and a smiling, heavily kohl-eyed hostess handed them embroidered slippers. The hostess led them down a corridor of tapestries, then lifted one up to let them in. All of the tapestries, Ruth realised, were doors to little booths, where you sat and ate in privacy. Their booth had a wooden table with cushions piled around on which to sit. The hostess gestured towards a leather-bound menu on the table, then spoke a stream of Farsi—it was Farsi, Ruth realised, not Arabic; it had a completely different sound. Then she left, lowering the tapestry door behind her. Their booth was a strange, almost claustrophobic place. It was big enough to sit perhaps six people, no more, and the ceiling was barely six foot high. An ornate ceiling fan, carved from dark wood, shuddered round, causing the hanging lamp to sway slightly and cast strange, soft shadows, so that you could almost be underground, in some deep cavern lit by flickering torches. The thick, dark wall hangings and rugs muffled all sound, so you could not hear any other diners.

Ruth settled Anna, unpacking a colouring book and crayons for her, and then she sat down herself, and turned towards Farid.

'Well,' he said, 'here we are.'

'Yes,' she said. Then she said, 'Thank you for coming.'

A bell tinkled outside. Farid turned and called a few words in Farsi, and the tapestry lifted to allow a waiter to bring in tall glasses of frothy, milky liquid on a silver tray. He bowed and set the tray down, then spoke to Farid. Farid replied, reeling off a rapid string of instructions, and the waiter bowed again and lifted the menu, left.

Farid had ordered, he explained, a series of typical dishes. Would this be all right for Anna?

'Oh yes,' Ruth said, and they both turned to look at Anna, who was absorbed in her scribbling. 'Oh yes, she eats anything, she'll eat whatever I'm having.'

She thought she could hear her heart pounding. She turned her attention to the glass in front of her, dabbed at the froth with the tip of her finger. It was flecked with tiny bits of green—she tasted one: mint.

'This is *doogh*,' Farid said.

'Is it alcoholic?'

'No.' He laughed suddenly. 'I am not trying to get you drunk. Taste, it is typically Persian.'

She took a sip. It was disgusting: thick, fizzy, fermented, minty yogurt. She put the glass down and tried not to gag. Farid started to laugh.

'I'm sorry,' she said. 'I wasn't expecting—well, that.'

'You said, once, that you wanted to learn about Bahrain, Bahraini food and culture. Well, this is what we drink when we are homesick for Iran.'

'I'm sorry,' she said again, 'I don't mean to be rude.' But he was still laughing, and something loosened inside her, and she laughed, too.

'Maybe you'll get used to it,' he said.

She looked at him. He had stopped laughing now. 'Maybe,' she said. 'Maybe I will.'

They said nothing else, for a while. It was difficult, with Anna there. The waiters came with food, dish after dish, and she accepted the spoonfuls Farid doled onto her plate—this a spicy couscous, this a seasoned sheep's milk cheese, this a yogurt with cucumber and mint, this a mashed fried aubergine. She had to force herself to eat, to swallow. All of the food tasted the same in her mouth, and the praise she gave each dish was perfunctory. The waiters brought more dishes: minced fried lamb with prunes and cinnamon, marinated chicken pieces with slices of peach, a bowl of pomegranate syrup, brought at Farid's request. He ate quickly and efficiently, moulding

186

the food with his right hand and scooping it up with ripped chunks of nan bread, keeping his head bowed close to the plate. She hardly ate at all. It was not until after the mint tea and sorbet—little gilded glasses and matching glass bowls—that she spoke.

'Farid,' she said. 'After Al Bander, when I said I didn't want to see you again.'

He looked at her, suddenly and completely still.

'Yes,' he said, softly.

And then she took a breath, gripping the table to stop her hands trembling, and said, 'I was wrong, Farid. I've been wrong, and I hope—if you do—if you can understand—how lonely I've been—how miserable—'

Her heart was racing and the words were lurching incomprehensibly from her tongue. But he understood. She could see by his face that he understood. And he reached over, and once more took her hand.

10

The Diary of Noor Hussain

Sunday, 23rd March 2003

Well, here we are, back home, and finally! After three days and nights at Amm al-Harun's I was practically begging for a stray American bomb to flatten the place. There are just <u>so many people</u> there, constantly people, talking, shouting, laughing, eating (<u>eating</u>), kids running from room to room, babies squealing and shitting their nappies. You do not get <u>one second</u> to yourself. If it's not the grown-ups hassling you to do this or that or asking you about school or all the rest of it (correcting your Arabic, refusing to answer you in English) it's a trail of giggling younger cousins following you wherever you go and shouting things they think are so funny. Their latest game: firing paper aeroplanes at your head and making noises like they've bombed you. I thought Farid might be my ally, but he was never around. He has his car, which of course is the perfect escape route. I asked him one day where he was going, and he looked vague, and just said, Nowhere. He was going to drive around in it, listen to music, that's all. He made it clear he didn't want me with him. Screw you, Farid!

Another thing: it is IMPOSSIBLE not to eat because they all eat together every day, it's the centre of the day, the main event: and someone's always watching you like a hawk. You've only had one koloocheh Noor come on azizam have another I baked them fresh, these ones have dates and these walnuts, take one of each. The first thing I did when we got back here, before even writing this, was weigh myself. And I have put on <u>two pounds</u> again. Imagine if we lived there full time?! Which it turns out is the plan: one of the extensions they're building is for Baba and me, and we'll be in by the summer, he says.

Yeah right, Baba!

Because (drum roll please)

THIS IS THE PLAN.

I'm going to go back to Ireland with Ruth and
Euan and Anna and live with them there. Mummy
won't mind, in fact she probably won't even
care. Her phoning to say she's worried about
me in Bahrain isn't about <u>me</u>, it's just a way to
get at Baba. Because I'll never be the daughter
she wishes she had. And Baba will be relieved,
too, because he never knows what to do with me
here. I'm in his way most of the time, and he just
stomps about and shouts at me, and it can only
get worse. I thought Bahrain was going to be a
fresh start, but it's as bad as England
ever was.

When I first had the idea at Al-Bander I thought it
was ludicrous, that it was just me being fanciful (Dr
Badawi: you have to control your fantasies, Noor).
But I've been thinking and thinking it over the past
few days, and I think it'll work!

I have enough money in my savings account to pay
for my flight back, and if I need more I can get
Mummy to sell off my Premium Bonds. And so my
flying back won't cost Ruth and Euan a penny. And
once I'm there, well Ruth is always talking about
the farm she grew up on and they're currently living
in 'one of the cottages on it' so I'm sure they'll be
able to find a room (if not a whole cottage) for
me. And if there isn't a room I can always sleep
on the sofa and make sure my bedding is all rolled
up neatly by the time anyone comes down in the
morning.

It's so simple, really, it's all so simple!

And I'll clean and I'll learn to cook and that so Ruth is free to do whatever she wants. And I'll look after Anna, of course, that's the main thing. I'll be just like an au pair. If money's tight I can get a part-time job, and I won't need much in the way of 'things' anyway. And we'll manage, because unlike Mummy and Baba and their constant squabbling over money, we'll know that it isn't money that matters in the end.

And I know I have to go to school, but only for another two and a half years because you can leave when you're sixteen. Even if I do have to be at school all day for the first couple of years I'll still be there to clean and cook in the mornings and evenings and at the weekends and during all holidays, and I'll come home (home!!) at lunchtime to see little Anna.

My heart is racing so fast as I write this! I think I need to go outside and have a cigarette to calm down. (N.B. I mustn't let Ruth or Euan see me smoking in front of Anna. In fact after I've finished this pack I'm going to give up for good. See what a good influence they are on me!)

How easy it is! How easy it all is!!

From the moment I first saw Ruth and Euan and Anna Armstrong it was special. I remember it exactly, seeing them go walking down the compound, each holding one of little Anna's hands and jumping her up and down, and it was so perfect, the most perfect thing I'd ever seen, and I so wanted to be part of it. Euan said the other night (how long ago that seems!) that with God there is a reason for everything. And now I start to see it! Why they're here, why I'm here, why everything.

There is one dark cloud on the horizon. I will have to confess to them—tell them everything—because I don't want them to find out later on by chance or gossip and think that I wasn't truthful from the beginning. And I've never been more scared in my entire life. But Euan said God forgives everything and who is anyone to cast stones when we've all got whole planks in our own eyes.

And in the meantime, I'm going to have to make myself indispensable. Looking after little Anna, being there, doing whatever Ruth wants or needs, so that when the time comes for her to leave she knows that she can't do without me.

Look how messy my writing's got! I'm shaking so much I can hardly hold the pen!

Now for that cigarette—the final cigarette.

I'm going to be a new Noor.

'Noor Armstrong'!!!!!

IV

1

The next two weeks are the happiest of her life.

Two weeks: a fortnight—such a short time, and yet an eternity, an entirety. The life of man, seen from the heavens; a handbreadth of days.

*   *   *

Farid picks her up each morning and takes her out, sometimes with Anna, but most often not, for Noor is happy to babysit all day. They wander the streets of downtown Manama—something that she could not do alone, a woman and a foreigner. In Ireland, she tells him, she used to go for long, long walks, across the fallow fields and down the rutted lanes to the waters, and she would walk all around the headland before looping back cross-country to the farmhouse. Sometimes she would walk across the cut-over bog, north-east of Kircubbin. You needed permission to access the bog, but she knew the rangers, and they let her walk through, so long as she kept to the tracks. There were Exmoor ponies there, three of them, and sometimes you could feed them handfuls of wild grass or Polo mints. And if you were lucky you might see otters, or a flash of a stoat, the white at its throat catching the corner of your vision. Once, sitting downwind, she had watched a family of foxes play, the mother nosing at her cubs, encouraging them to prance and fight. She exaggerates her stories, romanticises them:

Farid loves to hear her talk of Ireland. Even when Anna was born, she tells him, she would strap her in a sling and go walking, until the baby grew too big to be carried far. It is what she finds hardest about Bahrain, she says: her world so circumscribed. The compound is small—you can walk from one end to the other in less than five minutes—and the few times she has tried to go for a walk, the sentries have stopped her, or someone (Anjali, Trudy, Maarlen) has seen her and insisted she come back inside. There is nowhere to go, they tell her. And they are right: after two blocks of compounds and one apartment building, there is the cold store, and then the highway. If she wants, they will drive her to a mall, and she can stroll about there. Bahrain is not designed for walking. People go from air-conditioned houses in air-conditioned cars to air-conditioned malls: it is a lifestyle that turns its back on the outside world, which for so many months of the year is inhospitable, almost impossible to bear.

But this is still March, and although the days are already hot and getting rapidly hotter, you can still stand to be outside. The heat prickles into sweat beads on the back of the neck as soon as you climb out of a car, and within a few minutes of walking you are sweating and streaked with grime. But Ruth can bear this. She likes the strangeness of the air, the unfamiliar smells. The city is hot and pungent: exhaust fumes and dust and drains. You can feel the air as you breathe it in, drying the roof of your mouth, gritty at the back of your throat. And the noise: it is almost exhilarating, like another form of heat, bearing down on you. The blare of car horns and squeal of brakes, the rattle and hum of air-con units, the wail of Arabic music and shrill of Indian

196

from open-fronted shops, the clatter and whine of building sites and screeching of turning cranes, men shouting, gesticulating, scabby, sunken-eyed dogs snarling at each other.

She has never felt so alive as when she is exploring these streets with Farid, streets where few foreigners could—or would—choose to go. They walk through seedy, run-down textiles districts, where racks of faded saris and *shalwar kameez* trousers clutter the pavements, and ragged stretches of gauzy chiffon hang from washing lines stretched corner to corner. Alleyways where makeshift poles slung with T-shirts and bath-towels sag and bleach in the sun, and chipped mannequins draped with swathes of gold- and silver-sequinned cloth are suspended from upper-floor windows. Farid keeps up a stream of *imshee, imshee!* at the boys who run after them with open packets of cigarettes, stuffed toy camels, bobbins of thread, and at the shopkeepers who step out in front of them to push squares of fabric or handfuls of cheap, logoed T-shirts in their faces. The streets are a maze, and she cannot make sense of them: some seemed at first to be arranged in a grid, but just as she thought she had her bearings, or caught a glimpse of one of the iconic skyscrapers in the financial centre towards the north, the roads would twist and cluster together and seem to loop back on themselves. Alone, she would have been horribly lost, horribly panicked. But Farid knows his way. He shows her the Arab quarters, rows of coffee shops, flat-roofed concrete rooms open to the road, where men sit on yellowing plastic chairs drinking cans of Pepsi or tiny espressos, smoking hookah pipes or playing dominoes. Some are dressed in

197

trousers and polo shirts, others in full white *thobe* and *gutra*; some are old, some are young—but there are never any women. The air here is sharp and sweet with the smoke of the hookah pipes, appley, perfumed. It smells of sizzling meat, too; hot oil and spices from the rickety *shawarma* vendors shearing off meat into flatbreads or pitta breads, or frying strips of herbed lamb on hot plates. They stop, sometimes, to try the food, or to buy a juice or an ice cone from a street seller, and it is always the most delicious food Ruth has ever tasted: something to do with the heat, and the foreignness, and the daringness of it, the juices running down her wrists and the spices making her lips tingle and her eyes water.

He shows her the commercial district, too, where the streets are wider, smoother, and the buildings are glossy-fronted estate agents or travel agents or telecom companies. And they drive the length of the King Faisal Highway, past the ministries and the five-star hotels, the Sheratons and Hiltons and Ritz-Carltons, with their palatial driveways and lush, desert-defying landscaped gardens.

Once they have exhausted Manama, they go on excursions further afield. To the wildlife park at Al Areen to see the oryx and the zebras, the herds of adax and reem gazelle, protected Arabian species with delicate, long-lashed eyes and shy hoofs, like creatures from a story book. To the Qala-at Fort, where archaeologists are looking for Dilmun. To see the basket-weavers at Karbabad, where Farid buys her a sunhat and a shopping basket made by a blind man, who sits in front of his cottage all day twisting and knotting straw from a pile beside him, his callused, gnarled fingers moving with impossible

198

ease. They visit villages where old men still use donkeys, and water comes from wells. They go to the camel farm at Janabiya to see the sour-smelling, greasy animals being led out into the desert. They go to the beach at Al Jayazir, on the western side of the island, where the sea is so salty you can float in it without moving: you just spread your legs and close your eyes and the water holds you up. They go back to the Persian restaurant, and to others like it, and to Al Bander. They smoke hookah pipes in cafés where loud pop music plays and young people lounge drinking cans of soft drink or bright pink milkshakes, and rather than feeling too old, as she would if she came there with Euan, she feels young again, free.

She pities the limited world of the expats and Westerners, where weekends are spent in the malls or with day passes at the hotel spas, evenings drinking cocktails at the American Club, and eating steak *frites* or soft-shell crab. Their Manama is limited to the souk; they know nothing of the streets beyond. They drive, or have drivers to take them everywhere, they pass their time with coffee mornings and cocktail parties, the men playing golf and the women sunbathing at their husband's club. She has learned this from Trudy, and from several of the wives at church. She is grateful, now, that Euan has always declined their invitations to join in, because if she had had the distraction, the artificial whirl of that world, she might not have found this realer Bahrain.

*　　　*　　　*

At first, their relationship is innocent, chaste. They

cannot hold hands in public, and there are very few places that are private. The Persian restaurant, where they can kiss; discreet corners of Al Areen or the Corniche at dusk; the villages to the south where you can park the car under a banyan tree and, by paying a few fils to the young boys, ensure that nobody comes near.

Sometimes, Farid comes to the villa. But neither of them is at ease there: even if the maids are gone, and Anna is at Noor's, they feel at the mercy of visitors, and cannot fully relax. Nevertheless, it is here that they make love for the first time, on the floor, up against the divan. Farid pins her wrists behind her, covers her mouth with a cushion when she cries out. It is unplanned, or at least not wholly planned: they are not even fully undressed. But afterwards, Ruth feels a deep sense of relief, or release. That night, she presses the tender places on her arms, wondering if they will bruise, and thinks: I have been with another man.

*   *   *

After that, they make love more often: in the car, in the villa. Farid has no home of his own to take her to, and they cannot check into a hotel for an afternoon: even the hotels that offer hourly rates need passport details, identity, and this is something she is too frightened to risk. So they start to take precautions: Farid parks his Camaro in the cold-store car park, and comes in down the back passageway, through the utility room. There is a way, they discover, of getting in without alerting the sentries, a blind spot, where if you're quick in vaulting the low wall, you can be over and hidden from view before you're seen. She is grateful for the lack of windows: nobody can see what's going on, even outside their own front door, unless they're actually standing there. She gets used, too, to the banalities: if they eat in the villa, she makes sure the plates and forks and cups are washed and dried before Euan returns—not in the draining rack or dishwasher, but back in the cupboard or drawer, in their rightful places, so that he does not ask if Trudy or Anjali came over today and catch her out in a fumbling lie. She makes sure that the toilet seat, too, is put back down. When Farid leaves, she walks out of and then quickly into each room several times over, trying to see it with fresh eyes, with Euan's eyes: is anything displaced, awry, has anything been overlooked, that would give the game away? She tries to memorise the maids' rotas, but they are unpredictable, so she takes to locking the front door with the chain, so that at least they cannot get in without her knowing, without Farid having enough time to go.

It should feel sordid. But somehow it doesn't: only practical, necessary. And the curious thing is that she does not feel remorse: not at all, even when she is lying in bed with Euan. In fact, when she is lying in bed with Euan (who gets home late these days, and exhausted, too tired to make love or to want to) it is Farid she feels she is betraying. During the marriage preparation course she and Euan attended, she imagined that she would be wracked with guilt and regret if she so much as thought of kissing someone else. But it is not so. Here she is having an affair (*an affair*, she tells herself, several times a day, testing herself, marvelling; she, Ruth Armstrong, is having *an*

201

affair), and it should be wrong: it should be better to gouge out your eyes and cut off your limbs than even contemplate adultery. But being with Farid feels right—more than right: she feels *alive*. When he touches her, her body responds, and she feels a desire for him she has never known before, not for Euan, not for anyone, anything. And it is easy, so easy. Anna's mother, Euan's wife—they come out as needed, as if they are people within her who surface to play their role, and protect the secret, hidden her within. Because this, Ruth knows, is the real her. The other 'hers' just glide through the motions, distant, practised, capable. While inside, the real Ruth—the Ruth who is learning how to feel, how to live, how to be—is blossoming. That is what it feels like, blossoming: as if cramped, damp petals are unfurling in her chest, rising and swelling to fill the hollow places.

*   *   *

Farid introduces her to a woman named Maryam: his confidante, he says. Maryam is Iranian, only a year or so older than Ruth, with two small boys, Harun and Qasim. The boys are not-quite-four and three, young enough to be playmates for Anna, and on the days when they have Anna with them, they call in at her apartment. Ruth is shocked to discover, after their first meeting, that Maryam is Farid's father's second wife. She has read in her guidebook about Islam allowing a man to take multiple wives, and she knows the King of Bahrain has four. But she had not expected ordinary people—people she knew—people who were, to all other appearances, modern—to practise such customs. If she had not grown to trust Farid, she might have been repelled by it. But when he explains how it came about (his father married, soon after his mother died, a woman much older who could keep house, but who gave him no sons; Maryam fled from Iran with nothing after both of her parents were executed, and his father, a distant cousin, took pity on her and fell in love, married her and set her up in an apartment), it is so practical and matter-of-fact that Ruth finds herself understanding it. Maryam lives with her boys, and sees her husband two or three evenings a week. On holy days or family occasions, she joins the rest of the family in the compound—she is not a secret, or an outcast. In her spare time, she is studying for a business certificate, so that one day she can help Harun with his various enterprises. She seems happy with the set-up, and unembarrassed: from her point of view there is nothing salacious about it, Ruth realises, nothing of the stuff of dodgy late-night movies or tawdry travellers' tales. She had not known such other lives were possible.

Maryam's English is poor, but she is kind to Ruth, and they communicate through gestures and laughs, and Farid's translations. Maryam shows Ruth how to cook thick, salty Persian pancakes, on a gas stove on the kitchen floor, and she shows Ruth how to drape and secure a veil. When Ruth questions her about her life, here and before, in Iran, she tells of whole relationships conducted by text message and email, by long phone calls at night. You pass your number to a friend, written on a tiny, rolled-up slip of paper, and that friend will pass it on to another friend, and to another. Eventually, a boy might text you, and after a while you will email, exchange pictures, and then you might speak. You will never meet in person. You will do everything a normal couple might do—talk, fall in love, make love, argue, split up—without ever meeting.

Ruth's mind whirls with what she is learning. She had not known that so many other lives were possible, that so many other worlds existed.

2

Noor's plan was falling into place: just as if it was meant to be. Since returning from the al-Husayn compound, she had resumed her diet with a vengeance, allowing herself little more than a low-fat yogurt, an apple and one piece of toast a day. She was sure that Sampaguita knew: the witchy old woman always seemed to know everything, and she had started trying to foist bowls of *crema de fruta* or fried cassava with egg-yolk custard on Noor. But Noor was cleverer than Sampaguita: she would take the food without protest, go into her bedroom, leaving the door ajar, and make noises like she was eating it—clattering the spoon on the bowl, smacking her lips—then scrape the fatty mess into a shopping bag and later, when Sampaguita was gone or occupied elsewhere, flush it down the toilet. The crash diet was working: the weight was melting off once more.

Making an effort with her father was paying dividends, too. The politer she was with him, she was finding, the less he questioned her or watched her. By complying with a few of his simplest rules—that she dress modestly, that she not answer him back, that she give the outward signs of respect for him like bringing his indoor flip-flops, refilling his glass of tea—she was able to fool him into the sense that she was settling down, accepting her new life in Bahrain. She felt him relax, and relax his vigilance over her. He started to smile at her again, and once or twice even revived a silly childhood joke between them. Whenever he encouraged her to come along with him to the al-Husayn compound, she used the excuse that she wanted to study in preparation for her new school. Sometimes, she said she was going out with Farid—which was not wholly a lie—and one morning, when he frowned at her spending so much time with the missionaries, she hurried to explain that she hardly ever saw them at all, that it was the baby she was looking after—and it was good for her to have responsibility. This was a Dr Badawi idea, and she knew he couldn't argue with it.

'You're OK,' he said, tentatively, one evening. It was not quite a statement, but not quite a question, either. 'You're getting better.'

'I am, Baba,' she said. 'I really am.' And she was.

Best of all was the fact that Ruth was busy suddenly—with church, and outings with some of her churchgoing friends—and she was glad of Noor's help with Anna. It was almost, Noor wrote in her diary, as if she was being given the opportunity to prove herself, to prove how useful she was, how needed.

During the day, when Anna was having her nap—she slept for an hour or so after lunch—Noor would wander through the villa strewn with the Armstrongs' things, and let herself pretend that this was their house in Ireland, and they were living all together. At first, she confined her fantasy to the living room and central spaces. Touching Euan's books, tidying Anna's toys, draping over her shoulders a cardigan that Ruth had left lying around. But then, one day, she went into the bedroom. She didn't do anything, not then—she didn't even touch anything. She just stood there, breathing the air (which still smelt faintly of sleep, unventilated), her heart beating inexplicably fast. The next day, she sat on the edge of the bed, and the next she lay down on it, working out which side Ruth slept on, and which Euan. She found the T-shirt that Ruth slept in (how odd, to think that she slept in a faded old T-shirt! Noor had imagined her in something much more glamorous, silky pyjamas, perhaps, or a slithery nightdress) and inhaled Ruth's faint, soapy perfume. Then she folded it back under the pillow, lay down with the sheet pulled over her head, and let her fantasy roll: the fever, the helplessness, and Ruth and Euan being there.

Day by day, growing bolder, she took to looking at their things, riffling through them, touching them. She found Euan's ring-bound notebook, in which he planned his sermons. Ruth's Arabic phrase book, with a sheet folded inside: Muslim parables entitled *THREE STORIES ABOUT GOD*. The stories seemed vaguely familiar, but she could not place them. She put the piece of paper back exactly how she'd found it—she was always careful to do this. She didn't mean any harm, by looking. She didn't intend to take anything: just to know them, these scraps of the Armstrongs' world. She found a stack of Irish linen tea towels, which Ruth must have brought over to give as presents, some

206

with an Irish poem printed onto them, others with an illustrated map. The map she thought childish— but she learned the words of the poem, until she had them by heart. *May the road rise up to meet you, may the wind be always at your back. May the sun shine warm on your face and rains fall soft upon your fields. And until we meet again, may God hold you in the palm of his hand.* She found an envelope of photographs, too, of Ruth and Euan and Anna, of what must be Ruth's family farm in Ireland, the cottage they lived in, the lough. She pored over the photographs, until she no longer needed them to summon up the scenes in her mind.

*   *   *

Out of the blue one day, Ruth suggested that Noor might like to take Anna over to her own villa, and Noor wondered if she'd been found out: if she'd forgotten to wipe fingerprints from the photos, or to put something back exactly the way it had been. She stared at Ruth, searching her face for signs of anger, or displeasure. But Ruth's face was perfectly calm and kindly. Noor's villa was more comfortable, she said, its carpets and cushions were better for a toddler than her own, with its hard marble floors and sharp-edged tables. It might be easier to look after Anna there. Ruth was right. And Noor found she enjoyed having Anna in her villa, showing off—she could not help showing off—in front of Sampaguita, or her father, if he was there. How good she was with the child, how much Ruth Armstrong trusted her. Sometimes her father would snort and say, how come she showed no interest in her cousins' babies, her own relations? But she just laughed: of course he didn't, couldn't, understand how different this was.

*   *   *

In the evenings, when Ruth came home and collected Anna again, Noor would join them for Anna's supper. She loved these suppers. Sometimes, if Ruth ate, she even allowed herself to eat a little, too: sharing whatever food Ruth's maids had prepared. Noor would talk about the day, telling Ruth about the things she'd done with Anna—the pictures they'd drawn, the finger-painting they'd done, the games they'd played. And then she'd ask questions, questions she prepared and rehearsed each night, to show her interest in Ireland and in Christianity. One evening, Ruth gave Noor her very own Gospel of Matthew to read: and Noor was so taken aback by her kindness, by the meaningfulness of the gesture, that she almost started crying.

For a week, then, she read Ruth's Gospel of Matthew obsessively, long into the night each night. It gave her a peculiar thrill to be reading the same words that Ruth had read: *I know that sounds like a stupid thing to say,* she wrote, *because of course they're the same words, but you know what I mean!*

She appropriated a torch from the kitchen in case her father, coming home late from the hospital after some complicated surgery, or from smoking a pipe with her uncle, might see the light on under the bedroom door and catch her in the act. But on the nights that he came home late he merely kicked off his shoes, grunting, and shuffled slipper-footed to his room, not noticing or caring that Noor was still up.

208

The little book was worn, its pages thumbed soft at the edges and its imitation leather peeling. It was not a beautiful object. It was not made to last, either. It was a cheap, mass-produced edition, made for quantity rather than quality, its printing often fuzzy and its ink smudged. But Noor held and treated it with reverence, keeping it on a cloth on the shelf, as her cousins did the Qur'an, taking care to turn each thin page without dog-earing or ripping it further.

She read each chapter, each verse, not skipping a single word of the dull bits, the lists and litanies, mouthing the difficult words. After the exile to Babylon, *Jeconiah* was the father of *Shealtiel*, *Shealtiel* the father of *Zerubbabel*. She knew the story of the Nativity, of course, but she knew Luke's version: Caesar Augustus's census and no room at the inn; the little baby wrapped in swaddling clothes while the shepherds and angels watched the flocks. Matthew's account was swifter, scarier: the escape to Egypt, the killing of the baby boys—and suddenly, no mention of his childhood or questions at the temple, Jesus is grown and asking to be baptised and being tempted in the desert.

And then the Sermon on the Mount. The spine of the little book was broken at the beginning of the Sermon on the Mount, Matthew chapter 5, and in the margins was written, in faded biro, *This is the most important sermon ever given—these are all the guidelines you need by which to live your life.*

As she read, it made her shiver to think that these were Jesus's words—his actual words—and these were the words that Ruth had read, over and over, she had said, until she had them by heart. When Noor came to the Lord's Prayer, she tried to pray it with meaning, instead of rattling through the empty rhythms as she had done most mornings in house assembly. She read the Parables—the Parable of the Weeds and the Parable of the Mustard Seed and Yeast, the Parable of the Pearl and the Parable of the Net. She read each word fiercely, trying to understand them. She read about the Miracles, the walking on water and feeding the five thousand, the driving out of demons and raising of the dead. She read so intently, she almost cried when she reached the Crucifixion and the Death of Jesus: My God, my God, why have you forsaken me? In those nights, she almost felt that she had been there, that she was there: it was not difficult to imagine the hot and dusty Place of the Skull and the bushes of thorns, the vinegared sponge impaled on a stick and the sun beating down, the sweating of soldiers startled in the distance.

Every evening for the rest of that week, Noor talked with Ruth about what she had read the night before. Why should it be, she asked, that a man should be turned against his father, a daughter against her mother? When Herod declared that the babies should be murdered, why did God not intervene? How are people like salt? What happened to the poor farmers who lost their pigs, and why did the workers in the vineyard all get the same pay? Question after question: and Ruth answered them all.

And then, one day, when she had read the book of Matthew three times through, she knew it was time.

*   *   *

It was a hot, dry day nine days into April. Winds were blowing across from the Sahara coating Manama in fine red dust and Ruth had returned early from her excursion with her friends. Anna had been in the middle of her afternoon nap at Noor's villa, and they had carried her over the road without waking her up. Now she was napping in her cot and the maids were in the kitchen; it was just the two of them, alone in the living room; a perfect moment.

'Ruth,' she said, 'I think I want to be a Christian but I don't know how. Will you pray with me?' She gabbled the words too fast, and Ruth did not hear her; she had to repeat them, her face on fire. How many times she had said those words in her head, practised whispering them in front of the mirror!

For a moment, she thought that Ruth was going to refuse: to say that Noor was not ready, or not worthy. But then Ruth shrugged and said, 'Sure,' and gestured for Noor to sit down on the divan.

Noor closed her eyes and tried to block out the thin jabbering of the radio and the rumble of the tumble-dryer in the next room; to concentrate solely on the words that Ruth was saying. '*Our father*,' Ruth began. She placed the flat of her hand lightly on Noor's bowed head, and Noor was glad that she had washed her hair that morning.

'*Our father in heaven.*'

The hairs on the nape of her neck were stirring and she felt the skin of her legs pimpling. The velvet of the divan was pressing into the bare backs of her thighs; she could feel it, every tuft and fibre. Her hands were dampening in her lap. She tried again to concentrate, all too conscious of her physical body, of her proximity to Ruth. She could feel Ruth's breath on her neck, the warmth of Ruth's body, Ruth's sweet, clean smell. Her stomach was churning. It let out a gurgle and she squirmed, hoping Ruth hadn't heard.

'I am sorry for the wrong I have done in my life,' Ruth was intoning, *'and for those I have wronged. For all I have done, I ask your forgiveness.* OK, Noor,' Ruth said, making her jump. 'I want you just to take a moment to think about the sins you've committed, the people you've hurt. Reflect on them, and ask in your heart for God's forgiveness.'

'OK,' Noor said. Then she said, 'Ruth, there's too much to know where to start. I've tried to tell you before—I'm a bad person, I really am. I've done some terrible things.'

'We all have,' Ruth replied, distant. 'Just think on them, and ask God to forgive you, and He will.'

'OK.' Noor took a shaky breath, and let herself see Hong Chang Jones. The chubby face, the eyes that disappeared into her cheeks when she smiled, like a hamster, they all used to say. Hamsterface Jones. Her slightly protruding teeth and inability to pronounce the letter *r*, the way she said her own name, *Hoh-chah-joh*, they all used to whisper at roll-call, just loud enough that she could hear, but not the teacher. How they'd all laughed when she announced that she wanted to change her name to Rose. *Roh-hoh-chah-joh*, it had become then, until they tired of that and went back to Hong, which was easier to rhyme with Pong, and Mong. Noor saw them all following her down the corridor to the locker room, hunching their necks into their shoulders—Hong was short, and squat—and pulling their eyes into slits. Annabel Varley, raising her hand in history and asking, innocent-eyed, if it was true that Chinese people were only allowed one child and

212

they all wanted boys, so they tried to abort their girl babies, often very late in term, leading to hideous birth defects if the abortion failed? And then, that lunchtime, setting up a society to raise money for the poor deformed girl babies—asking the house mistress to announce a collection in house assembly, printing posters with Photoshopped images of dribbling, squash-faced Chinese babies for the society's noticeboard. Hong, all the while, knowing it was her, it was all about her, and unable to do anything. And Noor had joined in—Noor had joined in gladly. She had come up with all manner of small, clever persecutions: not enough for teachers to realise what was going on, or to get them in trouble if someone did realise what was going on, but enough for Hong to know. Asking the drama mistress to stage a celebration of Chinese New Year with Hong at the centre, working out that Hong's name anagrammed to Gang Chosen John, and spending a whole morning asking, Who have the gang chosen, Hong? and sniggering at her confusion, her pathetic attempts to laugh and pretend she understood. The truth was: Noor was relieved that the focus had moved away from her. Since September 11th, she had been the focus of the clique's attention. The societies they formed then had been Anti-Arab Coalitions—changed to Anti-Al-Qaeda when Miss Williams, the English teacher, had intervened and pointed out that Anti-Arab was a sweeping generalisation. When they had assemblies for the victims of the Twin Towers and their families, she knew that Lily Carrington-Villiers or Emily-May Brierly or whoever stood up to read, voice quavering just enough, a practised tear in the eye, was directing their words at her. *Hussain* was hissed in roll-call;

213

leering photos of Saddam appeared on the charities noticeboards. When Hong joined their year and the focus shifted to her, Noor leapt to join in. The house mistress had placed Hong under Noor's protection, asking Noor to show the new girl round and look out for her. Perhaps she had sensed that Noor, the fat girl always on her own when people paired up in lessons, was in need of a friend. But Noor could not allow herself to become friends with Hong: the new girl was too useful as a target, a foil. When Hong asked her to visit Beijing in their Christmas holidays, there was no way that Noor could accept—and she felt disgusted that Hong had asked, knowing that Hong's parents must have suggested she ask a friend home, and Hong did not dare admit that she had none. She told Lily and Emily-May and it became more fodder for their tormenting. Things had not let up over the holidays, either: they had worked out when she would be online at home and swamped her MSN Messenger in comments, put up recipes for dog soup in chatrooms she visited. And on the first day of term, Noor walked into the dorm room she shared with Hong and two other girls to see Hong hanging from the top bunk bed with a noose made from her tights, her face purple, a pool of urine spreading on the floor. Her eyes were open, bulging, staring straight at Noor. One of them was bright red: the capillaries had burst and it was swollen with blood. Hong's eyes saying: You did this. You.

*　　　*　　　*

Noor felt herself shaking. *Please, God*, she begged in her head. *Please forgive me. Please, Hong, forgive me. Please, Jesus. Please.*

214

'All right,' Ruth was saying, 'if you've reflected on your wrongs—'

'God can't forgive me,' Noor burst out. 'He can't, not the things I've done.'

'God can forgive anything,' Ruth said. 'Even the most heinous of crimes, if repentance is true, then God forgives. The blood of Jesus Christ Our Lord was spilled so that we may be cleansed, so that we may be washed white as snow, and enter the Kingdom of Heaven.'

'He will truly forgive me?'

'If you mean it in your heart, and ask Him, then he will forgive.'

'Truly?'

'Yes, Noor. Will we carry on, then? *Thank you God our heavenly Father for sending us your only son, Jesus Christ, to be born as a man and live as a man and die as a man, on the Cross, for our sins, and for the sins of humankind. In Christ we are all forgiven. From now on I will live my life by Him.*'

I will, Noor thought. I will: I promise I will.

'*I ask, now, for you to enter the heart of this girl, Noor Hussain, and to be with her, and to stay with her, and help her grow within you. Amen.*'

She had been holding her breath. She let it out in a long, shuddering gasp, and felt her body trembling.

'Amen,' she managed.

'OK?' Ruth said.

'OK,' Noor whispered. She felt so weak that if she tried to stand, she knew, her legs would buckle beneath her. 'Ruth,' she said, 'is that it? I mean— am I a Christian?'

Ruth looked at her with an expression Noor did not understand. 'Well,' she eventually said, 'you're

215

not baptised, so in that sense not officially. But yes, you have just asked Jesus into your heart.'

Noor's heart was racing but she did not feel any different. 'Shouldn't I feel it?' she said. 'Shouldn't I feel—or know—something?'

Ruth shrugged. 'Not necessarily. Some people feel calmer, more peaceful. Some people feel joy. But it doesn't necessarily happen right away. It might take time. You never know how the Holy Spirit will move in you. Some people might be moved to tears or laughter, but others . . .' She trailed off.

'What did you feel?'

'What did I feel?'

'When you asked—asked Jesus into your heart.'

'I don't know,' Ruth said, straightening up and turning away. 'I don't remember. It's different for everyone.'

Ruth seemed distracted, Noor thought. All she wanted was to stay there, to prolong the moment, she and Ruth praying together. But it was evident that Ruth was preoccupied. So she got to her feet—she did not think they would support her, but they did—and gathered up her things and went back home.

She was surprised at how weepy she felt, that evening: as if the slightest thing could set her off. A pat on the cheek from Sampaguita. The TV footage of Private Jessica Lynch being flown to Germany, and the joy of her family, played on a loop on CNN. Her own mother phoned and she found herself crying on the phone, even though they were only talking about the weather in England, a trip into London to see an opera with Jamie and his girlfriend, a scandal (Noor could not follow the details) at tennis club.

'Are you all right, Noor?' her mother asked, but Noor did not have the words to reply and she hung up the phone instead.

She tried to write in her diary how she felt, but she could not find the right words for that, either, and when she did find the words she could not seem to get them in the right order. And then, when the words started coming, she found they were not a diary entry at all.

The Diary of Noor Hussain

Wednesday, 9th April 2003

Dear Mr and Mrs Chang Jones,

I know it's no use me saying sorry but believe me I will be sorry ~~to my dying day and beyond~~ ~~for the rest of my life~~ always for what happened to Hong. I wish I knew then what I know now because truly I wouldn't have behaved in the way that I did. At the time it was me or her, I know that doesn't make it any easier for you and I know it doesn't change what I did or how wrong it was but that was the way it was you have to understand. If I had it all again I wouldn't do half of the things I did and I would be friends with Hong because she was really honestly a nice and sweet girl and I wish I had come to Beijing with her over the holidays like she asked because the honest truth is she is the only one who ever invited me to her home since I started at secondary school. And you won't know this but I saw you on the day you arrived at school, two days after it happened. I was in East Wing watching at the window for my mother to arrive and I saw your taxi pull up, and the two of you get out, and I saw you Mrs Chang Jones wobble on your feet and then straighten up and your husband had his arm around your waist and you stood there for a long time, well it seemed like a long time, maybe 2 or 3 whole minutes, just standing, looking at the school. And you looked up to the window where I was, only you didn't see me there. But I was watching you, and I swear to you, I would have killed myself there and then if it would have brought back Hong. And you didn't know what had happened or rather why it had happened because Hong didn't leave a note. But everyone knew. And I didn't even care that they all said it was me, because it <u>was</u> me, and what I did was worse than any of them because I knew how bad it was when you were on the receiving end. Some of them, I think they were just having fun. I know what that must sound like to you but what I mean is <u>they</u> didn't know how bad it felt and I did, so I should have protected Hong and been her friend and maybe we would have been ok, so long as there were two of us. I don't know—we'll never know—and I am so, so sorry. And there have been so many times I've thought I'd kill myself, too, that that was the only way, and I think I might have done it if it wasn't for Ruth Armstrong, who is the wife of a minister who has come to Bahrain, and who is showing me the truth and the way. And maybe this letter doesn't make sense to you and maybe you don't even want to know what I have to say because none of it makes any difference, really, because none of it can bring Hong back. And I can't ask for her forgiveness even though I dream about her most nights and I probably can't ask for yours because I can't imagine that you'd forgive me, so I won't, but again I just want you to know how sorry I am.

Yours Sincerely,

Noor Hussain.

Noor tore the letter out of her diary, carefully, using the edge of a ruler. She folded it up in a tight little packet and hid it in the basement, down the side of the packing crate where she used to keep her stolen cigarettes. She did not think she would ever send that letter. But she had written it. Somewhere, somehow, perhaps Hong's parents—or Hong herself—would know.

3

Her new life was an edifice built on sand.

It started to crumble with what seemed a chance remark. Maryam had promised to take her to a beauty parlour, and on the chosen morning Farid collected her, dropped her off, and took the boys for ice cream on the Corniche. Maryam led her through the backstreets and up a flight of stairs marked, at regular intervals, with *WOMEN ONLY* in Arabic, Farsi, French, English. Inside, Ruth was shocked to see the *abaya*-clad women disrobing: they shed their flittering veils like skins, and underneath they wore tight jeans, high heels,

219

and full faces of make-up. Maryam was having her face threaded: her upper lip and cheeks and chin, and Ruth had her eyebrows shaped. Afterwards, looking in the mirror, she was surprised to see how big and flirtatious her eyes looked, framed by teasingly arched brows. While she waited for Maryam's treatment to finish, she watched two Indian girls having *mehendi*: henna patterns applied on their hands. When they noticed Ruth's curiosity, they insisted on doing hers, too: not a full design, just the palm and wrist. It lasted up to six weeks, they told her, before it faded. Would she be back home by then? they asked. She could show all her friends, they giggled, and make them jealous.

She had a slight stab of fear when they said this, at the thought of where she would be in six weeks. Since the first lunch in the Persian restaurant, since *the affair*, she had not missed Ireland. For the first time ever, she had been faintly bored during her mother's conversation about farm life, had started to lose track of which cows had calved or died. The prospect of life back home seemed suddenly dull: colourless, adventureless, and she saw herself there miserable, with no escape from church coffee mornings and the mounting duties of a minister's wife.

She tried to dismiss the thoughts, but Maryam had seen her face, seen the panic flit across it. As they were leaving the beauty parlour—Ruth careful of her newly hennaed hand, smeared in Vaseline until the patterns dried—Maryam turned to her and said, 'Be careful of him, Ruth. I like him a lot. Please don't hurt him. He is only young.'

Ruth stared at her, felt her mouth open and close, uselessly. They had been careful to introduce her to Maryam as a friend, been careful not to touch or give any other indication of their intimacy in front of her. She suddenly felt foolish, and responsible.

'I do not think you are a selfish person, Ruth,' Maryam went on carefully. Later, she realised that Maryam had obviously chosen and learned her words, and she wondered if the whole beauty parlour trip had been planned for this purpose, for the opportunity to say them.

'I—' she said, and she stopped. 'It's not like that,' she tried. But her objections sounded lame, even to her own ears.

'There are punishments for adultery,' Maryam said, softly, not looking at her. 'It is a crime, Ruth, as severe as murder under sharia law. Bahrain is more liberal than most countries—than Saudi Arabia, say, or Iran, or even Dubai. In some countries, you can be stoned to death. Here, it will be lashes, or a term in jail. For Farid, the punishment will be greater, and the consequences of that punishment. Be careful, please.'

She had thought Maryam her friend, and Farid's: but now she saw that Maryam was a cover story, an alibi. It was a game, and she did not know the rules. No: 'game' was wrong. It was not a game. It had been a game—she had treated it as a game—but it was all too real.

*　　　*　　　*

Farid brushed away her concerns, when she raised them. She was careful not to say it was Maryam who had warned her—but an article in the *Gulf Daily News*, she said, that she'd happened to read.

221

They would not be caught, he said. Under the law, you needed four witnesses to catch you in the act. Unless the authorities had another reason, or unless they'd been tipped off and had to act, they would not bother to enforce the law. Why—he even laughed at this point—did she think they had taken so many precautions? It was not just for her husband's benefit, surely she had realised that?

They had lunch, but even in the cloistered cubicle of the restaurant she was jumpy. Farid reassured her, time and again. But the fears would not dissolve. They had plans for the afternoon— to drive up to Buddayi' Harbour and see the sailboats—but she asked him to take her home early. When he protested, she said it was not just the worry—she had a headache, brought on by the fumes in the salon, maybe. It was a pointless lie, and a bad one. There were things she had not told him, of course—about the bible-smuggling, the underground cell. The real reasons for their being in Bahrain. But these were omissions, not direct untruths. This was the first time she had lied to him, and he knew she was lying. He said nothing, but the reproach in his eyes was terrible.

Noor was surprised to see her back so early. When she followed Ruth into the house, talking, Ruth did not have the strength to stop her, or to turn her away. Noor had taken to hanging around, each day, after Ruth collected Anna. Even if Ruth tried to indicate that she would rather be alone— by going into the living room and switching on the television—Noor would follow her, copy her, and Ruth tried to tolerate it as the price for having a babysitter every day. She was starting, though, to dislike Noor: to feel uncomfortable around her.

Strangely, Noor was the only person who could make her feel guilty and deceptive about what she was doing. Noor swallowed every line Ruth fed her: about a sudden increase in church-related work, about meeting Euan for lunch, about outings with Rosa. It was as if, having made up her mind to think Ruth good and kind, she was incapable of seeing otherwise. When Noor asked her to pray, she almost said no. She had stopped praying, after the day at Al Bander, and stopped even trying to pray. Once, it had been as natural as believing, and the Holy Spirit as tangible as breath. Once, the words of the Bible had power: they were not only vehicles for the truth, they *were* the truth, the word of God, God. But now they just seemed words, loose, rustling, disposable. If Noor had asked on any other day, Ruth would have fobbed her off, found some excuse—telling her to ask Euan, perhaps. But that afternoon, something in her wondered—some tiny, residual voice—if she prayed for help, would God answer?

*   *   *

For the rest of the day, Maryam's remarks rang in her ears, and for the first time, she started to question what she was doing. What she and Farid had just done, without thinking or talking of what they were doing. They had been blithe, wild, free, caring only of their own pleasure. The last weeks had been a fantasy, a madness, the most liberating—liberated—days of her life. But suddenly the henna on her hand—blazing, scarlet and orange—seemed like a branding. That evening, she felt nervous lying to Euan about what

223

it was and where it came from, about where she had spent her day. She wondered if he knew more than he was letting on. She thought of the time she had come back sunburned from Al Jayazir. That night, as she applied aloe vera to the blistered skin, she had waited for him to ask what she had been doing to get so burned. Eventually, unable to bear it any longer, she had said herself, 'I got a bit burned today.' But all he replied was, 'Yes, you'll have to be a bit more careful.' She had thought, at the time, that she had got away with it. Euan was so engrossed in Saudi Arabia, so exhausted by it, that he had no time for Bahrain. He and the cell had been amassing Christian material to take on their trip: the gospels inside the pens and encoded on USB memory sticks, audio files of sermons and inspirational speakers, New Testaments in Arabic and Tagalog and Hindi and Malayalam. They were finalising their itineraries and cover stories, getting the necessary papers and signatures and stamps. Some documents needed as many as twelve or thirteen signatures, in a specific order, or they could be refused entry to—or worse, exit from— the Kingdom. They were memorising street names and addresses, phone numbers, safe houses and meeting points, places they could be safe if they were discovered or betrayed. They were learning code words and passwords for taxi drivers and compounds, being trained to take circuitous routes so that they did not draw undue attention to the places they were going. Their mission was to be the biggest, the most comprehensive, that any underground Christian network had undertaken in years. She was not supposed to know any of this. But Euan could not help telling her: it was an *I told you so*, she thought, a proof of the magnitude of the undertaking. He was trying to awe her into submission, because he still sensed that she was not supportive of him, had not yet forgiven him. She had listened, for the most part, in silence to his secrets; all the while cherishing her own. It gave her a strange, hot pleasure to think that he knew nothing of her secret world. But suddenly she was no longer sure: of this, or of anything. She had not considered—it sounded ludicrous, but it was true— what the consequences might be if Euan did find out. A squirm of fear twisted in her bowels. She tried to still it by telling herself that nobody did know; that Maryam had no proof of anything; that it would serve Euan no purpose confronting her. Of course he did not, could not, know. He was too dazzled by his Kingdom to see her shadows. She told herself this, ordering herself to calm down and stop being paranoid. But the doubt was there now, and that night she could not sleep.

*　　　*　　　*

The following morning, Trudy called by, and told Ruth that she and her husband were going home.

'As an American, I just do not feel safe here,' she said, 'and I do not feel safe with Patrick going out to work all day with Arabs.' *Ay-rabs*, she said, *Ay-rab*. 'You just can't trust an Arab,' she said, and she looked at Ruth with sly eyes. 'You have Arab friends here, don't you?'

Ruth realised that she should have kept up with the neighbours, endured the pumpkin pie and Indian sweets. For the last two weeks, she had been coming back to find notes on the porch, covered plates of food; and she had never gotten around to reciprocating, to returning the visits.

'Yes,' she said, keeping her voice light. 'I've found Bahrainis to be very friendly, actually.'

'"Very friendly"?' Trudy said, and giggled.

Ruth kept her gaze steady.

'Well.' Trudy shrugged. 'I sure don't trust 'em.' Then she said, abruptly: 'You've probably been too busy with your friendly Arabs to know that Anjali's in hospital.'

'In hospital?'

'So you didn't know. Oh, yes. It's the baby.' She paused for effect. 'It happened two days ago, on Tuesday. She had cramps, and bleeding. They rushed her in. There was an ambulance, and everything. They gave her drugs to stop the labour for as long as possible—they thought she was going into labour, you see.'

'And how is she now?'

'Stable. Well, I saw her yesterday, and she was stable. I'm sure she'd appreciate a visit from you.'

'Yes, of course,' Ruth said. 'That's awful. I'll go today.' She stood, helpless, while Trudy found a piece of paper and wrote down the name and address of the private hospital where Anjali was taken. She had preferred Anjali to Trudy, despite her affectations. They had joked, one day, about mother-in-laws—Ruth was not sure how the subject had come up, but all of a sudden she had found herself telling Anjali how Euan's mother disliked her, considered her not good enough, not educated enough, for her only son. How in the wedding photos, Euan's parents were standing apart from hers, and not smiling, not in a single one. How awkward Christmases were, and family gatherings:

how she often locked herself in the bathroom, to hide her tears. How even when they had called their baby after Euan's sister, who was in turn named for her grandmother, it had not brought the family closer.

'I didn't even like the name Anna,' Ruth had said, and it was the first time she had said it to anyone. Anna, playing at her feet, had smiled and looked up, and she had sighed. 'I mean I'm used to it now, she's definitely an Anna now. But I always wanted to call her Lorelei or Bethany, something exotic, you know?'

'Lorelei,' Anjali had said, curving her tongue around the strange syllables. 'For me—Maya or Mohini. But Maarlen and his mother are *con*vinced Baby is a boy.' And then she had talked about her mother-in-law, how she would come over one month before the baby was due, and stay for six months after that. They had both laughed, and grimaced, and commiserated over that. When Ruth left, they had promised to have another gossip soon: and Ruth had not, because then had come the day at Al Bander, and the war, and then Farid.

Now, she felt a surge of guilt, as if she had somehow betrayed Anjali, too.

*   *   *

Farid drove her to the hospital that afternoon. It was not far: on the outskirts of Manama town, just off the main roundabout. But it took a long time to get there: it was Thursday, the first day of the Arab weekend, and the roads were jammed. It took them almost five minutes to inch around the main roundabout alone. He could tell that something

227

was up, that something had changed, she could see that. He kept glancing at her, anxiously, and clearing his throat. She tried several times to make conversation, but everything she said sounded somehow stilted. She tried to make excuses—it was the tail end of her headache, it was concern for her friend—but she knew he knew she was lying.

He parked inside the hospital complex, and said he'd wait for her there. The small parking lot was lined with miniature palm trees, each one trimmed and manicured. The walkways were lined with *muhammadi* flowers, lilac and white and red, and on either side of the sliding glass doors was a Chinese hibiscus bush, bursting with frothy crimson flowers. The grass in front of the entrance was unfeasibly green: a network of pipes and sprinklers criss-crossed the ground to ensure that the plants were kept damp. It looked more like a boutique hotel, she thought, than a hospital. Inside was cool and quiet, marble floors and white walls, bare apart from a trio of portraits of the King, his brother, and his son the Crown Prince, all smiling benevolently from under checked headdresses. The staff were dressed in crisp white uniforms and peaked hats—like pictures of nurses from the First World War. Even the bellboys standing at the lift had white tunics with gold buttons and caps with golden tassels, and the security guards at the entrance wore smooth charcoal suits and discreet earpieces, like presidential bodyguards.

She gave her name to the receptionist, and asked if it was possible to see Anjali, and the receptionist asked her to be seated. The settees were leather and chrome, and there was a sleek stack of imported glossy magazines on a glass coffee table. American *Vogue*, French *Vogue*, *Tatler* and *Harper's Bazaar* and the most recent editions of *Hello!* Ruth thought of Anjali showing her around the baby's room for the first time, telling her that the inspiration came from *Hello!* magazine, and she felt a pang, imagining Anjali falling upon the discarded or out-of-date issues that Maarlen must have brought home.

She had a long wait. She was too distracted by her own thoughts to read any of the magazines, and she fell to thinking instead of the wealth that Bahrainis—or at least the Arab inhabitants, and the more privileged Indians—enjoyed. Farid had tried to explain to her the structure of society here. The sheikhs and sheikhas—there were hundreds of them, the relatives of the King—kept themselves apart. Unless you were one of them, you rarely saw them or interacted with them. You might see their cars—recognisable by the special number plates, with fewer digits than anyone else—and you might catch glimpses of them, crossing the lobbies of the more expensive hotels or being ushered into nightclubs through side doors. But you never met them, or got to know them. Bahrainis who were not related to the royal family came next: and they too lived a pretty good life. Low taxes, good wages, plenty of household staff for their villas and gardens. They holidayed often, in Dubai or America or Europe; their children studied at the top universities abroad. And then, Farid explained, there were the non-Bahraini Arabs: the Kuwaiti or Iranian emigrants, like his mother, or Maryam, who had fled the country for fear of persecution. There were the wealthy Indians and Filipinos— although, he emphasised, even if you were born in the Kingdom or married a Bahraini, as a non-Arab you would never have equal status. And then came the economic migrants, the Africans and subcontinentals who laboured on the building sites or worked as indentured servants. Expats and Westerners, he teased her, were not so high in society's stratification as they liked to think: but she was all right, as long as she stuck with him.

When she questioned him further, as fascinated by the rigid layering as he was by the difference between Protestants and Catholics, he had used the analogy of prostitutes. The Saudi boys would pay thousands of dinar for an Arab girl, he told her, thousands and thousands. Then a pale-skinned Westerner, English or French. The Russians were cheaper, because they were a lot more ubiquitous. But they were usually beautiful, so they cost more than the Moroccans or the Filipinas. Cheapest of all were the Indians and Eastern Europeans.

He would take her into any bar, he said, in any hotel, and she would see the prostitutes, working in packs. There would always be a blonde one, a dark one, a plump one, a thin one—different nationalities and body shapes to cater for different tastes. You could sit in a hotel bar and watch them circle, watch the men debate their merits and then signal the one of their choice; disappear, and return an hour later.

She had protested, disbelieving, and he had laughed at her naivety, her innocence, he called it. At the time, it had seemed a game. But now, she suddenly realised how little she knew him, and wondered if he had used prostitutes before. It was an unpleasant thought. Perhaps it was being in a hospital that was making her think such things, but they had not always been as careful as they might have been.

Stop it, she told herself, sternly. Stop it. Two days ago—only two days—she had truly believed she had never been, could never be, happier.

She sat there, feeling sicker by the minute, until an orderly appeared to take her up to Anjali's room.

The room was on the sixth floor of the clinic, looking directly out over the glittering skyscrapers of the financial district and the executive hotels beyond. Maarlen was there, standing by the window, twisting the cord to turn the slats of the blinds outwards and back in. Light slanted across the room, thinned, disappeared, blazed again. He turned when Ruth entered, took a step towards her, and stopped.

'Thank you for coming,' he said, and he attempted his usual bow. Then he said, in a low voice, 'It means a lot. Anjali does not have many friends in Bahrain. I know you have been a good friend to her. She talks of you often.'

Anjali was propped up immobile in bed, pale and exhausted, with pads and wires attached to her stomach, monitoring the baby's heart rate. Ruth kissed her cheek then sat down on a chair beside the bed, stiff and awkward with pity for Anjali, that she should have no better friends to call on.

Anjali spoke about what had happened—the stomach cramps, the blood, the rush to hospital, the tests and more tests, the drugs to delay labour. She was going to stay in hospital, she said, until the baby was born. She paused then, and looked sideways at Maarlen.

'The baby,' she said, 'it is a she. I mean to say,

231

she is a girl. They did ultrasound tests.'

'Congratulations.'

'I say to Maarlen, a girl is not so bad. Look at Ruth's beautiful girl.' Anjali attempted a laugh. 'Ruth, where is little Anna?'

Ruth explained that she was with Noor, Dr al-Husayn's daughter.

'Really?' Anjali said, and she frowned. 'Dr al-Husayn is a good man, a very good man. He is an excellent doctor, and he has been very kind to Maarlen. He find us our house on the compound—when first we arrive we are in a nasty apartment, very noisy. He is a good man. But his daughter—she is troubled, no?'

'Troubled?' Ruth said.

'I do not know the details, I must confess. When she come out here to live, it is only'—she turned to her husband—'February? Valentine Day? Anyhow'—turning back to Ruth—'she come here because there is some problem, she is expelled from school. That is why she lie around the house all day, not go to school.' Anjali stopped. 'Oh, but Ruth. I do not mean to alarm you. I am sure your little princess is completely all right.'

'Noor has always been perfectly pleasant, perfectly normal,' Ruth said. 'I wouldn't leave my daughter—'

'Oh, no, but of course not,' Anjali said. 'I am sorry, Ruth. Forgive me.'

There was a momentary silence. Ruth could feel her mind hiving with sudden doubts and fears. Almost every day, for the past few weeks—

She must not think like that. Anna was fine, Noor—whatever might have gone on in her life—was capable, devoted. She had seen Anna with

232

Noor. Anna was perfectly happy, perfectly safe.

But she wondered, even so, if it was too early to take her leave of Anjali. She was suddenly anxious to get back: to curl up with her daughter and close the door and not let anything, anyone else in. Her heart was beating fast, as if it was trying to keep her body afloat. Suddenly, everything she had ignored, held at bay for the past few weeks was closing in on her: she could feel herself sinking, submerging. The ground she had thought to be solid was not at all.

She stayed a few more minutes, then made her goodbyes.

*   *   *

In the car, she says to Farid: it's no good. We can't do this. I can't do this any more. He does not understand what has happened. What's changed? he keeps asking her, what's different? and he thumps the steering wheel in frustration, so hard the car swerves across two lanes and almost causes an accident.

'I love you, Ruth,' he says. It is the first time either of them has said it, said those words. *I love you.*

Something tightens within her. 'You love me?' she repeats.

'Don't you love me?'

'I don't know,' she says. They have not talked of love. Maryam's words, her warning, suddenly echo in Ruth's ears.

'I didn't know—' she tries. 'I didn't think—'

In her bag, her mobile phone starts ringing. She takes it out: it is Euan. She stares at the screen, frozen. She does not answer. He rings off, then

233

immediately starts to ring again.

'Pull over,' she says to Farid. 'Please pull over. It's my husband.'

He jerks the car off the highway and onto the scrubby verge. She opens the door and scrambles out. The air hums, pulled tight by heat.

Fearing the worst, she takes the call.

*　　　*　　　*

The preparations were finished and the trip was set for Monday. He was to go at first light, returning for the Maundy service on Thursday, all being well. Now—the calm before the storm, he tried to joke— he was free to spend some time with them.

'Where are you?' he asked. 'Are you outside?'

'Oh,' she said, vague, 'I've just been to see Anjali at the hospital, I'll tell you about it later.'

'I'll be home shortly,' he said. 'I was going to surprise you, but I just couldn't wait.'

They only just beat him home.

*　　　*　　　*

It was painful to see Euan making an effort those last few days: he was more loving, more attentive, than he had been in weeks. He hired a car for two days to take them around the island: to the gardens at Al Areen, to the camel farm, even out to Al Bander to watch the sunset—all places she had discovered with Farid. Being there with Euan seemed a mockery of all she had felt, or thought she had felt, with Farid. She felt sick the whole time, in case someone—a waiter, a parking attendant— would recognise her and make some innocent

234

comment, which would give away everything. Bahrain had seemed limitless: a playground. Now, she understood how small it really was: how bounded and circumscribed are all imagined freedoms.

*   *   *

Sunday was Palm Sunday. The service was joyful, spectacular. A procession of children strewed palm fronds along the aisle to the altar, and there was even a real, live donkey led in on a rope. They sang Psalm 118: *Let Israel say, 'His love endures for ever!' Let the house of Aaron say, 'His love endures for ever!' Let those who fear the Lord say, 'His love endures for ever!'* and for the children they sang a hymn of which Ruth had always been fond. *Tell me the stories of Jesus I love to hear, Things I would ask him to tell me if he were here, Scenes by the wayside, tales of the sea, Stories of Jesus, tell them to me.* It had always summed up, for her, the gladness and simplicity of faith. She had sung it to Anna, often, as a lullaby. But now the words felt facile, sentimental and saccharine, and she mouthed rather than sang them. She felt unspeakably sad as she did so: apprehending what she had lost, of earlier, innocent times when she did not realise that she was unhappy. After the service, everyone was laughing, clapping, applauding the children and the donkey. How long, she thought, could she keep this up, this façade?

*   *   *

That night, Euan asked her to pray with him. They

had fallen out of the habit, since coming to Bahrain: he had been arriving home so late, she had taken to going to bed without him, or pretending to be already asleep when he got in. But now, there was no excuse.

'Ruth?' he said.

'I'm sorry,' she said.

As he gazed at her, she wondered if he knew, or suspected. But his eyes were bright, steady. His belief in who he was, in what he was doing, shone so fiercely that it obliterated—made impossible— any shadows. He did not know a thing. He thought her struggles were struggles of faith, not knowing she had passed that, was beyond that now. His incapacity to see, she realised, was a naivety, a kind of innocence, and all of a sudden she felt hollow with sorrow for him. She thought of how he had looked at her on their wedding day, of the private promises they had made each other, on top of their public vows. How nothing could and ever would come between them. Sadness tightened around her chest. It was something, she knew, that she would carry with her always.

For a moment, the resentment and guilt and discontent towards Euan she had amassed and nurtured over the past few weeks melted away. It was just her and him, the man she had loved. And he, she realised, in his innocence, blinded, had no idea, no idea at all. For a moment, she wished with all of her heart that they had never come, that they had never left Ireland, that they were safe in the cottage by the lough.

'I'm sorry,' she said again, and she tried to put into those small words an apology for everything, for all that had happened, and all that was to come.

'Jesus said,' said Euan, still holding her gaze, ' "I am the resurrection and the life. He who believes in me will live, even though he dies; and whoever lives and believes in me will never die." '

Her frustration with him flared again. She said nothing, did not even move, but he felt it; she saw him feel it, like an arrow. He closed his eyes, and ducked his head. When he looked up at her again, his eyes were glinting. 'I love you, Ruth,' he said.

The way he said it sounded as if he was saying goodbye: and she realised that in a way, he was. Both of them were. To everything they had known before: to how, or who, they had been.

As she looked at him, she had a fleeting vision of Paul at Miletus, taking his leave of the Ephesians. *I am going to Jerusalem, not knowing what will happen to me there.* Paul is eager, in his outward words, to suffer pain and martyrdom and die. *Now I know that none of you among whom I have gone about preaching the kingdom will ever see me again. Prison and hardships are facing me, but I consider my life worth nothing to me.* But suddenly she saw him in a new light: gaunt and frightened in his travel-worn robes and dusty sandals, hauling himself onto a rocky outcrop to address the people thronging on the harbour by the boat, his foot slipping on the sea-spattered stone. He is trying to convince himself, as much as them. He does not want to go, she realises. He knows he has to, but he does not want to go.

Lord, take this cup from me: yet not my will, but yours.

How had she not seen this before? For all of Euan's rhetoric, for all the ease with which he talked of death, he was scared of pain, and scared

237

to die, just like anyone.

It's too late for that now, she wanted to say.

She turned and left the room; left him to his prayers.

She had not told Farid about Euan's trip, not even with the line Euan had given her: that he was going to a conference in Qatar for a few days. Over the course of the weekend she had managed to text him sporadically from the bathroom. But it was risky—turning on the phone, waiting for the signal, composing the message, sending it—and turning the phone off immediately afterwards, in case Euan should hear it beeping or see the flash of a new message and ask who it was from.

Now, in the kitchen, she thought: I don't care if Euan walks in and sees. In fact, some small, selfish part of her almost hoped he would, so that he could understand he was not the only one who suffered. She turned on her phone and wrote a message. *E's leaving tomorrow for 3 whole days. I'll meet you at the usual time.* When she tapped in her usual *X, X*, each one felt like a nail. She pressed the button to send the message. There: sent. It was done.

4

The Diary of Noor Hussain

Monday, 14th April 2003

Ruth said no. She said no. SHE SAID NO.

5

When the banging on the door came that morning, she immediately assumed the worst. Euan had left while it was still dark. The disruption had woken Anna, so she had taken her into their own bed, and the two of them had only just fallen back asleep. Ruth lurched out of bed, her heart thudding, and went to answer it.

It was a shock to see Noor there. She was wild-eyed and jumpy, as if she had not slept, and Ruth noticed for the first time how unwell she looked, how thin she was getting. Anjali's words rang ominously in her head.

'Is everything OK?' she said, relief jostling with annoyance.

Noor took her glasses off and rubbed them on her stomach. 'I know this isn't a good time,' she said. 'But can we talk?'

'Can we talk?' Ruth said, incredulous. 'It's barely eight in the morning, Noor.'

'I've missed you,' Noor said. 'The last few days, not seeing you, or Anna—and I wanted to go to church with you yesterday, I waited on the porch for you to pick me up, but you didn't.'

'I'm sorry,' Ruth said. 'It's been a busy few days, as you know'—she had a moment of misgiving, but she had already started talking—'with Euan going to Qatar, we—well, we had lots of things to do beforehand.'

'Oh,' Noor said. 'I thought—oh Ruth—I thought I'd done something, and you didn't want to see me again.'

'Don't be ridiculous,' Ruth said. 'Why would I think something like that? In fact—I might need you to look after Anna again today, if that's all right?'

'Oh, of course, Ruth! Of course, any time, you don't even need to ask!'

'OK, then.' Ruth went to step back and shut the door, but Noor did not move.

'Ruth, when are you going—I mean for good? It's soon, isn't it?—Sampaguita said the villa was only rented until May.'

'That's right.'

'Well—there's something I've been wanting to ask you, Ruth. You and Euan. And—well—I think we'd better talk about it now, because there isn't much time left, because today's already the fourteenth of April. There's less than two weeks, that means. Can I come in?'

Bemused, Ruth held the door open and let Noor in. Noor stood there in the hallway for a moment, then took a breath and launched into a gabbled, rambling speech about a girl at school, and how it was all Noor's fault, and how her mother hated her. Ruth could barely make head or tail of it.

'Hang on—' she tried a few times, but Noor was in full flow, unstoppable. And suddenly she was talking about Ireland, and Anna, and sleeping on the sofa, and Premium Bonds, and –

'I'm sorry,' Ruth finally managed to interrupt, 'but I'm not sure I understand—'

'I'm not explaining properly, I know I'm not, but all I'm trying to say is that it won't cost you a thing, not a penny. But it takes eight working days for the investment to be cashed in, and that's once they receive the form, so you have to allow an extra five

240

days in the post even if I send it this morning, and eight days and five days is almost two weeks and two weeks is May and that's when you're going so we have to plan it now.'

'Wait a minute,' Ruth said, not sure if she was hearing it right, 'you want to come back to Ireland?'

'Yes!' Noor cried. 'I've got it all planned, Ruth—'

'You mean for a holiday, or . . . ?'

Noor blinked at her. 'For ever,' she said. Her voice faltered.

'You want to come back to Ireland,' Ruth said, not even trying to stifle her incredulity, 'and live with us there?'

This time, Noor just looked at her.

'I'm sorry, Noor,' Ruth said, 'but—I mean, I just don't think that's feasible, do you?'

Noor whispered something that Ruth did not catch.

'Beg your pardon?'

But Noor would not repeat it.

'Listen, Noor,' Ruth said, making her voice jovial. 'I think, somehow, you must have gotten the wrong end of the stick. Because—'

'But the way I've looked after Anna,' Noor interrupted, 'and the way you've prayed with me, and taken me to church—and taken me out with you, to Al Bander that day, and all of our suppers and talks—I thought you liked me, I thought'— her voice was breaking down, now—'I thought you might—you might—'

'We might what?'

'Adopt me,' Noor finished.

The absurdity of it almost made her laugh aloud. 'Adopt you?' she said. 'Us, adopt you, and bring

241

you back to Ireland?'

They stared at each other.

'Noor,' she tried again. 'But Noor—'

Before she could continue, Noor had turned and was gone, her sandals slapping as she ran, banging the door behind her.

*   *   *

After that, Ruth could not leave Anna with Noor—and with both of the maids there that morning, Farid could not come to the villa. She walked with Anna to the cold-store car park, and when she saw him, she realised with a rush how much she had been wanting to see him, how much she had missed him. Despite what had happened outside the beauty parlour and with Trudy, and at the hospital. Euan was going away and perhaps—she had told herself—perhaps they could have three whole days, three blissful days of being together, as it had been at Al Bander, at the beginning. But when she tried to kiss him, he pulled away from her.

'I want to talk,' he said.

'I know you do,' she said, 'but please, not now. We have three days, Farid—three whole days. Let's just try and enjoy them, forget about—everything.' But even as she was speaking, she knew how hollow her words sounded.

They drove to the Adhari Amusement Park. The gardens there were deserted during the day: it was one of the few places they had found where, on certain days of the week, they could almost be alone. They bought Anna an ice cream, then walked down past the Log Flume and the Pedal Boats, huge swan shapes, bleached yellow in the sun, bobbing on the artificial lake. They walked past the Dodgems and the Flying Carousel, its spiderlike arms contracted and stilled. Ruth had never noticed, before, how faded and sorry for themselves the rides looked in the glare of the mid-morning sun. At the far end of the complex were the Pleasure Gardens, where you could talk in privacy, in the shade of a few gnarled banyan trees. They found a bench and sat. And Farid started talking.

He was glad that this had happened, he said, that things were being brought to a head, discussed. He was not happy with the way things were—snatched afternoons in car parks, or on the outskirts of deserted villages, hasty lovemaking on the divan when the villa was empty. At first it felt secret and sexy, he said, but now it was just base. He wanted them to be really together, truly. He knew Ruth was not happy with her husband. He knew she no longer believed what her husband believed. He wanted her to leave her husband, ask for a divorce, and be with him, Farid.

'Divorce?' she said.

He grabbed her hands, his eyes imploring and earnest. He knew he was younger than her, he knew he had no home for her at present—but he would work, he would get a job, any job, provide for her. He would build a house for her—his family would help him build a house. He had never had reason to work before, to work or study, he had just drifted. But now he had met her, she was his reason. He wanted to work so hard that he would be too exhausted to stand up any more, and all of it would be for her.

'Please, Ruth!' He was on the verge of tears. 'I

love you. I know it will be hard, but if we love each other we can do it.'

'Farid,' she said, helplessly. She had been expecting goodbyes, expecting them to lay things to rest, to kiss or make love one final time. She should have known, she thought, when he said he loved her in the car. She should have known then, but she had dismissed it as spontaneous, hot-headed.

Suddenly, she started to laugh. Farid drew back from her, appalled. 'Your cousin came to see me this morning,' she managed, through gulps of laughter. 'She wanted us to adopt her, and take her back to Ireland.'

'Us to adopt her?' Farid said. 'But I don't understand.'

'Euan-and-me us, not us us. She wanted'— Ruth was doubled over now, laughing so hard she thought her stomach might rip—'she wanted—'

Farid beside her, and Anna playing in the dirt at their feet, both watched her until her fit had passed.

Then she said, 'So I would spend the rest of my life in Bahrain? And what about Anna—she would be brought up here?'

'Why not?' he said.

'Why not? Her father, for a start. He would never allow—'

Farid cut her off. 'Her father,' he scoffed. 'Her father never sees her. Even I see that much. He is gone first thing in the morning, back when she is going to bed—if that. What does he do, say a prayer and pat her forehead?'

'Stop it,' Ruth said, 'it's not like that.' But it was not untrue, what Farid said. And she thought back to the night they arrived, the realisation that Euan was ready to sacrifice not only her, but Anna too.

244

He had been prepared to lose her, then.

Farid was watching her closely, the expressions chasing each other across her face.

'You see?' he said, softly. 'I do not mean to be unkind, Ruth, but you know I am right.'

'But—' Her words failed, at the enormity of it, the impossibility. She threw her hands up. 'Farid—'

'Bahrain, or anywhere,' he interrupted. 'We could go back to Ireland.'

'We couldn't go to Ireland. Everyone would know, it would be a scandal. It would be unbearable.'

'Dubai, then, we could go to Dubai. Or Europe, or anywhere. Anywhere in the world, Ruth.' He was getting frantic now. Anna would be with them, no problem, and go to her father for holidays, if he insisted on seeing her. And they would have children of their own, in time.

For the first time in the weeks they had been together, she felt the weight of the age difference, every day of it.

'You're not even twenty,' she said.

'I knew you'd say that,' he said, almost triumphantly. 'But it hasn't been a problem so far, and it won't be, once I am working and providing for you.'

There was nothing she could say that he had not already thought of, had not already got an answer for. And when he said, 'So what is the alternative, Ruth? You go back to Ireland, with a man you don't love, to a life you don't believe in?' she had no reply.

*   *   *

It was getting too hot to stay outside. They drove to a hookah bar, one they had been to before, a cavernous mass of lounges and corridors, all draped in bright fabrics. It was usually crammed with young people, but at midday on a Monday, few others were there. They had a lounge to themselves.

They ordered soft drinks.

'I've missed you,' Farid said. 'These last few days, when I couldn't see you—I didn't know what to do with myself, Ruth. I realised how much you mean to me. I realised I am in love with you.'

'It's only been a few weeks,' she tried. But he replied: 'Don't pretend these few weeks haven't changed your life, too.' Then he said, 'I understand you can't say you love me back. That would be a commitment. But I know you feel it, Ruth. I know you feel the same.'

They stayed in the hookah bar until lunchtime, when it began to fill with young people from the nearby college, and two girls asked to share their sofas. They got back in the car, then, and drove to the Marina Mall for lunch. Neither of them ate much. They wandered about the mall for an hour or so, until the maids would be gone. Every other person, Ruth thought, seemed to be someone from church, or someone she knew. At one point, she was convinced she saw Rosa's head, in the queue for the ladies' room. She turned and hurried back out, so abruptly she almost knocked over the woman behind her.

Back home, she insisted that once he had dropped them off, Farid park the car by the cold store and come back in through the alleyway. Even with Anjali in hospital, and Trudy gone, she did not want the Camaro in front of her villa.

It was barely six o'clock, too early for Anna's bedtime. But she had not had a nap, and so Ruth tried to get her down, hoping she would be tired enough to sleep anyway. Anna did not want to go to sleep. She screamed and flailed, throwing such a tantrum that Ruth eventually gave up and set her down in front of the television set to get some peace. She was not being a very good mother today, she thought. They had smoked in front of Anna in the hookah bar—she had not dared to ask Farid not to, and she had felt that she needed it herself—and now this. Then the irony of the thought hit her: she was sleeping with a man not her daughter's father, practically in front of her daughter, and allowing him to discuss divorce, and she was worried about smoke and Nickelodeon? She almost laughed; but then she thought, instead, Who have I become?

In the kitchen, they opened a bottle of wine, and Farid repeated, almost to the word, everything he had said earlier, going over and over each argument. Sometimes, for a moment—a shard of a moment—she wanted to believe him, wanted to believe that it was possible. But she knew it was not.

When the wine was finished, she went to check on Anna. She was sprawled asleep on her pile of cushions, lurid shapes and colours flickering across her bare skin. Ruth scooped her up and laid her in her cot. Farid as Anna's father? That was the sticking point, she thought. If it were not for Anna—

She was immediately ashamed at having such a thought, even just for a moment.

She went back to the kitchen, where Farid had opened a bottle of whiskey—the gift-wrapped Bushmills that Euan had brought over from

Ireland. Half of the bottle was gone, and it was long past midnight, when Farid finally accepted that this was it: that this was the end.

Now that there was no more to say, they made love—wordlessly, almost violently—on the divan, and afterwards they were both sobbing. He, because he did not want to lose her. She, for everything she had lost.

*   *   *

She makes up the camp bed in the spare room for them to sleep in. He has refused to sleep in her bed—her and Euan's bed—and he is in no fit state to drive. The spare room is clean—the maids mop and wipe it down weekly—but it smells sterile, unlived-in. Once the metal frame of the bed is wrested into place, the thin mattress flattened out and bedding found, he strips off his clothes and gets in, and she gets in with him. The bed is too small for both of them to lie comfortably. If one turns, the other must, too. Farid lies facing the wall, and she holds him. She feels him crying, silently, his shoulders quivering. She fits her body to his—how odd, that it can so easily take on the contours of another—and thinks: she has loved him, after all, in a way.

The final hours of the night pass, minute by minute. She drifts off, somewhere not asleep, but not quite awake, and wakes now and then with a jolt. Farid is asleep, breathing heavily, through an open mouth, like a child. He does not wake until the sun slants in through the window, sharp and white. It is even more intimate, Ruth realises, to wake with someone than it is to sleep with them.

She watches him wake and feels the tug again, the helplessness, the love.

'I do love you,' she says. 'It's not a commitment, and it doesn't change anything, but I do love you, Farid.'

When he has gone, she crawls back into her own bed, stiff and exhausted. The sheets are flat and icy, unwelcoming. She cannot get comfortable, cannot get warm. She wonders if she should have said yes, after all. She knows it's impossible—but she can't help wondering what life with him would have been like, could have been.

6

When Noor saw her cousin emerge from the Armstrongs' villa at just after six in the morning, she finally knew.

She sat there for a long time after he had gone, her legs chilled numb, incapable of motion. The sun rolled up, but she could not feel its heat. She had been sitting out all night, outside the empty villa, watching, waiting. She did not even have a blanket, just her cold-store cigarettes to keep her warm, and they had been smoked hours ago, one after the other, in a grim, mechanical sort of pleasurelessness. Her mouth was dry; her tongue fibrous; there was a strange, slow shrieking in her head. The teachers from number seven left for work, and then Dr Maarlen. Her father would be up soon: she had to go in before he saw her outside. She swayed to her feet, steadying herself against the rough wall. She turned to look one last time at the Armstrongs'. Its blank face stared back at her. Chevrons of pain were darting up and down her legs. Each movement was like walking on knives. Keeping one hand on the wall, she rounded the corner and made her way back to her own villa.

Her diary lay on the floor of her bedroom, its cover snapped in half. It had borne the brunt of yesterday's shame and rage. She picked it up, laid it on the bed. Pages fluttered from it, ripped, mutilated. She had torn handfuls from it, gouged her pen through particularly humiliating passages. On Sunday 13th, the penultimate entry, she had copied out from the church service sheet the words from one of the hymns they had sung, underlining the phrase 'the lovelight of Jesus' face'. Underneath, she had written: *Ruth's face. The lovelight of Ruth's face.* It had seemed, as she wrote it, a perfect word, a perfect description. The lovelight of Ruth's face! How could she ever, ever have written such a thing?

Her elation after the service had been what spurred her on to act. Palm Sunday, she had not realised, was the last Sunday of Lent—Easter was just one week away. Euan and Ruth had only come to Bahrain until Easter; at the start of May they would be returning to Ireland. She checked this with Sampaguita, who knew everything that went on: and yes, Sampaguita confirmed it. Their villa was only rented and their maids only engaged until the end of April. She had not realised she had so little time. The Premium Bonds website said that eight working days were needed for monies to clear if you wished to cash in your bonds. That gave her barely enough days to get hold of the money, buy her flight to Ireland, sort out her things and announce her plan to her parents. As well as convincing Euan and Ruth. Ruth, she was sure, would not need much convincing, but Euan might. She was slightly in awe of Euan. She should ask Ruth first, she decided, on her own, and then together they could tell Euan. She knew he was going away on Monday, to Qatar for several days: Ruth had told her so when she collected Anna on Thursday, because she would need extra help with Anna. So Monday was the time to do it. She hardly slept on Sunday night, and got up on Monday to wait for morning. She saw the car come for Euan, and she saw him leaving. She had planned to wait until after breakfast, but by eight o'clock she could bear it no longer.

As soon as Ruth answered the door, she knew that she had made a mistake. Ruth's eyes were screwed up from sleep and her hair was messy; she wore nothing but the T-shirt. She had still been asleep, and Noor had woken her. And even worse, she was glaring at Noor with an expression Noor had never seen before: an expression she had never thought possible on Ruth Armstrong's face. It was angry, and scathing, even disgusted, all at the same time. Noor panicked. And from then on, everything went from bad to worse.

*   *   *

Back home, Sampaguita found her crying in a heap on the bathroom floor. The old woman hauled her up—she was surprisingly strong, her bony arms hard and stubborn—and marched her into the kitchen, sat her down at the table and made her

251

drink a milky bowl of coffee drenched with sugar syrup. Sampaguita plucked at Noor's arms and at her stomach, and Noor almost started laughing to think that Sampaguita thought she was crying about her weight. She was not: she had lost the stone she intended and half a stone more. But when she tried to explain what was wrong she managed only to say Ruth's name before the tears came again.

Sampaguita had made it clear she didn't like having Anna in the house. Whenever she saw the child she would narrow her eyes and click her tongue and mutter in Tagalog. Once, she had gathered up the things of Anna's that had accumulated in the house—nappies, baby wipes, a few soft toys—and heaped them up on the veranda in the dust. Noor had been furious then, and Sampaguita had called her a fool for looking after the Irishwoman's baby and thinking the woman liked her. Now, Sampaguita repeated what she had said: the foreigners were bad people, and Noor should stay away from them. And then she said something more. The Irishwoman, she said—she did not call Ruth by her name—the Irishwoman is sleeping with your cousin behind her husband's back.

Automatically, Noor protested. Sampaguita had got it wrong, she misunderstood: Farid was helping Ruth learn Arabic, and about the culture of Bahrain. They had been on a few excursions, but it was for Ruth to see the island. Sometimes they took Noor and Anna along with them. And recently, Ruth hadn't had time to see anyone, she had been so busy with church business.

The old woman laughed. Liweiwei and Maria had told her everything, she said. About how the

Irishwoman had taken away their keys, so they could not come in without her knowing. About the extra towels to wash, and the dirt walked into the kitchen through the back alleyway— what innocuous visitor would frequent the back alleyway? About the bundles of tissues placed directly into the outside bin, the stain on the divan and the underwear in a corner of the room. Small things, meaningless in themselves, but together they told the full story.

With every excuse Noor made, at every protestation of Ruth Armstrong's goodness and kindness and innocence—the beliefs were ingrained deeply—Sampaguita cackled harder. Her English, Noor realised, was suddenly fine. And Noor could not keep at bay any longer the knowledge that Sampaguita was right.

*   *   *

That evening, she was watching as Farid brought Ruth and Anna back to their villa. They exchanged a few words, quickly and furtively—she could not catch what was said—and Farid shrugged and got back into his car. Noor was sure that something was going on. The way Ruth had leaned in to speak to him, the hand on his shoulder. It was obvious—so obvious. How could she not have seen it before? And Farid, of all people—*Farid*?

She watched as he turned the car around and left the compound. Ruth had gone inside and closed the door. She ran out of the compound, ignoring the sentry, and watched the direction the car took. It indicated left after only two blocks: the cold-store car park, of course. Noor jogged along the road to the cold store. Sure enough, there was Farid's Camaro, parked at the far side. She ducked behind a Hummer and watched as he came out of the store, carrying a brown paper bag, and walked straight past his car. He was going, on foot, back to the compound. Noor's heart was hammering so fast she thought she was going to be sick. She needed cigarettes. She had not smoked a thing in weeks. But now she needed one. She had just enough change for a packet, and a lighter.

She walked slowly back to the compound, settled down at the side of the empty villa—where she could see both the Armstrongs' door and the entrance to the back passage—and waited for Farid to come out. She would wait all night, if necessary, she told herself. When she saw, with her own eyes, Farid leaving Ruth's house, on the night that Euan had gone away, then she would know for sure.

What she would do with that knowledge, she did not yet know. But at least she would *know*.

*   *   *

Now, as she sat on her bed and flipped through the tatters of the diary, she did not know what to do. The diary was page after page of Ruth. Page after page after page. How stupid she had been. How utterly, utterly stupid. Ruth had used her, just like Sampaguita said. To mind the baby while she went gadding about with Farid, having an affair, not caring who they hurt. How they must have laughed at her, stupid, gullible Noor, she could just imagine it. And church, and Christianity, and everything—it was all a sham. She had believed: she had believed

254

in Ruth. But now she knew the truth, and she did not know what to do.

7

As the morning wore on, the feeling that she had made the wrong choice only increased. She thought back on the times they'd had, her and Farid, the brief, precious days, everywhere they went and everything they did, how happy they were. She had never known such happiness, such carelessness, such freedom. She thought, again and again, of the life that was in store for her with Euan, and it seemed impossible that she could go back to such a life, knowing now what she had known. It would be a long, grey line of Sunday schools and services, coffee mornings and counselling, endless, inexorable. When she thought of it now it seemed preposterous, impossible: no less so than staying in Bahrain. She thought of being back without Euan—separated from him, perhaps, living with her parents and Anna. She could help out on the farm again, begin to take over. But she knew as soon as she thought it that this would not work, either. The village was too small, the scandal—Reverend Armstrong's wife leaving him— would be too much, her parents would not be able to hold their heads up in church; *she* would not be able to hold her head up. No, the best chance was another life—a completely new life, far away, where she could start again. But here, Bahrain, Farid? Her head was going round and round, too fast. What if this was her one chance at life, at happiness? What if it was her one true chance, and she was letting it

255

go, when she should be seizing it? She had done the wrong thing, her heart was telling her. She had made the wrong choice.

*   *   *

She went to the bathroom and was sick several times. Afterwards, splashing water on her face, she felt clearer-headed. Last night's discussions had been frantic, whiskey-fuelled, unbearably sad. They needed to talk it all through again, as calmly as they could, in the light of day. She needed to see if there was a way—however slim—that it could work. Where they would live, what job Farid would get. Whether he did, truly, mean all that he had said.

*   *   *

She phoned him; he came over straight away. He looked haggard.

'You can't do this to me,' he said. 'You can't keep doing this to me.'

'Please,' she said, 'this is different, Farid. I've thought about what you said.' And she told him that she wanted to talk things through, once more.

They went into the living room; she put a DVD on for Anna, with the volume low. The maids were both still there, cooking, ironing fresh sheets. She asked them for some coffee. For a moment, she thought they were laughing at her behind their deferential faces. But she shrugged the thought off: what did it matter, what did the maids matter?

One of the maids brought coffee on a tray; tiny cups, the coffee treacle-thick and sweet. Ruth sipped hers; Farid knocked his back in one. The

256

maid came back in with glasses of water, biscuits on a plate. The DVD jammed and Anna cried. It was impossible to talk. It was such a delicate, such an important conversation, she had not wanted to have it at Adhari, or in a hookah café, or even in the Persian restaurant. But it was clear they could not have it here.

'Let's drive somewhere,' Farid said, but she recognised the mood Anna was in—needy, whiny—and she knew how Anna would wriggle in the car and scream; it would not be possible to talk with Anna there.

'What about Noor?' Farid said.

'I can't leave her with Noor,' Ruth said, helplessly. 'I told you about yesterday, how odd she was.'

'She is a teenager,' Farid said. 'She behaves oddly one day, so what?, teenagers do. Listen, Ruth'—he held up a palm to silence her objections—'I will ask her myself. She is my cousin, she will do it as a favour to me.'

'All right,' Ruth said, reluctant. 'But we'd better go together. I want to make sure she's really OK with it.'

When Noor opened the door, she took a step back and blinked, pushing her glasses up her nose as if she could not believe what she was seeing.

'Noor,' Farid said, *'bent I'am*. Will you mind Ruth's daughter, for one hour?'

Noor just stared.

'Noor,' Ruth said hurriedly, 'it would be such a favour to me. You've been so good with her, and I know I've asked an awful lot of you, too much, probably—but this would be the last time, I promise. And I'll pay you,' she added, 'I should

257

have been paying you all along for your time, I realise that, now, I'll make it all up to you.'

'You want me to come over and look after Anna?' Noor said, her clipped tones lengthening in disbelief, drawing out the vowels of Anna's name.

'Or I could bring her here. Just for an hour. Please, Noor.'

Farid added something in Arabic. Noor looked from Ruth to Farid, and back again, and Ruth suddenly thought: does she know?

They gazed at each other for a moment. Noor's eyes were red-rimmed and her face was drawn.

It was wrong they had asked her. Desperation had driven her to agree, but it was wrong.

'Look, it's all right. I can see you're in the middle of something,' Ruth started to say. But Noor cut across her.

'No,' Noor said, suddenly. 'No, I'll look after Anna. All right. OK.'

*   *   *

Farid drove a short way along the coastal highway, and they pulled in on some wasteland on the outskirts of Manama. Once again, they went through everything. And he did seem to have the answers. They could not be openly together, he said, not at first, not until Ruth was officially separated, at least, and had started divorce proceedings. But until then Ruth could stay with Maryam, in her spare room. Maryam was like a sister to him, a best friend: she would be glad to help him. His family were moving to a new compound in a few weeks' time, where there would be lots of room, enough room for the three of them. As soon as the divorce

258

came through, she could move there—and in time, they could get their own apartment. His father would employ him: he had been trying to convince Farid to take a job for months in one of his various business ventures. It would be amply paid. His father could employ Ruth, too, nominally, or act as her sponsor, to assist with her visa application. His family would rally around, he knew they would. They would take Ruth in, treat her as one of them. Alternatively, he said, he had another plan. Ruth could go back to Ireland and sort things through, then come out to Bahrain in the summer, properly.

'No,' she said, 'not that. If I stay here, I stay, at least for the first while, anyhow, at least until things have blown over.' If she went back, she knew, the filaments that held them, the threads, were so fragile they would snap. If she left, she would never come back—never be able to come back.

'You really are sure, aren't you?' she said. And despite everything—the emotion, the exhaustion, the upheaval—something inside her flickered with excitement. 'You really think we could do this?'

'I love you,' he said simply. 'It will be hard—it will be very hard. I am not blind to that. But I love you, Ruth. I love you.'

'I love you too,' she said. And it was true. Fleetingly, then, she thought of her namesake. *Where you go I will go, where you stay I will stay. Your people will be my people*, that Ruth had said, *and your God my God.*

'What are you thinking?' Farid said.

She started to explain. But then she thought of Boaz, later on—she knew the picture from Anna's illustrated Bible, the grey-bearded man sitting, while the slim young woman knelt at his feet,

259

half-hidden in Naomi's borrowed shawl. *You have not run after the younger men, whether rich or poor.*

'It doesn't matter,' she said. And this, too, was true: the freedom of it not mattering, of deciding that it *did not matter*. Then she said, again: 'I love you.'

*   *   *

When the hour was over, he took her back to the compound. Inside, the villa was strangely still. The maids had gone, and they could not hear Noor, or Anna. Noor must have taken Anna back to hers, she thought. But something was not right. She could feel it. She turned and walked back out through the hallway, retracing her steps in.

On the table by the door, propped up against the phone, was a ragged-edged piece of paper, folded in half, RUTH written in spiky capitals. She must have seen it when she came in, without really registering it. She picked it up, unfolded it. Farid was behind her. What is it, he was asking, what is it, Ruth?

His voice seemed to be coming from very far away. She did not answer him.

For a moment, her eyes could not seem to focus. And then her vision snapped back and she started to read.

~~Dear Ruth,~~

No. <u>Dear</u> is wrong because you're not dear, not
dear at all. You, of all people, are just the same as
anyone else. When I first met you I thought you
were different. I thought you were special. The
first time I ever saw you is seared into my brain.
You and Euan were walking down the compound
towards the empty swimming pool & tennis court
and you were each holding one of Anna's hands
and playing one-two-three-jump! with her and it
was the most perfect thing I'd ever, ever seen. The
two of you, and little Anna the cutest baby ever.
You were <u>perfect</u>. And I thought you were so kind
to me—I thought you liked me, too. But you didn't.
You were just using me—means to an end—means
to <u>Farid</u>.

And I mean: Farid?? How could you throw away
everything—everything you've got—for a fling with
him?

You obviously don't know your Bible as well as
you pretend to because in Matthew it says that it is
better to cut off a part of your body than commit
adultery and go to hell. And what about the other
part, the part that says, There is nothing concealed
that will not be disclosed or hidden that will not
be made known? And I am quoting exactly, Ruth!
How could you? What were you <u>doing</u>?

You're not fit to be a mother to poor little Anna
you know. You're just as bad as my mother, worse,
even, because on the outside you pretend to be so
religious and good. She had an affair, that was why

261

she and Baba got divorced and I got packed off to
boarding school while she moved into a little flat
with her 'lover' who was also married at the time.
But I was <u>twelve</u> at the time and little Anna isn't
even <u>two</u>! How can you do that to her—just dump
her with me all day while you run around having <u>sex</u>
with Farid. And even today?!! I was so, so shocked
to see the two of you there—so brazen, together.
Brazen—that's the word for you, Ruth Armstrong.

Poor, poor little Anna is all I can say, having
a mother like you. She doesn't deserve it. She
deserves far, far better. And your behaviour today
just <u>proves</u> it.

Ruth read the letter, shaking. Much of it was
incoherent: the writing was so messy that she could
hardly make out individual letters, let alone the
words. And the last few lines were indecipherable.
But she understood as much as she needed to.

'Anna!' she yelled. 'Anna!' and she pushed past
Farid, who was still trying to finish the letter.

In Anna's boxroom, the cot was made neatly,
as the maids had left it. But Anna's toys were
gone, and her blanky and—by now Ruth was in
the kitchen—her beaker. And—running into the
bedroom—Noor had gone through their wardrobe,
too, and taken Anna's clothes. Handfuls seemed
to have been snatched from the shelves at random;
several little T-shirts and dresses lay on the floor
where they had been dropped, and empty hangers
littered the wardrobe floor.

'She's gone,' Ruth shouted. 'She's gone—Noor's
taken Anna!'

8

Noor could not believe it when she answered the door and Ruth was there, and Farid, brazen, asking her to look after Anna. She looked from one to the other and thought what a laugh they must have had at her expense. Stupid Noor, they'd say. Poor stupid, ugly Noor. She doesn't even know what's right before her eyes. And the way Ruth insisted: for an hour, she said, only for an hour—as if that made things better, as if Noor had no idea what sordid things the two of them were planning on doing. She almost slammed the door in their face. She almost spat at their feet, or swore, or told them what she really thought of them. But then: All right, she found herself saying, without even knowing that she was going to say it. All right, I'll take Anna.

Anna was pleased to see her. She ran to her, jumped up at her, covered her face in sloppy kisses, stroked at her hair. She lifted Anna up and they stood on the Armstrongs' doorstep, watching Farid's car pull away. When it had left the compound, Noor turned quickly and went back inside. Bile was spilling up from her stomach— she could feel it, burning her chest, the bitter taste of it in the back of her throat. She made it to the bathroom and retched over the toilet. Nothing came out—there was nothing to come out, only acrid, acidic saliva. Little Anna beside her was big-eyed with concern: she kept trying to hug Noor better. Noor sat back, her head spinning, her mouth slimy and foul. Anna scrambled onto Noor's lap and patted her cheeks. Noor hugged her, tight.

Little Anna was so soft, and warm. So loving. All Noor's fantasies of going to Ireland and living in Ireland came flooding back. She would have looked after Anna, brushed her hair each night and sat over her until she went to sleep, told her stories and sung her songs. She would have taught her how to read and walked her to school each day, baked with her, been like a mother and a sister. And instead, all Anna had to look forward to was a cheating mother, a lying, cheating, two-faced, hypocritical mother who probably wouldn't think twice about packing *her* off to boarding school so she could run around having affairs left, right and centre. Anna did not deserve that. Ruth did not deserve Anna.

Suddenly, without even thinking about it, almost without knowing what she was doing, Noor was on her feet and in Anna's room, gathering up clothes and toys. Anna capered after her, laughing: she thought it was a new sort of game. They went through the villa room by room, gathering things they might need. There was no plan to it, no forethought. Noor realised they would need a bag and she ran back to her villa to find a holdall, stuffed it with handfuls of her things: T-shirts and jeans, a washbag, her diary. Then she went to the safe and took all the currency she could find, US dollars and GB pounds, thanking her lucky stars that it was Sampaguita's half-day. She ran back to the Armstrongs'. The maids were packing up and leaving: she suddenly panicked that they would realise what she was doing, but they barely acknowledged her. They were used to her coming and going with Anna. She shoved and pummelled Anna's things into the holdall and zipped it closed.

264

Last thing was to write a note for Ruth: she ripped a page from her diary and scribbled on it, her hand shaking so much she could hardly keep hold of the pen. She left the note where Ruth would be sure to see it, as soon as she and Farid returned. Then she strapped Anna's sandals on and heaved the holdall over her shoulder. Nobody must see them leaving the compound: the sentry would be sure to stop them. But that was not a problem: there was the back alleyway. It gave her a grim, bitter satisfaction using the same underhand way that Farid used to get in and out of the villa. She had to lift Anna over the dustbins, and over the little walls dividing each villa, but Anna still thought it was a game. They waited at the end of the passageway, crouching metres from the sentry box, until she was sure the man was looking the other way. She picked Anna up and they ran for it, clumsily, Anna's legs kicking and the holdall bumping against her back. And they had made it. There they were, out on the highway—they had done it!

She had no idea where they were going. It was just happening, so suddenly, without any time to think anything through. She put Anna down and started to walk. Left, there was nothing but the six-lane highway, so they turned right in the direction of the cold store. After only a few metres Anna started grizzling. She wanted to be carried. Noor rearranged the holdall and heaved Anna up onto the other hip. It made for slow progress. Anna played with her hair and kicked and the holdall kept slipping; she had to put Anna down, adjust the straps of the bag, then pick Anna up again. And it was hot: almost thirty degrees, with the midday sun glaring down. By the time they reached the cold store, Noor was sweating and her legs were trembling. She went inside: the cool of the air con and the shade was a relief. Anna started running about, colliding with racks of potato chips and pretzels, and screamed when Noor tried to catch her and make her stay still. Noor bribed her with an ice cream—using up a few precious fils—and Anna promptly dribbled it down her dress and blew messy raspberries over Noor's T-shirt. Noor saw the owner of the cold store looking at them. They made an unlikely couple, she realised: the Arab-looking girl with the little blonde toddler.

'Anna,' she said, in best, poshest voice, 'thank heavens your mummy will be collecting us soon. You look such a mess. She'll think I'm a terrible nanny and it'll all be your fault.'

Two men and a woman were looking at them now, as well as the cold-store owner. She felt her face burning and tried to seem oblivious.

'I really'—*raihlly*—'don't want to get the sack on my first week, Anna,' she said, loudly. Then she cursed herself, realised that she'd said Anna's name, twice. People were sure to remember them now. She had to get out of here, fast. She turned her back on the people watching, so they could not see her face, written with panic. In front of her was the magazine rack, and she pretended to be studying the imported glossies, her mind racing. One of them, a travel magazine, had a Gulf hotels special. And suddenly she had an idea. She took out her mobile phone and, moving into a corner where nobody was in earshot, rang the number of one of the taxi firms advertised in the window—one that accepted American dollars.

'Good afternoon,' she said, still in her best tones.

'I would like a driver for'—she cast about wildly for an address, then settled on the street address and the name of the cold store—'going to a hotel in downtown Manama, please.'

'Yes, Ma'am. Which hotel, Ma'am?' the operator asked.

'The—' She racked her brains for the names of hotels. 'The Ritz-Carlton, if you please.'

'The Ritz-Carlton. Which Ritz-Carlton would that be, please?'

'Which Ritz-Carlton?'

'Yes, Ma'am. The Ritz-Carlton Seef District, the Ritz-Carlton Manama, the Ritz-Carlton Hotel and Spa—'

'That one,' she chose at random.

'The Ritz-Carlton Hotel and Spa?'

'Yes.'

'All right, Ma'am.'

'And please be quick, my niece'—she looked quickly around again, to make sure nobody had overheard—'is very tired and needs to get back for her nap.'

She hung up, then wandered back within earshot of the cashier. 'Yes,' she said, pretending still to be talking to someone. 'You're sending a car for us, you say? That's wonderful, we'll wait right here.'

She was making an awful hash of it, she realised. She almost decided to go back, then and there—before Ruth could return and find them gone. But then the thought of what Ruth was probably doing, right now, with Farid, stiffened her resolve again.

The car came within a few minutes. If the driver was surprised to see how young his passengers were, he did not show it: he was well-practised in prudence and tact. A Gulf taxi firm had to cultivate a reputation of utter discretion if it wished to retain the custom of clients who might not wish their journeys—to where and with whom—to be observed and remembered. That, at least, was on her side.

He drove them through Manama, and to the 'Hotel Strip'—a highway along the north coast where the city's most exclusive hotels were situated. His meter was ticking at an alarming rate. Noor did the currency conversion in her head and worked out that this trip alone was using up most of her stolen dollars. But it was too late to turn back. The driver pulled up at the front of the Ritz-Carlton, she handed over the bulk of her money, and liveried bellboys came to open the door and help her out. They, too, masked any surprise they might have felt at seeing Noor and Anna. One of them lifted her holdall, but she wrested it back from him: as soon as he asked what room she wished it to be taken to, she would be found out.

'We're, uh, just going to—' she mumbled, seized Anna's hand and walked quickly away from the main entrance. She soon realised there was nowhere else for them to go, no other way into the building. She thought about just marching confidently in—but staff were sure to stop her and ask what room, what name. She wondered if they could try to tag along with another family—but someone was sure to notice them. Her mind was whirling. She was feeling sick again, as if she might throw up, any minute, into the sculpted bushes or flower strips. And Anna was lagging behind, dragging her feet, pouting and threatening to burst into tears.

Her mobile started ringing. It was Ruth. *Ruth*

Armstrong, Ruth Armstrong flashed up on the screen. Noor froze. She couldn't say she had just gone on an excursion because of the bag of clothes—and the money stolen, and the letter. The letter. She had written it in such a fit of rage, she could hardly remember what she had said in it. The phone stopped ringing, and immediately started again. *Ruth Armstrong, Ruth Armstrong.* She could answer, confess. But then she imagined what her father would say, imagined trying to explain to her mother, hysterical and furious on the phone. It was too late to go back. *Ruth Armstrong, Ruth Armstrong.* She pressed the button to reject the call, and turned her phone completely off. They could still track phones, though, even if they were turned off—couldn't they? She looked around to see if anybody was watching, then dropped the mobile into a flower bed, right beside a sprinkler valve. She nudged it in under the flowers with her toe. Then she turned, picked up Anna and the bag, and made her way as quickly as she could out of the hotel grounds. At the exit, she turned left—towards the city, away from the sea. Anna started crying, thrashing out and drumming her fists against Noor's back.

'Please,' Noor begged, and then, for the first time ever, she shouted at Anna. 'Shut up. Shut up or I'll give you a *reason* to cry.' Anna stopped, momentarily, stared at Noor, then started howling again, twice as loud as before. Noor thought she might burst into tears herself. 'Please, Anna. Please!'

But Anna would not be soothed, now. She writhed and kicked until Noor was forced to let her go, and she lay on the sidewalk, red-faced, convulsed with sobs.

'Come on, Anna-pet. Come on, Anna-banana,' Noor pleaded, trying all the pet names she had ever heard Ruth or Euan use. 'Come on, wee love.' But none of it was any good. Anna screamed until Noor was sure that one of the passing cars was bound to slow down, stop, and ask what was going on. But none of them did: and slowly, Anna's tantrum blew itself out. Her screams turned to sobs, her sobs to whimpers, and finally she let Noor pick her up again, and lay limp across Noor's shoulder. It was almost three o'clock, now. Noor was covered in dust and sweat, exhaust fumes from the cars. And she was suddenly terrified that Anna would be seized with heatstroke. They needed to get inside. She tramped along the strip until they came to the turn-off for the next hotel along. This time, she took the risk of walking straight into the lobby. When a bellboy came up to her, Noor said, with as much dignity as she could manage, 'We're meeting my uncle for afternoon tea.' The bellboy looked dubious, but he pointed Noor in the direction of the restaurant. She walked through, pretended to be searching for someone. By now, the waitress had seen them, and she could feel the bellboy still watching. There was nowhere to hide. She stopped, tried to think. Nearby, two middle-aged men were eating plates of sandwiches and bowls of soup. The smell of food made her feel faint. She had not eaten, she realised, not at all, in more than twenty-four hours. She scrabbled for her purse and counted her dinar and fils. There was not much, but there was enough for a sandwich. She found a secluded banquette and sat down, letting Anna slump across her lap, and without even waiting for the menu she ordered a plain cheese and tomato sandwich and a Diet Coke. She could not tell if the waitress was looking at them suspiciously or not, so she made a point of strewing her dinars on the table and saying, 'I'd better not eat too much, our uncle is taking us out for dinner tonight.'

The waitress stared and smiled a smile Noor knew to be fake.

'Can I have your room number, please?' she said.

'Oh, we're not guests here,' Noor said. 'We're staying—we're staying at the Ritz-Carlton Hotel and Spa, just down the road. But we're meeting my uncle, my cousin's father, here later on, he's resident but I don't know which room.' She felt herself start to gabble. But the waitress did not ask any more questions. The sandwich came, garnished with crisps and parsley, and she savoured every salty, fatty mouthful. It was the most she had eaten in days. She could feel her stomach start to curl up in protest at the sudden influx of food. She eked it out as long as she could. Anna fell asleep, breathing hot, fast little breaths into her lap. She did not want to move, did not want to wake Anna and risk another scene. But the waitress was watching them, and she saw her conversing with another waitress, both looking in their direction. They might call the police, she thought, and then she would be arrested for kidnap.

Kidnap. She realised, in a panic, that was what she had done. She had kidnapped Anna. That was a crime: she could be thrown in jail for that. She stood up, bumping Anna's head and waking her. Anna was white-faced and sleepy, a dead weight. She picked her up—it took both arms—and managed to get her left arm through the straps of the holdall. She left the restaurant, with all of her dinar still on the table. She had almost nothing, now. A few dollars, a few useless pounds—that was all. A group of businessmen were getting into a lift and she followed them in. They were English. One of them asked her a question—what was she doing, was that her baby?—designed to make the others laugh. She stared blankly back at him and spoke a few words in Arabic, hoping that Anna was still too sleepy to start babbling in English. The businessmen got out at the third floor. Noor pressed the button for the fifth, at random, and the lift went on up. When she got out, the corridor was deserted, but for a cleaning trolley. She wondered if they could slip into an empty room, stay there. But all the rooms were locked, except for the one the maids were making up. She walked round the corridor—it was shaped like a horseshoe, with the lifts in the middle of the curve—and back again. She heard voices, and ducked into the staircase, went down a floor. But the voices followed—they were in the stairwell, too—and she had to hurry down another floor, and another. Right at the bottom the stairs led to a corridor with toilets, male, female and disabled, and a baby-changing room. She went into the baby-changing room and closed the door behind them. It was a small room, with a changing mat folded against one wall and an armchair against the other, a sink and toilet sectioned off at the back. It had a door that locked with a bolt. She slid the bolt across and sank down, shaking. Her arms were almost dead from carrying both Anna and the bag. Anna wriggled, and started to whimper. It was cold in the baby-changing room. She made a nest for Anna out of all their clothes, and as they both curled up in it, Noor wondered how on earth there could ever, ever be any way back.

9

The villa is Peter's gloomy dungeon, the darkness his chains. She is lost; there is no hope; her child is gone from her. That night, she knows hell.

*   *   *

At first, Farid had been calm. 'She is a silly girl,' he said, 'a silly, silly girl.'

'You don't think it's malicious, then? You don't think—' Her words, mind, would not continue.

'I think she found out about us and flew into a rage, no more. She can't have gone far. We'll find her.'

They searched the villa, room by room, then went across to the al-Husayns'. But it was closed and its front door locked. They knocked and knocked, but no one answered.

'She could be in there, hiding,' Farid said. But Ruth knew she was not.

They searched the compound, the swimming pool and tennis court, the alleyways behind the villas. But it could have been dead, a ghost town, as uninhabited as one of the traditional villages she had seen with Farid, where reconstructions of old-style houses gathered dust, the only people in them plaster, frozen blank-faced in imagined or approximated tasks. They questioned the sentry-man, but he swore he had not seen anyone go in or out. This meant nothing, Ruth thought bitterly. They had evaded him themselves countless times, thinking themselves clever, resourceful. Now it was coming back to mock them.

'Well,' Farid said, 'she can't have gone far. We'll get in the car and go looking for her.'

'But—what if she comes back?'

He shrugged. 'We'll leave *her* a note.'

On the back of some pages ripped from Euan's notebook, Ruth wrote, in large capital letters: *NOOR—ALL IS FORGIVEN. RING ME. RUTH.* Her hand shook as she wrote *forgiven*. They propped one page up on the telephone table, by the door, where Noor had left hers, then pinned another to their front door and a third to the door of the al-Husayns'. *NOOR—ALL IS FORGIVEN. RING ME. RUTH.*

It was only then it occurred to her.

'Farid!' she said. 'We're being so stupid—we're not thinking straight. We can try ringing her. Maybe she'll pick up, and we can get through to her!'

Her hands shook so much that she could barely scroll through the names in her contacts list. But she found Noor—*Noor Anna* was the hurried entry, which made her almost vomit when she saw it—and managed to jab the call button. After an agonising few seconds, the phone rang. It rang—wherever Noor was, her phone was still on: she was still reachable. Maybe all of this was a horrid mistake—maybe it could be a horrid mistake. But Noor did not answer. The line clicked, and there was Noor's voice, flat and sullen, *This is Noor, leave a message*, as pop music played in the background. She hung up and tried again. The same. And then again. Please, Noor, she thought. Please, Noor, please, Noor, please. This time, the phone flipped to voicemail in the middle of a ring, after ringing only a few times. Noor was there. Somewhere, she was watching her phone ring, and not answering Ruth's calls—and now she had just rejected a call. But she was there! Ruth dialled again—but the phone went straight to voicemail. What if Noor was trying to phone her back? she thought, but even as she thought it she knew it was not true. She rang again: answerphone. Again: answerphone. Noor had turned her phone off.

They got in the car, then, and drove off looking for her. Round and round, a larger loop each time. Noor wouldn't have had time to walk more than three miles, Farid calculated, in the time they'd been gone—and they had to remember she had Anna and presumably a bag or a suitcase with her, too. Whatever progress she made would be slow. There was nowhere for her to hide: he was sure they would find her walking down the side of some highway. Ruth felt sick at the thought of Anna, toddling along the verge of the highway, the huge cars thundering past. But she felt even sicker when they didn't see them.

What about buses, she suggested, could she not have taken a bus? But nobody took buses, Farid said, buses were for labourers or immigrant workers. She could have taken a taxi—but where would she have gone? One of the malls, maybe—in which case she would be forced to return home as soon as they closed for the night—or the family compound, but he did not think she would turn up there with Anna in tow. He phoned his stepmother, anyway, just to check—but of course she was not there. Don't worry, he said, his hand on Ruth's knee. Bahrain was small. She would be seen, she would be found. There was nowhere really for her to hide, nowhere she could go she would not be found.

His words were meant to be reassuring. But Ruth began to shiver. *There is nothing concealed that will not be disclosed, nor hidden that will not be found.* It was a warning, not a comfort.

They drove in circles until dusk, when it was difficult to see any more. Then they went back to the compound, hoping against hope that Noor would have returned, that they would walk into the villa to find her there, hot and dusty after some foolhardy adventure. But the villa was even emptier than before.

Farid went across to check the al-Husayns', and then said he'd better phone his uncle.

They sat on the veranda until Dr al-Husayn arrived, on the swinging chair, in silence. Images of Anna spooled through Ruth's mind. Her little face, so sweet and trusting. Her warm smell, and fat cheeks, the way she'd clap her hands and giggle, the soft weight of her when she crawled into bed in the mornings. *How can you do that to her?* Noor had asked, and Noor was right. How could she? Anna had been an annoyance, an obstacle—she had been all too ready to hand her over, to be free of her. Now, she promised that when Anna was found— it was when, not if, she could not allow herself to think *if*—she would never let her out of her sight again, would never, ever do anything to hurt her.

Now it was nightfall. It was night-time, and Anna was alone, lost and probably terrified, with an unstable teenager, goodness knew where. Farid

276

tried to put his arm around her, but it was an unbearable weight. She shrugged him off, and he did not try again.

Dr al-Husayn arrived. They did not tell him—not exactly—what had prompted Noor to take off with Anna. They did not show him the letter, either. They simply said they thought Noor was upset with them. He said nothing. But Ruth could feel him looking at her, judging her, sizing her up. She did not care, she realised. All of a sudden, she did not care who knew, or what anyone thought, so long as she got her daughter back.

Dr al-Husayn begged her not to call the police— not yet, he said. The Bahraini police could be harsh, very harsh, and they would not make a distinction between adult and teenager. Noor had gone through a very hard time, lately—he was not making excuses, but please would Ruth understand—and he hoped the matter could be sorted out privately, and he and Noor's mother would deal with Noor.

Then his eyes narrowed. Besides, he added, he was sure she would not want the police involved. He looked her up and down as he said it. She tried to stare him down.

'And what exactly do you mean by that?' she asked.

He shrugged, and she saw a hint of a smile. You bastard, she thought. She thought once more of Farid's words: the police wouldn't do anything unless they had an ulterior motive, or a specific complaint had been made. If she went to the police about Noor, he would tell them about her and Farid, force them to act. Would he do that, she thought, to his own nephew? Or was he only bluffing?

The abruptness of his next question sent her reeling.

'Where exactly is your husband right now?' he said. There was no trace of a smile now, only a cold, calculating stare. He had her, and even if he did not know exactly how, he knew it, and he knew she knew it, too.

She stammered out the Qatar line; visiting acquaintances, uncontactable—he had left his phone behind by mistake. This he had: though not by mistake. All of Euan's things—his passport, wallet, mobile phone, the fish-shaped lapel pin he always wore—were in the combination safe in their bedroom. For the first time since Euan had been gone, she felt a real stab of fear for him, too, defenceless and illegal in Saudi Arabia. She could not call the police, she realised. Quite aside from protecting Noor—or herself, from the accusation of adultery—if the police were involved, they would check on Euan's whereabouts, test out her Qatar line, and it would be exposed as a lie under the slightest pressure. A phone call or two would be all it took.

But this was her daughter. This was Anna. That she might face imprisonment, that Farid might face lashes, hardly seemed significant in comparison.

Noor had until the morning, Ruth said. If by first light she had not turned up, or been found, then Ruth was calling the police.

She thought, suddenly, of the choice Euan had made: between them and his mission. Now, she knew: she would have to sacrifice him, and Christopher and Rosa, and all the others, and the Christians in Saudi Arabia, and who knew who else, all for the chance of getting Anna back. The Kingdom of God for her child.

'This is my daughter we're talking about,' she said, as much to herself as to Dr al-Husayn. 'My daughter.'

Dr al-Husayn stared at her. 'It is my daughter too,' he said. 'I love my daughter, and if anything happens to her, if she comes to any harm at your hands—'

'Harm at my hands?' Ruth felt her voice rising out of her control, almost breaking into a laugh.

Farid, who had been standing silent to one side, stepped forward and put a hand on Ruth's arm. She saw Dr al-Husayn notice it. He looked at her, then turned and spat on the ground.

'Uncle,' Farid said, and she knew he was speaking in English for her benefit. 'Please, Uncle. Conflict will not solve anything, now.' Dr al-Husayn turned back to them, and Farid spoke a long, urgent burst of Arabic. Whatever he said seemed to mollify the doctor: he turned away and climbed into his car, without another word.

*   *   *

Now, Farid went back out driving too, while she stayed in the villa, the door wide open, watching the compound, for Noor to return with Anna.

The night passed so slowly it seemed not to pass at all. Each minute was a thousand years, each hour an eternity.

At one point, the deadest part of the night, Ruth found herself on her knees praying, trying to strike a deal with God. If there is a God, she prayed, I ask Him for help. It was better not to have known the way of righteousness, she knew, than to have known it and then to turn her back on the sacred command. If there was a God, He would not pity her. Like the rich man in Luke, looking up to Abraham and praying in vain for a fingertip of water, there was no comfort for her. She had received her good things, had her measure of earthly joy, and now there was a chasm between her and salvation. It was no good repenting. But nonetheless she tried.

If you return Anna, she said in her mind. If you return Anna, I will never sin again. I will give up Farid, and go back to Ireland. If you return Anna.

She knew that you did not—could not—make deals with God, that you should not presume to make deals with God. But still she tried, over and over, trying to fix her mind to God, to keep on praying, *as to a light shining in a dark place,* Peter had said, *until the day dawns and the morning star rises in your hearts.*

If you return Anna, she said, I will believe in You again, or try to, to the best of my ability.

If you return Anna, if you return Anna, if you return Anna.

*   *   *

Her phone rang at five that morning, just before dawn. Farid and Dr al-Husayn had rung at intervals during the night, but this was a new number, a Bahrain-coded number, a number she did not recognise.

'Hello?' she managed.

'Good morning,' a sing-song voice said at the other end. 'Would that be Mrs Ruth Armstrong

280

with whom I am speaking?'

'Yes,' she said. 'Yes?'

'This is Paresh here, calling from the Elite Seef Residence, Avenue 38. Oh dear oh dear, Mrs Ruth Armstrong. You have two girls here in a bit of a sorry state. Are you able to come and collect them?'

10

Maundy Thursday, the Reverend Day's sermon.

The word *maundy*, he explains, comes from the Latin *mandatum*, from which we get our English *mandate*. Mandate: to give, to entrust, to order.

On the sunlit hills of Galilee, by the silvery lapping waters, it is easy to hope, or to believe in hope, and the promise of a life to come. But in Jerusalem, in the fierce and unremitting midday heat, where the glare of the light on the bleached white walls and dusty pathways pains the sight and makes the eyes water, truth, like the light and the heat, begins to seem a stark and terrifying quality: it will skewer you, helpless and wriggling; sear you to nothing if you come too close. In the relief of the darkened rooms and the faint breezes of inner courtyards, people grow uneasy and defensive, and begin to speak mutinously against the man who talks of nothing but suffering and servitude.

Faith is not gentle, and more than a gift it is a command, because it is a necessity, and it more than anything is the one thing God demands of us.

Hope is not gentle, and it too is a command, a necessity.

And Love: Love is the greatest and most

281

terrifying commitment, and obligation, of all.

*   *   *

Anna on her lap, Euan beside her, both returned to her safely. She has no choice but to listen, as intently as possible, every fibre in her body quivering and straining to hear, to know, to understand. She is exhausted. Euan is exhausted. Both of them have new creases etched in their faces, from their separate trials; ever so faint, but there nonetheless, the sign of lines to come. Only Anna, thank God, seems unaffected by the last few days. And in four days' time, Easter will be over and they will be going home.

'You mean the world to me,' Euan had said that morning, taking her into his arms and hugging her, almost crushing her, uncharacteristically tight. 'You and Anna. If you have ever doubted, Ruth—and I know you have, I know you must have—then please know now. I love you. At one point'—his voice caught—'I thought my number was up. I was baptising two young men and a woman, and suddenly the *Mutaween* were at the door. We heard their voices, and there was nowhere to go, and I thought that was it, we all thought that was it. One of the men went to answer the door, but by the time he got there they had moved on—and he thought at first it was a trick, a trap—but they really did go away, for no discernible reason, and we were saved. And all my thoughts were of you and Anna, and I just wanted to get back to you, then, and get you away from here.'

His body, as he let himself collapse against her, had felt a dead weight, and she had felt herself

282

stagger. She was certain, then, that she would have lost him: him and Anna.

Now, she thinks to Euan beside her, to Anna: You are my life. Maybe another day, another moment, I will once again feel the way I did about my husband and my child: the ambivalence, the exasperation, the resentment, the burden of them. Maybe when life is restored it will seem to lose all value once more. But now, in this moment—and I must try and carry the memory of this moment inside me, always—in this moment, I know that they are all that matters.

And all of a sudden she finds that thanks and relief and profound gratitude are streaming out of her, as if she is praying without trying to, praying without words, and she thinks: I promised to believe in you, God, and I want to believe in you, and maybe that's as far as we can ever go. Prophecies will fail, tongues be stilled, knowledge will fade away, but love, somewhere, even if we cannot see or feel or apprehend or understand it, love, somehow, remains.

*   *   *

Graham Day is taking a different tack, now. And yet, he is saying, and yet: should it be complicated, should it be difficult, to love? Jesus's final commandment, is it not?, is to love: Love one another, he says, even as I have loved you. Love your friends, love your enemies, love all who know you and those who do not. That is all: God is Love, and it is simple, and perfect; and perhaps it is we in our flawed and human anguish who demand to struggle and to suffer.

283

* * *

She has lost the thread of the sermon. What he said at first does not seem to relate to what he is saying now. She must not allow her thoughts to wander. She must not think of Farid.

* * *

They rise to sing, the sixty-third Psalm.

> *O God, you are my God*
> *earnestly I seek you;*
> *my soul thirsts for you,*
> *my body longs for you,*
> *in a dry and weary land*
> *where there is no water.*

Everything is meaningful.

* * *

Tonight, when the service is over, they will go back to the villa, and Euan will tell her a little about Saudi Arabia, the people, the place, the Word. She will not tell him what has happened to her. She will never tell him. She has thought about it, briefly, but something tells her there is no need. She has learned what she needed to know. This is what she tells herself.

Noor's father has taken his daughter to the family compound, where there will be people to watch over her, until her mother arrives from England and they decide what should be done with her.

Farid she will never see again. He had taken her to pick up Noor and Anna, he and Dr al-Husayn both. Afterwards, back in the villa, Anna bathed and safely asleep, she had told him she could never see him again. This time, he had not cried, or protested his love.

'You can't do this to me,' he had said. 'Again and again, Ruth, you have said it is over, then changed your mind, and I have come running. This time, I am serious. You tell me to go, and I will go, and you will never see me again.'

She had looked at him, and for a moment she had wanted to fall into his arms. But she had made her promise.

'I will always love you,' she whispered.

'Fuck you,' he said, 'damn you,' as he turned and left.

Friday, Good Friday, will be spent at church all day. Saturday packing. Easter Sunday, then last things on Monday, then Tuesday home. It was meant to be a fortnight on Tuesday—May—but Euan is glad to change their flights, when she suggests it, now that he has done what he needed to do. He is shaken, she can see, in ways that he will never fully explain to her. Both of them are; changed; both with their own silences.

Home.

*   *   *

It does not happen quite like that. She does not see Farid again, but she does hear from him. He rings and texts her on Easter Sunday, several times: she can feel the phone buzzing against her thigh, again

285

and again, and she has to ignore it, to pretend to ignore it, because Euan is beside her, and even if she took it out to turn it off he would glance over and see the name, the volume of messages.

It is a shock to realise that she has not quelled the habit of having her phone always on her, set to silent and vibrate, even after everything, all of her promises and resolutions. The Communion wafer is dust on her tongue, and sticks to the roof of her mouth.

After the service (so joyful, the Bishop of Cyprus and the Gulf himself conducting, the purple cassock and ceremonial mitre, the exultant music, the congregation singing as if their hearts might burst, and Christ restored) she makes use of the jubilance and general confusion to slip outside, to the smooth marble courtyard and the white heat, and round the back of the building.

Farid has left two voicemails on her phone, and several text messages. They are sending him away, is the gist of it. They have been too lax with him, his uncle has decided, too lenient; he is to go to some second cousins in Esfahan, Iran.

'They will send me to Iran, Ruth'—his voice cracks and pleads on her answerphone—'even though my mother fled from there in seventy-eight. That's how angry they are, how little they care about me. They say I must leave Bahrain, next week. Please, Ruth. Please, we belong together, I know we do—'

Shaking so violently she fears she might be sick, she cuts off the message and deletes it. If she listens to one more second, she knows, she might give in. She tries not to look at the text messages as she deletes them, too. Then she turns her phone off:

she will leave it off, she vows, for the next two days, until they are back in Ireland.

She has made her choice, she must uphold her side of the bargain. There is no other way. He will know that her silence—her failure to answer—is her answer, is all she can answer.

She must go back inside. She has been out here too long. She will say it was her mother on the phone, calling from home.

Home, she thinks again.

She must go back. She must go back now. She must. She will. It is over, she tells herself. Over.

V

Seven years pass. Ruth is the age Euan was; Farid Ruth's: although she does not allow herself to think this, to think of him. She had loved him: that she now knows. It was real, what they had, and true, however brief it was. But it is Euan she loves now, faithfully; in mind and deed, as best she can. She has done so every day of the passing years, to the best of her ability, even through the difficult times. Especially through the difficult times. He is in charge, now, of a congregation on the outskirts of Belfast, and they live in the manse house nearby: an airy, elegant detached house with gardens front and rear, a garage, a cat. Anna is a skinny, anxious girl of nine, and they have two other children: Luke, who is six, and Joshua, four. She was pregnant with Luke when they left Bahrain, although she did not realise it then. And the months of her pregnancy were sleepless, hellish. She had slept with Euan only twice in Bahrain: the day of the storm, she remembered that, and on Maundy Thursday, when he returned. Neither time had they used contraception; but the baby, she was convinced, could not be his, because she had made love with Farid almost every day for weeks. Countless times she was on the verge of confessing to Euan, admitting—and wondering too if she could contact Farid and tell him. But every time, something stopped her: and when the baby was born with blue eyes and reddish hair, and unmistakably Euan's nose, she made herself give thanks.

Her mother is delighted with her brood of grandchildren; her father, feeling the first signs of the rheumatoid arthritis that will slowly cripple and eventually kill him, talks increasingly about selling up, buying a house in Belfast to be nearer to them. With nobody to take over the farm, he has sold it off, in bits and pieces, to the neighbours; one a farmer, another a property developer. Little remains, now, but the farmhouse and barns; the sea-meadows and one or two fields kept for families who stable their horses there.

She is kept busy by her children, by her parents, by the demands of being a minister's wife. There is grace, she has learned, in the most ordinary, the humblest of things. In the chopping of onions for a stew, in the deboning of fish and boiling of eggs for a fish pie. In the folding of warm, tumble-dried sheets in winter, or the pegging of washed sheets out on a breezy spring day, when they billow and swell in raptures. In such things, there is a certain grace, the keeping of these rituals of the ordinary.

This faith is not her husband's, nor something she can ever say to him, or try to explain. But what she has come to understand is simpler, deeper than his: living itself is an act of faith.

It is only in the last few months, since Joshua started school, that she has had any time to herself, for idle thoughts. She has read the poem of Gilgamesh, slowly, laboriously, at first, for its words and rhythms were arcane to her, inhospitable. The slim yellow volume with its spotted and yellowing pages she found in Euan's study, untouched by him, or by whoever owned it first, because several of the pages were joined together, and she slit them open with a knife. Now she knows the Sun God Shamash, just and benevolent, and the beautiful, terrifying Ishtar, goddess of Love. She can see the temple at Uruk, the outer wall shining copper, and

292

the masonry burned brick. She can see the statue of Enkidu, its breast of lapis lazuli and gold, holding a bowl of carnelian filled with honey. Lapis lazuli: an azure blue semi-precious stone; carnelian: a reddish form of chalcedony; chalcedony: a type of quartz. At first, she had to chase the words through dictionaries, follow their threads, but they are hers, now. She does not feel the sense of outrage she might once have felt that the warrior Enlil, rather than Noah, should be warned of the deluge and told to build a boat, and take in the seed of all living creatures. Just as these words and this story are become hers, so her stories must be allowed to others. The serpent senses the sweetness of the flower, and rises to snatch it, and sinks back to the depths. This too is true. All things that happen have happened many times before; no love is lost; and all that dies comes again. The wind blows over us, but we are not gone; we are the places we have been, and the remembrance of them.

But mostly, she tries not to think of Bahrain. When she does, she always thinks of it as something that happened to her, an experience as well as a place, like the sort of lands in the fairy tales she read to Anna, and now reads to Luke and little Josh, that exist only at a certain time, given a certain convergence of shore and sea, a certain slant of light. She thinks of it, of her time there, of what happened there, as like a pebble, buried deep in her solar plexus. A smooth, round pebble; basalt, maybe, a not uncomfortable weight, the sort you might pick up on a shore and weigh in your hand, enjoying the solidity of it, the quiet certainty of it, calmed by the centuries and warmed by the sun. It is not a rough, jagged-edged sort of rock that causes you pain, a jabbing, shortness of breath. A scruple, Euan told her once (an amused, throwaway sort of comment, something he was reading, tossed like a bauble for her to catch), used to be the word for the insistent sort of stone that worked its way into your shoe and would not easily be shaken out. Hers is not that, not a scruple; not a misgiving, or regret. But it is there, nonetheless, deep inside of her, somewhere behind and below her heart, in the place her breath comes from. God, she hears Euan saying to Luke one day (quick, serious little Luke, already struggling to understand the world and his place in it), is closer than your next breath. She tries this out, makes herself conscious of her next breath, the moment before it happens, the moment before it comes. She imagines God in the breath, rushing up and through her body, around the pebble, around the hidden nicks and cuts and scar tissue of life, the wear and tear of living; and there is something deeply calming, deeply reassuring in the thought. She does not believe, these days— although of course she does not tell Euan this— in an interventionist God, one who restores your child to you, averts the tidal wave at the last possible moment. Why should He, when He takes the children of others, deaf or careless to their pleas, their anguish? But yet she does believe, in something she does—doubtingly, questioningly, it is true, but yet she does, she does believe. The act of trying, she sometimes thinks, is belief itself. There is no good (she reads this passage in the book of James often) in saying to a starving man outside in the cold, Go, I wish you well, I wish you warm and fed. You must work at faith. It never gets easier: but there is a grace, too, in this; for she would not want it easier, diminished.

*   *   *

When she saw the Bahraini stamp and postmark on the letter, she put it away in her handbag before Euan had a chance to notice. It was a dull morning, a chilly April day. She had taken the children to school, fed the cat, gone to do some errands— food shopping, renewing the tax disc on the car— and Euan was at home, working in his study. She was glad he had been too absorbed in his work to hear the postman come, to wander into the hallway and sift through the day's letters. She called out to him that she had forgotten something at the shops, and she got back into the car and drove to the big supermarket nearby. As she drove up the hill, she saw the fields of the countryside beyond, dull green, and she remembered seeing Ireland from the plane, as they returned, as it banked and descended. The lurid green of the grass, and the grey-green tinge of the sea. She had felt numb, then, and empty, as if life was over. But it wasn't, of course, that was just the exhaustion, the anticlimax of it all. As her mother said to her the next day, no wonder you're a wee bit down in the dumps, sure haven't you been living the life of Riley out there.

She parked at the far end of the car park. It was raining heavily now; nobody would see her sitting in the car, or wonder what she was doing. They would just think she was waiting for the rain to ease off, to make a dash for it.

The envelope was stiff, thick—as if it contained a packet of photographs. She held it in her hands, turned it over, taking in the heft of it, the weight.

295

There was no address or sender's name on the back of the envelope. The writing was neat and slanting, black ink, fountain pen. It was not how she imagined his hand to look. It could be Anjali, she thought—it took her a moment to remember Anjali's name—but although she visited Anjali once more in hospital before they left the country, and swapped email addresses, she had never heard from her since.

She noticed her fingers trembling as she slit open the envelope and took out the contents. There was one cream page, written on both sides, folded around a pamphlet of some sort. She unfolded the page and her vision blurred; it was a few moments before she could read the letter.

Dear Ruth Armstrong,

I hope that my writing out of the blue and after all these years is not an unwelcome intrusion.

I thought it would be difficult to find you, but it was not, after all. The chaplain gave me the phone number of the secretary of the Bishop of Down and Dromore, and he was able to find the Reverend Armstrong's parish and address, all within a few minutes.

I have thought of you often over the years.

I have wanted to apologise to you, for a start. In fact I have apologised to you so many times, Ruth, that you would not be able to count them. I hope I am forgiven for what I did.

I have often wanted to let you know, too, that somehow, the spark of faith you gave me stayed with me for a long time. I am ashamed to admit that I am less and less sure of it now, these days—

but it got me through a lot over the next couple of years. In fact, I think it is no exaggeration to say that it <u>got</u> me through the last few years. I was in a very bad place, Ruth, a very, very bad place. After everything that—shall we say, 'happened', I finally confessed to my parents all that had gone on at school, and the rest of it. I think I had been too humiliated to admit what had really been going on: I was very badly bullied myself, for years. It took a good year of counselling for me to accept this, and to forgive myself, and learn to like myself again. And with this, God—Jesus— faith—whatever the right term might be—it helped. It even made me friends in the next school I went to, back in England, because I was able to join the Scripture Union Society and a couple of other bible study groups. I think that the fact that I was Muslim—or that my father was, at least, and my name—made me even more of a coup as a convert, and everyone went out of their way to be nice to me, and include me in things, which believe me was a first.

I have often wanted to make contact with you and tell you this. I still—can you believe this?—have the little old Gospel of Matthew you gave me. After all these years! It is pretty battered now . . .

I hope that you and the Reverend Armstrong and Anna are all well. Anna must be almost ten by now? And maybe you have other children too? I send you all my best wishes and hope that everything in your life is wonderful.

Things are good with me. You will see I am writing this from Bahrain: I am here, visiting my father and his family for my Easter holidays, before going back to university to take my finals.

I have not yet decided what to do afterwards. I might do a Masters, I might travel for a while—who knows . . . I write poetry. That was something I started during my time in Bahrain, at the suggestion of my counsellor, in fact, but I have kept up the habit, over the years, and have started to make something of it. A few of my poems have just been published, and I hope it's not too much of a liberty to be sending you a copy.

Ruth felt for the pamphlet, which had fallen into her lap. *Dilmun*, it was called, and underneath, *Noor Fairbridge Hussain*. Dilmun: in Dilmun the raven does not croak, the lion does not kill. The lines flashed through her mind as clear and sharp as if she was there, now, reading them, back in the museum, back in that day, that moment.

She forced herself to open the booklet, skim through it. 'The Life-Tree', the first long poem was called; 'Locusts', another; 'On Grace'; 'Dilmun'.

Slowly, her heart stilled.

Do you remember the day we visited the Tree of Life,

Noor's letter went on,

and how disappointed you were at the mess and the graffiti? For some reason that made a great impression on me, and that's the title poem and theme of the collection.

I hope, once more, that my sending this is not unwanted, or an imposition, and if it is then please accept my sincerest apologies.

I hope you understand everything I have been trying to say. If I do not hear from you, I will not

298

contact you again.

The letter finished there, with an address printed at the bottom.

Noor.

Noor at university, Noor a poet.

She had never wondered what happened to Noor. *Ashamed* was the word Noor used in her letter. Well, Ruth too had always been ashamed to think of Noor, ashamed of how she treated the girl, how she disliked her, but used her nonetheless. Noor was not to blame, really, for what she had done. It had been Ruth: everything had been Ruth.

She wondered if she would write back to Noor; if she would ever be able to say any of this, or if thinking it—knowing it—was enough.

She reread the letter, then folded it back around the pamphlet and slid them back into the envelope. As she did so, something stuck, jammed; they would not go. She tried again, more carefully: and this time noticed another piece of paper. It was lined and punched, taken from a file pad, and the writing was not in neat black ink but biro. She took it out and smoothed it open. It was Noor again: but this time no dear, no preamble, just a few scrawled lines.

I can't decide if you'd want to know or not, and I'd decided not, but here at the post office I've changed my mind again and unsealed the envelope to include this. Because I know it's none of my business, and it never was, and probably it means nothing to you, but if it was me I think I'd want to know.

299

Farid. Noor's hand was loose and messy, hard to decipher in parts, but the name leapt out. Ruth thought, fleetingly, of tearing the paper up, turning away right then: but it was too late, she was already reading on.

Farid has stayed in Esfahan. He doesn't keep in touch with any of us, much, apart from my brother Jamal, who he emails occasionally. For the past couple of years he's been working for Irancell, the mobile phone company, and he is married, with two small daughters. My uncle wants him to leave the country, with the American talk of war and the rioting, but he says he'll never come back to Bahrain. I know this only because Jamie tells me.

Anyway, I'm running out of room, and the post office is closing for lunch, so I have to go. It isn't much to report, but I thought you'd like to know, and if you didn't, please rip this up and forget I ever wrote it.

Time has stopped. She feels a hard, bright sense of loss for him, then, and is momentarily unable to breathe.

But she is used to this now. The first time it came, a few days back in Ireland, she had thought she would die. The pain had risen until it was almost unbearable, a noise rather than a sensation, a howling, hopeless shriek. But like the swells and contractions of childbirth, it had ebbed and gone, expelled from her body, just when she thought she had reached the peak, the precipice. We are capable, in our bodies, of surviving more than we can imagine. This pain, she fights to tell herself, it too will pass, and seeing Euan, her children, will be a balm, a salve.

She struggles back into herself. It is not a real wound: just the ghost of an old one.

It is almost midday: time to collect Josh from school, and half an hour later, Luke. Before she starts the engine again, she tries to form her mind into a prayer. An unbeliever, she tells herself, struggling to wrap her mind around the words, to make her thoughts the words, to the exclusion of all else, an unbeliever watches a flower unfolding in a garden.

ACKNOWLEDGEMENTS

My deepest thanks to Peter Straus—reader, advocate, agent extraordinaire—and to Jenny Hewson and all at RCW. Thank you to Rowan Routh for her insightful readings of the manuscript at every incarnation. Thank you to Natalie Abrahami, Mike Brett and Nick Harrop for reading early drafts; to Maureen Caldwell for reading every draft; to Peter Caldwell for so many extra-literary matters.

To Roopesh Ravindran, Mohammed Abdulla Awadi and the Awadi family, also Yasmin, Charly, Paaresh, Habiba, Sonali, Jason and all those who showed me such wonderful Bahraini hospitality: thank you, shukran, khayli mamnoon, nanni, dhanyawaad.

Thank you also to Alice and the Careys for Mill Farm; to Ronnie Hetherington of the Union Theological College; to the Alpha Course at Christchurch, Spitalfields; to Steve King and Frank King; to Julia Shepherd. Thank you to Damon Wake (formerly of the Press Association); to Kevin Bakhurst and Nick Marcus of BBC News 24; to Faisal Bodi (formerly of Al Jazeera).

I thank Gemma Seltzer and Arts Council England for a grant which bought the time and space to finish the novel.

Thank you to the most sensitive and brilliant of editors, Angus Cargill, and to the fantastic team—family—at Faber.

And finally, Tom, to whom this book is

303

dedicated: without your support, strength, and the surety of your belief in me, I couldn't have written it. Thank you, thank you, thank you.